Mirrored

A Keone Boyd Mystery

By Rick Ludwig

2-9-2015

Rick Ludwig (signature)

Mirrored
A Keone Boyd Mystery
First Edition
Copyright © 2014 Rick Ludwig
Published by Babylon Books

ISBN-10: 0989378985
ISBN-13: 978-0-9893789-8-7

For Christy

CONTENTS

ACKNOWLEDGMENTS

I'm blessed with a collection of wonderful people who read and commented on this book while it was incubating. Ken Andrus, Elaine Gallant, Doug McLellan, Laurie Hanan, Bill Bernhardt, and Christy and Jennifer Ludwig plowed through one or more versions of this book and provided valuable feedback. Dr. John H. Draeger provided information on psychiatric conditions. Sergeant Audra M. Sellers, Maui Police Department and Chief Scott Fleuter, Ashland, Oregon Police Department, (Ret.) provided valuable input on Maui Police Department structure and law enforcement procedures.

Any errors that remain are mine

Thanks to the great authors in Write On, Maui! for valuable input and especially Marti Wukelic for getting us started. I also thank my colleagues in William Bernhardt Writing Seminars whose talent inspires and encourages me every day. Special thanks to Greg Field, Kent Reinker, Bill and Judy Fernandez, JoAnn Carroll, Danielle Bergan, Lynette Chun, Kathy McCullough, Diana Hindman, and Taressa Watson.

My daughter Jennifer Ludwig created a beautiful draft for the front cover. My friends and neighbors Rick and Shirley Lantz helped turn ideas in my head and words on a page into social media sites, submission ready manuscripts, and attractive covers. Kindle Direct Publishing and Create Space provided directions, templates, specifications, and distribution— priceless to a first time author.

The Maui, Hawai'i, and Aloha Writers Conferences gave me the chance to meet and learn from a number of authors, editors, and agents. I especially thank William Martin, Yvonne Medley, and Les Stobbe for their encouragement.

I'm forever indebted to William Bernhardt, a fantastic writer, teacher, mentor, and friend, who has taught me more about writing than anyone deserves to learn.

Christy, Jennifer, and Jonathan taught me everything else.

A NOTE ON THE SPELLING OF HAWAIIAN WORDS

Since moving to Maui, I have learned a great deal about the history and culture of the Hawaiian Islands. It is my desire to respect this ancient and vibrant culture in everything that I write in this beautiful place. But I am not a native Hawaiian or a speaker of the language, although I have learned a few phrases that I am not too embarrassed to speak aloud. This created a challenge for me when it came to spelling Hawaiian words.

Two characters are used in proper Hawaiian spelling that may be unfamiliar to those new to the language. These are the 'okina and kahakō.

The 'okina can be represented by an apostrophe, but is an actual consonant and represents a glottal stop. It may occur at the beginning or in the middle of a word and changes the pronunciation and meaning of words. An example familiar to many non-Hawaiians is the name of the island Lana'i (Lah-nah-ee), which is very different from the word for a veranda or covered patio, lanai (Lah-nigh). Throughout the novel I have used an apostrophe to represent this important consonant.

The kahakō indicates vowel length, which changes meaning and the placement of stress. In other languages it is referred to as a macron and represented by a line over a vowel. An example of how this impacts meaning in a Hawaiian word is the word kāne (kaa-nay) which means male while the same word without the kahakō, kane (ka-nay), means skin disease.

In this novel, I have elected to use the 'okina, but omit the use of the kahakō. I apologize to Native Hawaiian readers for my limitations. As I become more knowledgeable of this beautiful language and how to represent it in a computer file, I hope to do a better job of sharing it accurately.

I have also attempted to use the standard method for distinguishing non-English words, using italics for the first occurrence of such words, except for place names.

Part I: Left isn't Right

If you don't know where you are going, any road will get you there.

Lewis Carroll, author

Chapter One

Friday, March 15, 4:40 PM

For the first time in his life, Keone Boyd felt completely content.

He blew through eighty miles per hour on the one stretch of Maui road where that was possible. He just happened to know that no cops would be patrolling his route at this particular time on this particular day. He'd waited eighteen months for his brand new Morgan Roadster to be constructed and delivered dockside in Kahului. Now it was his.

Driving through the cane fields of central Maui with the top down, the wind whipped his mop of black hair. He knew he'd have to slow down to make the turn onto Honoapi'ilani Highway but savored his short burst of freedom.

Keone just missed the light, which allowed the traffic from the airport to catch up and fill both his and the inside lane. He shrugged and glanced in his side-view mirror. There must have been twenty cars waiting patiently for the light to change. He planned to be first in line when they reached the signal at Ma'alaea.

As soon as the light turned green, he gunned the three-liter

Ford Duratec V6 engine and matched the specs of zero to sixty in four-point-nine seconds, leaving all the other cars still waiting to turn. As he'd predicted, the light at Kapoli Street changed before he could get close enough to imagine it was still yellow. He drummed his fingers on the leather covering his steering wheel while the long line of cars caught up. Four pulled up behind him into the left turn lane and twice that number crammed the lane to his right. Looking left, he saw the green roofs of his condo complex. He and his Morgan were almost home.

Out of the corner of his eye he caught rapid movement.

What the hell?

A black Hummer approached at full speed, aimed directly at the cars stopped beside Keone. When the wrong-way driver saw the cars, he tried his best to swerve right and turn onto Kapoli. But the Hummer couldn't handle the sharp change in direction and began to tumble sideways into both lanes of stopped cars.

All Keone had time to ponder was, *Why now?*

The sound of the crash was tremendous, but stopped rapidly for Keone as the other vehicle crushed his beautiful new roadster with him inside.

Chapter Two

Friday, March 15, 6:29 PM

Detective Sergeant Keone Boyd burst through the automatic doors into the emergency room of Maui Memorial Hospital. In his mind two words described the scene. They were far more colorful and vulgar than the two he actually wrote in his notebook: *utter chaos*. The island hadn't dealt with an accident of this magnitude in its history. The wrong-way driver not only disabled fifteen other cars on the island's major east-west artery, he first totaled one pristine Morgan roadster. Keone was damn well going to find out why.

Seventy-four minutes earlier

Keone amazed the firemen who carved him out of the wreckage by being both alive and conscious. A brawny arm reached in to help him crawl out. He glanced at his watch to find it stopped, retrieved his notebook from his hip pocket, and wrote: *Time of collision 4:49 PM.*

"What time is it now?" he asked a fireman.

"5:15 PM. Sir, we need to take you to that ambulance to evaluate your injuries."

"I know the drill. I'm MPD."

The fireman's partner spoke up. "We know Sergeant Boyd.

3

We've worked together before."

Looking more closely at the two firemen, Keone smiled. "Kelly and Scottie. Sorry I didn't remember right off. Howzit?"

"Busy. You better check in with EMTs, Sergeant."

The EMTs were standing by an ambulance that Keone was not about to take a ride in. He recognized one of them. Eldon Miranda, pressing a thick layer of gauze against a young woman's lacerated cheek. Miranda looked up. "Hey Sarge, you okay?"

"Yeah, I was only out a couple minutes."

Miranda glanced at what was left of Keone's car and back at him twice before saying, "Yeah, right."

The efficient EMT finished affixing the bandage to the young woman, then smiled and nodded for her to get in the ambulance before turning to examine Keone.

In five minutes, Miranda had completed his examination. "You should be dead, you know. I'll cut you loose, Keone, but only if you promise to stop at the hospital and let them check you out. And I mean before you go anywhere else, even home." A doctor in the Philippines, Eldon worked as an EMT on Maui while studying for his U.S. license. Keone had worked numerous cases with him and respected his expertise.

"Don't worry doc, I'm going straight to the hospital. I need to see a man about a Hummer. I assume you guys sent the two from the Hummer directly to the hospital."

Eldon looked at his own notebook. "Yeah. Guy named Loftus was the driver—first name Samuel. The passenger was...uh...Marder—first name Leroy. They were both unconscious."

"Thanks, Eldon."

Keone walked over to three patrolmen on the scene and asked for the keys to the first man's car.

"Sure, Sergeant Boyd. I'll catch a ride back to the station with Manolo. You headed for the hospital?"

"Yeah. Hey, while I'm there you want me to take care of some of the grunt work for you guys?"

"Hell, yes. We're up to our asses in work right here."

4

"No worries. I'll square it with my lieutenant and your watch commander, then shoot you a copy of my supplemental statements."

"*Mahalo*, brah."

"Mahalo, Keali'i. I'll take good care of your ride." They both glanced at the scrap metal that used to be Keone's ride. Keone added, "Better than I took care of mine."

Friday, March 15, 6:30 PM

Keone flashed his badge at the first person that approached him in the ER. The expression on his face must have clued the young nurse that he was not up for polite conversation. She retreated from the pissed-off, six-foot-seven, two-hundred and seventy-five pound Hawaiian invading her space.

Keone could see most of the injuries were minor, although some elderly patients seemed to be having more trouble than the rest. Probably the shock of the collision set off existing heart, circulatory, or lung conditions in those folks. One kid, about three years old, had severe facial lacerations.

When would people quit ignoring the seatbelt laws?

As he passed the third treatment cubicle on his right, he noticed a wall clock. 6:35 PM. He'd made good time. He overheard a conversation coming from the cubicle that commanded his attention.

"Sammy was driving just as normal as can be, griping about all the damn tourists on the other side of the road coming from the airport. He got this weird look on his face—like he was about to hit a brick wall or something. I remember him saying, 'My God, everything's changed.' Then he swerved to the wrong side of the road just before the stoplight at Kapoli.

"He tried to swerve back at the light to miss all the cars. But the Hummer started bouncing down the road sideways. I didn't know whether to shit or go blind. I saw the front half of the car headed for the left turn lane. That first car in line was sure a beaut. It looked brand new.

"My half of the windshield was pointed right at the driver

before the Hummer bounced up and steamrolled the back half of his car. I'll never forget the look on his face.

"I sure hope his airbag worked. Sam's knocked me silly, but it saved my life. Next thing I knew I woke up here."

Keone pulled the curtain open to find a man of about sixty years propped up on the bed. A grey-haired, no nonsense nurse that Keone knew well from previous visits to the ER was cleaning abrasions on the man's face, chest, and arms with disinfectant.

He flashed his badge at both of them, flipped open his notebook, and spoke to the man.

"You're Mr. Marder–Mr. Leroy Marder?"

"That's me. But call me Lee, okay?"

"You were riding in the car with Mr. Loftus when the accident occurred. Is that correct?"

"Yes, I was. Scariest damn thing I ever saw."

"Could you tell me exactly what happened?"

"Well, like I was telling this lovely young lady here, we left work at four-thirty, like we always do on Aloha Fridays. Most of the trip from Lahaina was as normal as could be. Sam had his usual Friday CD playing. He had a different CD for each day of the week. This one started with the Aloha Friday song. You know:

It's Aloha Friday,
No work 'til Monday,
Doot de doo,
De doot de doot de doot de doot de doo."

"Yes, I know the song. What happened next?"

"He played some Bruddah Iz, some Keola Beamer, some Keali'i Reichel—"

"No, I mean when did the drive get less normal?"

"Well, right when we passed the harbor entrance, just before that big old restaurant...uh, Buzz's, everything got wonky."

"Wonky?"

"Well, this thing happened, then Old Sammy swerved into the wrong lane. I call him Old Sammy cause he's so much younger than me, get it?"

"Yes. You say he swerved?"

"Yeah, but when he saw all them cars lined up in his lane, he tried to swerve back at the signal to miss 'em. His big old hummer had too much momentum and started to roll. Damned if we didn't end up hitting both lanes."

"What thing happened?"

"Huh?"

"Before he swerved the first time, you said 'this thing happened.'"

"I'm not exactly sure, because it only happened to Sammy."

"Did he say anything?"

"He sort of cringed at first, then he said he was on the wrong side of the road and swerved into the wrong lane."

"Did he say anything else, Mr. Marder? Think carefully."

"Yeah, right after he cringed he said, 'Did you hear that pop?'"

"Did you?"

"No, there wasn't a sound."

"Can you remember anything else?"

"Well, Sam said, 'Did you hear that pop?' Then he started talking weird."

"Exactly what did he say?"

"He said, 'It was like a huge soap bubble. My God, everything's changed. I'm on the wrong side of the road!' Then he swerved onto the wrong side and.... Hey. Aren't you the guy that was in the first car we hit?"

Keone nodded.

"Your face was the last thing I saw before I woke up here. Thank God you're okay."

"Thank you, Mr. Marder. Here's my card. If you think of anything else, give me a call."

"You're a detective? Boy is Sam screwed."

Chapter Three

Friday, March 15, 6:50 PM

After his interview with Marder, Keone asked the nurse to take him to Sam Loftus.

"I have to stay with my patient, Sergeant. Why don't you ask someone at the desk which cubical he's in?" She pushed open the curtain indicating he should leave.

Keone left but avoided the desk and grabbed the arm of the next doctor to walk by. Glancing at the man's nametag, he said, "Excuse me, Doctor Wayne?"

"Yes. How can I help you."

"I'm Sergeant Boyd of the Maui PD. Could you tell me where I could find Mr. Samuel Loftus? I need to speak with him."

"No problem. I'm Sam's family doctor. Just got here myself. They called my office once they identified Sam. He's supposed to be in the fifth cubical on the left."

"Before we see him, is there anything I should know about him? Does he have any medical conditions that could have contributed to the accident?"

Dr. Wayne ran his fingers through his thick, black hair,

pushed his glasses up on his nose, and cleared his throat before speaking. "I've been Sam and Janet's doctor ever since they moved to Maui."

"Janet?"

"Sam's wife."

"I see."

"To answer your question, I just gave Sam his annual check-up last month and all his results were fine."

"What about any emotional problems or odd habits?"

"No. He's relatively reserved. He exercises regularly and maintains a healthy diet. He's very meticulous, but that comes with the territory when you're an accountant."

"Is he on any medications?"

"Nothing unusual for a man his age."

Keone didn't expect to get a straight answer but was paid to ask.

"Nothing then that could explain the crash?"

"No. May I see my patient now?"

"Yeah. Let's go." Keone knew he wasn't going to get anything else of value from Wayne. Nothing unusual. The doctor was clearly worried about his friend and patient.

Keone followed the doctor into the designated cubical to find an attractive, impeccably-dressed woman of about thirty standing at the side of an emergency room bed. The man in the bed had a lump on his forehead and appeared confused. He looked about the room anxiously. "How did I get here?" he asked.

Keone guessed Sam Loftus had just regained consciousness.

The woman at his side leaned over and kissed the patient on his forehead. Her honey-blonde hair fell across his cheek. "It's good to have you back, Sam."

He stared at the woman for a moment and said, "Janet, how nice of you to come by. I had an accident, didn't I?"

"Yes, but you're in the hospital now." Janet squeezed his hand. "They'll fix you up as good as new."

"How long was I out?"

Janet glanced at her watch, "They told me the crash was right before five o'clock and it's nearly seven now."

"Two hours. Everything's so strange. Has anyone told Julie?"

"Uh...no, I came here as soon as they called. I'll call everyone as soon as I'm sure you're really okay. Why are you so concerned about my sister Julie?" She glanced at Dr. Wayne, who shrugged his shoulders.

Sam laughed. "Well, I think my wife should know about this, don't you?"

"I do know. I'm right here."

"And, I'm very grateful, Janet, but you aren't my wife and I really do need to see her."

Keone watched Janet's look of concern turn to one of fear.

"Stop this right now, Sam Loftus. If you think this is funny, it isn't—"

Dr. Wayne touched Janet's arm to calm her. "Sam, do you know who I am?"

"I ought to, Bob. I beat you at golf every Saturday, let you deliver our babies, and very occasionally let you treat me when I'm sick. I guess around this place I should call you Dr. Wayne, sorry."

"Sam, I'm glad to see that you know me, but you're talking kind of strangely. What kids did I deliver?"

"Our kids, of course. Cindy and Timmy."

"You and Janet don't have any kids."

"Of course we don't. I prefer to make babies with my wife, not her sister. That would be kinky."

"Have you been taking your medications as prescribed?"

"Ah, a trick question. You know I'm strong as a horse. I don't need any magic pills, at least not yet. Hell, I'm only thirty-six."

"Yes, you are. Just rest for now, Sam. I'll be back in a little while."

"Okay, but bring Julie next time. I really need to let her know I'm all right."

"I'll let her know right away." Dr. Wayne motioned to Janet

Loftus and Keone, guiding them out of the cube. Before he left the cubicle, Dr. Wayne stopped to talk with the nurse. He then walked Janet and Keone to the far end of the ER.

Chapter Four

Friday, March 15, 7:15 PM

They departed the surrealism of Sam's bedside for the relative normality of the ER hallway. Janet slowly raised her hands to her face and began to cry.

Dr. Wayne cupped her shoulder with his hand. "Janet, Sam suffered a head trauma. On initial examination, the ER doctors thought his injuries were minor. His behavior just now suggests it's a bit more serious. I don't want you to worry, though. Disorientation and even temporary amnesia are quite common in injuries like this. Remember, he's conscious and able to speak, so his prognosis is good. The fact that he recognized you and me, even though he confused you and Julie, is actually a good sign."

"A good sign? He doesn't even know I'm his wife." She glared at the doctor through tear-glazed eyes.

"He's disoriented. I'm sure twenty-four hours from now he'll be back to his old meticulously accurate self. In the meantime I'm going to get him up to a private room and give him a mild sedative. I'll perform a complete exam tomorrow and schedule a battery of tests—if he still needs them. After a good night's sleep, he may well snap out of this temporary disorientation."

"I pray you're right. Can I go back in with him?"

"I need you to hold off until tomorrow. I know you want to be with him, but we can't risk upsetting him. It's critical we do nothing to enhance his disorientation. The best thing you can do right now is go home and get a good night's sleep. Do you still have those blue pills I prescribed last month?"

"Yes, but I—"

"Take one—just to take the edge off—about a half-hour before your regular bedtime. Trust me, Janet. I'm the doctor." He gave her a hug before placing his hand on her back and gently guiding her toward the exit.

Keone watched this exchange with increasing interest. He waited until the wife was gone before speaking to Dr. Wayne. "I understand why you wanted her to go. But I need to ask Mr. Loftus a few questions before you sedate him—for my report."

"I understand. I've worked with the police before and know the drill. But it'll have to wait until tomorrow. I'm afraid he's already been sedated."

Keone remembered the discussion Wayne had with the nurse as he ushered them from the cubicle. If he'd worked with the police before, his actions could suggest a hidden agenda.

"Let me get him moved to a private room and through the night. Then you can ask him any questions you want, as long as you keep it brief."

Not satisfied, Keone held himself in check. He knew Wayne was seriously concerned about his patient's ability to get through the night with what remained of his sanity. Though his detective side suspected Wayne was isolating Sam from interrogation for some other reason.

"You're concerned about him."

"I am. His physical condition doesn't explain his confusion."

"Aside from the obvious things, did you notice anything unusual about him?"

"Well he seemed more gregarious than usual, and wittier. It could just be the result of adrenaline producing nervous energy. He also seems more muscular than when I saw him for his check-up. I'll have to ask Janet if he's been working out."

"If you hadn't told me about him before I went in, I would have thought him surprisingly lucid for having just suffered such a severe trauma."

"Every patient is different. Sam's world is very ordered. And he was just confronted with the ultimate in disorder. It's essential he avoid facing additional challenges right now. I'm sure his neurons will be firing more normally in the morning."

Keone backed off. "I understand, doctor. I know you want to do what's best for your patient. You say you've worked with the police before?"

"Yes."

"Then you understand that my lieutenant expects an interview with such a key witness within twenty-four hours of the incident. I'll be back tomorrow morning at ten to question him."

"Agreed."

Wayne re-entered his patient's cubicle, leaving Keone no choice but to head for the exit. He reached the doors he'd so recently plowed through before a hand grabbed his shoulder.

"Sergeant Boyd. Why am I not surprised to see you once again in a restricted area where you have no business?"

"Dr. Lloyd. Nice to see you again."

"Wish I could say the same. You cannot be in the Emergency Room."

"I'm just leaving."

"That's not good enough. After your last escapade, Lieutenant Alcala promised me you would never again disrupt the critical activities of this emergency room. I'm reporting this."

"I was just in a car accident. The EMT told me to get checked out in the ER before going home."

"I didn't see your chart in the rack."

"The doc looked me up and down and said I was fine. Given the number of other patients you have in here tonight, I didn't want to keep him." Keone wasn't anxious for another negative report to reach Lieutenant Tony Alcala's desk.

"Oh. Well, just see to it this doesn't happen again." With that Lloyd walked off. Keone hoped he'd talked his way out of another reprimand.

Chapter Five

Saturday, March 16, 7:25 AM

Sam Loftus opened his eyes to find he was lying on a cool, firm bed in a sparsely decorated room. He recognized the odd flat shape against his right upper arm as a blood pressure cuff, suggesting strongly he wasn't in a cheap hotel. As the pale dawn light crept through a gap in the window blinds, scattered memories from the day before crept into his awareness. A wild, spinning sensation. A man's face filled with surprise in a shiny new car. A loud crunch. Severe pain.

He instinctively reached for his forehead and touched the tender lump above his right eye. His chest hurt, as well. Pulling down the sheet, he saw a diagonal bruise.

A car accident.

In the ER, the same face from the shiny car studying him while Bob Wayne talked foolishness. Julie's sister trying to convince everyone that she's his wife.

The pieces slid together at last, but the image they created was disturbing. It must have been the drugs they gave him. Today everything would return to normal. Order would be restored to his life.

Looking around the room, Sam began to notice individual objects. A bedside table stood solidly to his left. One of those little over-bed tables was on that side too, turned away from the bed but waiting patiently on its wheeled base. Looking up, his eyes followed the U-shaped track for a privacy curtain, which was pulled all the way back to his right. Beyond the privacy curtain, adjacent to the door, he saw a chart on the wall marked with some scribbles he couldn't read. The pale round face of a clock looked down on him from across the room. As his eyes focused on the numbers, he flinched.

"What the hell?" His voice echoed in the empty room.

As if in response, a nurse entered his room and said, "So you've decided to join us this morning. Can you tell me your name?"

"Sam Loftus."

"Good morning Mr. Loftus."

"Good morning. Are you my nurse?"

"I'm one of them—the best one. Do you remember why you're here, Mr. Loftus?"

"I seem to recall an accident. A car accident?"

"Yes. You were involved in a car accident. How do you feel?"

"I feel like my face was crushed by an airbag. How do you feel?"

The nurse came over to his side, straightened his arm, and fiddled with the blood pressure cuff before sticking her stethoscope's earpieces into her ears.

Sam decided conversation could wait until she finished.

He spotted her nametag and received his second shock of the morning. He couldn't read it. After a bit of study he realized why. It was in mirror writing. Slowly he translated, discovering his nurse's name was Gwen Tanaka.

When she finally deflated the cuff and removed her stethoscope, Sam asked, "Is this backwards day, Gwen? Surprise, I can still work out your name."

Gwen's face displayed only confusion.

"And where'd you get a clock with the numbers increasing counterclockwise and a movement that runs in reverse? A friend of mine in college had a watch like that, but it had Goofy on it. It's 7:35 AM, right?"

Gwen glanced at the clock and back at Sam. "Yes, Mr. Loftus." She removed a small penlight from her pocket. "Could you please look at this light for me."

Sam looked at the light and followed it with his eyes when she moved it to each side. She walked to the back of Sam's door and retrieved his chart. She flipped open the chart and busily inscribed his blood pressure readings and whatever her penlight had disclosed. Sam winced when he realized everything she wrote, and everything else in the chart, was in mirror writing. She continued in this exotic script with no more effort than if she'd been writing normally. He managed to translate the last two words, *extremely disoriented.*

Before he could comment on Gwen's bizarre behavior, she slipped from the room, leaving Sam flummoxed.

What the hell is happening to me?

Part II: Examinations

All this time the Guard was looking at her, first through a telescope, then through a microscope, and then through an opera-glass. At last he said, "You're traveling the wrong way," and shut up the window and went away.

Lewis Carroll, author

RICK LUDWIG

Chapter Six

Saturday, March 16, 9:35 AM

Two hours after Sam's encounter with the nurse, Bob Wayne entered the room, pasting a big smile on his face. Inside Bob felt nervous as hell. Sam's behavior last night was the strangest he'd ever encountered.

Patting Sam's shoulder, Bob said, "Good morning Sam, welcome back to the real world. I trust that a good night's sleep helped get all the neurons firing properly. I'm sure you still hurt a bit, but I'd like to do a brief exam before I let you have any more pain medication, okay?"

"Okay, but don't take all day."

"The first portion of the exam may seem a bit silly to you, but after a head injury like yours we have to check everything. Do you understand?" Bob said, using his most reassuring family doctor voice.

"Sure. But let me tell you right off that my name is Sam Loftus and I was born on September 7th, a tad over thirty-six and a half years ago—if today is indeed March 16th, as I assume it is."

"It is indeed, Sammy. You answer the rest of my questions like that and I'll have you out of here before you know it. Do you remember much about yesterday?"

"I remember driving home from Lahaina with Lee Marder and having a traffic accident. From that point until this morning, I'm not sure what was dream and what was real. You must have given me some good stuff in that IV."

"The next series of questions regards things you know that I know, but please humor me, all right?"

Sam nodded.

"Where were you born?"

"Newport Beach, California."

"Where did you go to high school?"

"Newport Harbor High School. We were the Sailors."

"Who were your parents?"

"My dad, Joseph Loftus, was a Computer Systems Analyst and worked in Irvine for a medical device company. My mother, Frances, was a librarian—she would say library scientist—who worked at UC Irvine. She was born here in Hawai'i."

"Brothers or sisters?"

"I'm an only child."

"Who is your closest friend?"

"Dave Walden's been my best friend since college. His wife is my wife's sister and the four of us spend most of our time together."

Bob nodded and made an entry in the chart:

Confusion from last night seems to be resolved. Answered all questions about background accurately. Exaggerated a bit about relationship to Walden, but consistent with earlier, closer relationship.

"What is David's occupation?"

"David? Aren't we being a little formal? You're Dave's doctor, too. Dave's a lawyer."

"And?"

"And a damn good ocean kayaker, but not as good as me."

"I meant does he have any other job?"

"Do you think he needs one?"

"No, of course not."

Bob now had the answer to a question that had troubled Dave Walden enough to call Bob and send him rushing to the hospital after the crash. Bob remembered his surprise at Dave's call. He was even more surprised when Dave told him about Sam's accident. How did he learn about it so quickly? Bob knew Dave had a broad network that included members of the police force, but didn't realize he was this well connected.

Last night, seeing how disoriented Sam was, Bob thought it best to sedate him before that nosy detective could ask him any questions. Walden had thanked him when Bob reported back after he left Sam.

"When did you last see Dave?"

"I think it was Christmas."

Bob paused at that and made another note:

Memory lapse noted, but it is recent—the last six months—not unusual after such trauma. Check with Walden about ocean kayaking.

He decided to get right to the area of Sam's confusion from the night before.

"Tell me about your family."

"I'm married. We celebrate our thirteenth anniversary in June."

Good.

"We have two children. Cindy is eight and Timmy will be five next month. I spoil them both, but Julie keeps them in line."

Oh shit.

Bob struggled to maintain his neutral expression and plowed ahead.

"Tell me about your wife."

"Julie is brilliant and beautiful. She's a fantastic pediatrician, as you well know, and was named Chief of Pediatrics at this fine institution last month. A well-deserved promotion which I'm sure you helped along."

Bob ignored the comment. "Who is Janet?"

"Janet is Julie's sister, Janet Walden, Dave's wife. They have two children as well, named Rain and Mist. They're four-year-old twins. I remember how happy they all were when the adoptions became final. I don't know if all Korean girls are beautiful, but these two could melt your...What are you writing down? You know all this stuff."

Bob looked up from the chart, where he had just written:

Delusions include fantasy children for friend as well as self. Still believes sister-in-law is wife and vice versa. Also believes sister-in-law is a pediatrician instead of a writer.

"I need a comprehensive record of this examination, especially the stuff I already know. Let's get back to you. What is your occupation and where did you receive your training?"

"I got a degree in accounting at Indiana University followed by an MBA at IU Kelley School of Business. An international property management group headquartered in Indianapolis, called Resorts Unlimited, hired me right out of grad school. I moved to the Maui branch eight years ago, where I'm currently CFO. My office is in Lahaina and I live in Pukalani."

Bob wrote again in the file.

Knowledge of education and occupational situation mostly unimpaired. Dates his move to Maui to two years later than it was.

"Okay. Let's move on to the physical exam. First I'm going to touch you in a few places, gently. You tell me if anything is tender."

The poking and prodding went on for about five minutes with no unexpected findings. If anything, Sam was exhibiting less head, face, and neck pain than Bob had expected.

"Now, let's check range of motion. Can you lift your head a couple of inches off the pillow? Not too far. That's good. Now turn your head to the left."

Sam turned his head to the right.

"Ah, okay. Good. Now turn it back to the middle.

Excellent. You're moving smoothly. Are you having any pain in your neck?"

"Not much."

"Good. Now turn your head to the right."

Sam turned his head to the left.

Struggling to suppress a frown, Bob said, "Turn your head back to the middle and let it fall back onto the pillow slowly."

Sam did.

"Okay. Let's check your arms and legs. Lift your left arm."

Sam lifted his right arm.

"Point your index finger down."

Sam did.

"Up."

Sam did.

"You can rest your arm now, Sam"

Bob wrote in the chart:

Right-left inversion appears complete. No evidence of up-down inversion.

"Lift your right arm this time and point up and down."

Sam lifted his left arm and pointed up and down.

"Put it back down and we'll check your legs."

Bob was not surprised that Sam showed the same inversion for his legs, movement of his eyes, and identification of locations touched on his body.

"Sam, do you see the clock on the wall?"

"Yeah, and what's the joke? Why is it backwards?"

"Can you tell the time?"

"Sure. It's ten, uh A.M., I assume."

"That's right."

"Are we about done?"

"Almost. Let me show you something. I'll be right back."

With that Bob left Sam's room and went to the nurses' station. He found the item he needed and noticed the police sergeant from last night had arrived. Bob held up one finger to indicate he'd be with him in just a minute.

When he returned to the room, he asked Sam, "Do you know what this is?"

"Uh...yes. I believe it's called a newspaper. Are you all right, Bob?"

"Humor me. Can you read it?"

"Not easily. It's written in mirror writing, you jerk. What kind of test is this?"

"Let's try something," Bob said, as he moved the cross-bed table in place and opened the hinged section on the right to display a mirror. Pointing the paper at the mirror he asked, "Can you read it now?"

"Of course. **Maui police baffled by wrong way driver. Injuries surprisingly minor.**"

"How about that small print on the bottom...uh...right of the page?"

"**Remains of museum destroyed by terrorist bomber. AP photo.**"

Bob wrote in the chart.

Patient expresses difficulty reading newspaper, but surprising fluency reading mirror image of the same newspaper.

Bob returned to the physical exam. When he was done he said, "Physically you are recovering very nicely. I'm still concerned about your short-term memory. I need to run a full battery of tests just to be safe."

"What kind of tests?"

"You know MRI, EEG, a few neuromuscular tests, and memory and perception tests. They're pretty routine for a traumatic head injury like yours."

"Okay, but get on with it. I don't plan to spend much longer in this hospital, or this bed."

"We'll be getting you up by tomorrow at the latest. Today, just relax and let us check you out top to bottom."

"But mostly top, right? Is there something seriously wrong, Bob? Tell me the truth."

"On the whole you're doing very well for someone who

just rolled a car and smashed into two lanes of traffic. There are a couple of things I want to look at further, but they may well be gone by the time we test for them. Just concentrate on getting better."

"Okay, but when you're sure, you have to tell me if there's something I need to know."

"I will. I will. You're not just a patient. You're a friend. I have two more questions to ask. I'll tell you if you get them right, okay?"

Sam nodded.

"What hemisphere is Australia in?"

"The southern."

"Where does the sun rise and set?"

"The sun rises in the east and sets in the west."

"Absolutely correct. I'll see you tomorrow. And get some rest."

"Can I see Julie?"

"Very soon."

Chapter Seven

Saturday, March 16, 10:10 AM

Keone Boyd was waiting at the nurse's station when Dr. Wayne returned. Last night, on a hunch he'd examined Dr. Wayne's interactions with the Maui PD, before finally heading home to bed. The good doctor didn't have a serious record, but he'd been investigated a couple of times for questionable prescription practices. His file also contained hints of a flirtation with methamphetamine abuse. He was never charged, but the name David Walden appeared associated with his file as *amicus curiae*. Keone also discovered that the E.R. staff had not called Dr. Wayne last night. He'd just shown up.

"Hello, Sergeant Boyd. I suppose you want to see my patient."

"Yes. I appreciate your help in expediting this. My lieutenant would have my ass if I waited too long to take this statement."

"All right. I'll give you ten minutes before I re-medicate him, but you need to do something for me. He's still saying some things that suggest he has a brain injury. If he says or does anything unusual, please don't do anything to make him aware of his behavior. After you finish, let me know what you observe, okay? That way, I can get the unbiased impressions of a second individual."

The doctor's words struck Keone as odd, but he agreed to the conditions after bargaining to be allowed fifteen minutes with Loftus.

As he entered the room, he heard Dr. Wayne say, "Fifteen minutes, no more," to the nurse.

"Good morning Mr. Loftus. I'm Sergeant Boyd of the Maui Police Department. I have a few questions for you regarding the accident yesterday." Keone flipped open his ID and handed it to the man.

"Weren't you in the first car I hit?" Sam replied, returning the leather case.

"Yes, but that's not why I'm here."

"I'm sorry about your beautiful car. It was a Morgan, wasn't it?"

"Yes, but I—"

"My Uncle Bob had one of those. I think he loved it more than he did my Aunt Terry. A beautiful little car."

"I only have fifteen minutes, Mr. Loftus. Do you remember leaving for work yesterday morning?"

Loftus closed his eyes and concentrated. "Yes. I walked out our front door and waved goodbye to Julie before driving off. Just like every morning."

Keone noticed Sam said Julie instead of Janet. "Was it a normal day at work?"

"Perfectly." Again Loftus closed his eyes and concentrated. "I parked in my regular spot, and walked up the stairs to my office. While I was opening the door, Lee Marder came by to ask me for a lift home. We joked about the crushing boredom of our jobs before I walked into my cubicle and started right to work."

Keone noted the level of detail in Sam's answer. "And where is it you work?"

"I'm CFO for Resorts Unlimited's West Maui office."

"And Mr. Marder works there, too?"

"Lee is responsible for the entire complex. It includes retail outlets and restaurants as well as offices like ours. He can fix anything. He spent years as a contractor in Denver doing remodeling."

"What happened on the drive home?"

"I was driving from Lahaina to Pukalani, just like I do every day. Lee and I were talking and listening to music, when I had the strangest feeling."

"What sort of feeling?"

"I felt like I passed through a kind of film, like a clear bubble, and heard a loud pop."

Keone wrote in his notebook:

Story corroborates Marder's observation.

"Was it just your body that passed through or the entire car?" As weird as this sounded, Keone acted as if passing through a clear bubble was the most natural thing in the world.

"That's a good question. You know, I think it was just my body. The bubble seemed to move inside the car and wrap around me. It didn't seem to touch Lee either, so I asked him if he heard the pop."

"What did he say?"

"He said he didn't hear anything. That's when I noticed everything was wrong."

"What do you mean wrong?"

"We were on the wrong side of the road. I was on the wrong side of the car. The road signs were unreadable. I swerved to the right-hand side of the road. But you were there...and all those other cars. There was nowhere to go. I tried to turn left around the corner, but started rolling over and over..."

Keone looked into Sam's eyes. "You say you swerved to the right."

"Uh-huh. I discovered I was on the left-hand side of the road and moved over to the right."

"Which way did you turn the wheel?"

"To the right, of course."

"Close your eyes. I need you to imagine you are in the car driving along before you hit the bubble."

"Really?"

"Humor me."

Keone watched Sam put out his hands and grasp an imaginary steering wheel.

"Okay you hit the bubble, now."

Sam flinched.

"You realize you're on the wrong side of the road and turn the wheel."

Sam made a sharp turning motion with his hands. Keone noted he turned the wheel to the left, as he actually did to enter the wrong lane. Not the right as he'd claimed.

"And then you try to turn to miss me and the others?"

"Yes," Sam said, jerking the imaginary steering wheel sharply to the right.

"What way did you just turn the wheel?"

"To the left, just like I told you."

"You can open your eyes now."

"That's enough," Doctor Wayne announced upon entering the room. "I must ask you to please leave—now."

Keone refrained from commenting on Dr. Wayne's edict. "That's okay, we were wrapping up anyway. Thank you for your time Mr. Loftus."

Keone left the room but paused outside the door. Intrigued at the interaction, he flipped open his notebook and wrote:

Who is Sam Loftus, really? What was he like before the crash? Does he really think his right is his left or is he a great actor? Most important is he criminally responsible for the crash?

Chapter Eight

Saturday, March 16, 10:30 AM

After the detective and Bob Wayne left, Sam began to review his three recent interactions: the nurse, Bob, and Sergeant Boyd. Something was odd about this. Why were they all so obsessed with left and right? Why were they showing him all these weird reversed images, the clock, the newspaper? Why had all those cars been parked at the stoplight on the wrong side of the road?

"What the hell's going on here?" he asked the empty room.

He noticed there was an inhalation therapist sitting outside his room reading a paperback book. *She must be waiting for her next appointment.* Sam decided he needed to see the cover of that book, but the therapist's back blocked his view. Ringing the call button would just bring his nurse and not cause the woman to turn the way he wanted, so he started banging his head on the over-bed table. Before the nurse could run in and shut the door, the therapist turned to look at the commotion. The book in her hand had a familiar cover. Sam recognized it at once as one of John Lescroart's excellent thrillers, *The Hunter.* Unfortunately, on the cover he saw The Hunter was in mirror writing along with all of the other words.

In that brief instant, before the nurse could close the door he glanced into the room across the hall and saw the television was showing *The Price is Right.* The camera focused on a stage prop with increasing amounts of money. The amounts were all in mirror writing.

That was too much. They couldn't have carried the joke this far. Something was wrong with the rest of the hospital. Maybe more.

Nurse Tanaka hurried to the bed and pulled him back from the bedside table. "What's going on, Mr. Loftus? Are you troubled?"

"I'm simply fabulous."

"But you were banging your head on the table."

"Was I?" Sam temporized. "Ow, yes, my forehead hurts. Do you think I just fell asleep and my head banged on the table?"

"No, I heard three distinct bangs. When I came in, I saw you bang it the fourth time and your eyes were definitely open. Don't you remember?"

"Damned if I don't. Maybe it's a reaction to one of those drugs you're giving me through this plastic tunnel in my arm. I do have a few allergies."

"I'll ask your doctor. For now, I'm going to remove the table from the room. Do you mind?"

"Do whatever you need to keep me safe. I'm sure glad you came in when you did. I could have beaten myself senseless."

The nurse looked as though she didn't buy what Sam was saying. But he was so sincere about it she let it go.

"Okay I've moved the table outside and pinned your call button next to your right hand. If you need me, call me. I'll be right back. I want to talk with your doctor before I take you for your tests."

Sam guessed his little bit of acting would mean a few more tests, but didn't care. Getting wheeled around more of the hospital would just provide him more opportunities to glimpse the outside world.

Sam couldn't help noticing she'd pinned the call button by his left hand. Something was clearly wrong here. And he was damn well going to find out what.

Chapter Nine

Saturday, March 16, 12:00 PM

After debriefing Dr. Wayne, Keone drove straight to Lahaina. He didn't tell the doctor the additional details Sam had shared about the accident but did confirm Wayne's observation that Sam seemed to have his left and right confused. He wasn't anxious to share anything more with Dr. Wayne, until he learned about his connection to Sam's brother-in-law.

He reached Lahaina at noon to find Resorts Unlimited didn't open until 1 PM on Saturday. *Welcome to Maui Standard Time.* Keone knew that on Maui people are in when they're in.

He was happy to discover that the complex that held Sam's office also housed a favorite hangout of his during the days he worked out of District Four in Lahaina. Lahaina Fresheners was just downstairs from Resorts Unlimited. From the outdoor seating area Keone could keep an eye on the entrance to Sam's office. The owner/bartender, Max, had been a friend for years and knew pretty much everything that went on in West Maui.

Max poured Keone his usual, a mango cooler (non-alcoholic), before greeting him with "Howzit?"

"No good. My new car got hammered at Ma'alaea."

"No shit? How'd it go down?"

"Wrong-way driver."

"God damn tourists!"

"No, a local guy. He works around here."

"Was it Walden?"

"No, a guy named Loftus, Sam Loftus. Know him?"

"Just to say hi. He's okay I guess, but pretty boring and he's got, how you call dat, COD."

"OCD. Yeah, I've heard that about him. Who's Walden?"

"He's sort of related to Sam. His wife and Sam's are sisters or something."

"Oh." Keone opened his notebook. "Janet and Julie."

"Yeah. Julie, that's Dave Walden's wife, she's quite a looker, but real sweet. Walden, he's a player. She deserves better."

"What about Loftus? Is he a player?"

"No. Like I said, he's boring. Spends all his evenings at home with his wife. She's pretty, too, but a little stiff. He brought her in here once, but she turned her nose up at the friendliness of some of our regulars. They never came back."

"What about Walden?"

"He's here most afternoons, drinkin' and shmoozin'. Always seems to be entertaining guys from out of town."

"One particular guy?"

"No. That's just it. Lots of different guys from all over. East coast, west coast, Australia, even Europe."

With that Max headed back to the kitchen to create Keone's regular grind, one of his special monster burritos. Keone knew these babies were not for the squeamish.

While he waited, he wrote in his notebook:

Dave Walden. Best friend (?) and brother-in-law of driver. Looker wife. Player. Interesting contacts. Follow up.

Sam Loftus. Boring life. Stiff wife (?) Stays home a lot.

"Why we don't see you 'round here so much no more, Keone?" Max asked as he placed a burrito the size of a large cat in front of him.

"Once I made detective, I was assigned to Division One in Wailuku. I'm part of CID."

"Criminal Investigation Division. I got an uncle wid that

bunch. Terrell Mason." Despite his island boy speech pattern, Max knew what was what. He had degrees from UH and the Culinary Institute of America.

"I know him very well. I didn't know he was your uncle. He's a good detective," Keone said, then poured a thick layer of Max's homemade hot sauce on the burrito.

Seeing this, Max poured Keone another mango cooler. "I'll keep deese comin'."

Keone smiled as the first, fiery bite reached his tongue. Strong men had been reduced to tears by a drop of Max's hot sauce, but Keone loved it. The secret to survival was to take it slow and savor each bite. He knew he had enough time to do it right.

Keone finished his burrito and wiped his mouth—a key step—before dousing his throat with the rest of his fourth cooler. He then sat back, fully satisfied and observed a young woman jog past, bounce up the stairs, and unlock the offices of Resorts Unlimited. He'd get around to Sam's boss and co-workers, but always preferred to start his questioning with the person at the front desk. Receptionists always seemed to absorb more of what was going on than those stuffed away in private offices or cubicles and were generally anxious to talk.

"Thanks, Max. See you on the other side." Keone tossed down fifty percent more than the cost of his lunch.

"You know it, brah," Max said as he scooped the money off the table. It wasn't a good idea to leave loose change on the outside tables.

Keone introduced himself to receptionist. Kimberley—Kimmey—Kanamalu, a lovely island girl of about twenty. Island girl was a term Keone liked. It recognized that she was from the islands, but didn't try to sort out her ethnicity. Hawai'i is the melting pot of melting pots. Keone was Hawaiian, Portuguese, and Scottish. Most of his friends on island were also complex mixtures of the different waves of immigrants who settled on these islands

"Kimmey, tell me about Sam Loftus. I'm interested in what he was like before the accident," Keone began.

"Oh, everybody loves Sammy. He's a sweetheart. He always wishes everybody good morning. Every day. And he brings in food to share from home. His wife loves to cook and Sammy loves to share."

"Does he often work late or come in early?"

"Not really. He's always ahead on his work. He works steady all day, but never seems stressed out. He's very, very organized. All the other guys respect him for that. I don't think I ever heard Mr. Casey criticize Sam for anything."

"Did he ever praise him?" Keone asked.

"You know, I don't think I ever hear him praise Sam, either. Sam doesn't like compliments. He likes to stay out the spotlight, yeah? On his ten-year anniversary with the firm, they planned to make a big deal about giving him this special pen, but Sam found out. He begged Mr. Casey to give it to him privately. I just think he's kinda shy, but very sweet."

"Does he have any close friends at work?"

"Well he and Lee talk a lot at lunch. I hear Sam and Dave Walden, his brother-in-law, were best friends when Sam moved here. But they had some kind of falling out right after Sam came. They still get together because they're *'ohana*, but not too close anymore."

Keone's own *'ohana*, Hawaiian for family, was very large but they remained close. 'Ohana was important on Maui.

"Dave's a lawyer. He had an office in this building, until he became his wife's agent full-time, about six months ago. Since then he's been winding down his practice. I think I saw Dave packing some stuff in his old office this morning."

"Where's Dave's office?"

"Right down the hall on the left. See, the door's still open."

Keone decided to postpone his interview of Sam's boss until after he talked with Dave Walden. Kimmey said he could meet the boss in an hour. So he agreed to return then. He headed across the hallway to attorney David Walden's former office.

Chapter Ten

Saturday, March 16, 1:00 PM

Sam was fed up. After a morning of being poked, prodded, and visualized with everything from sound waves to X-rays to some kind of radioactive crap, Gwen finally rolled him back to his room. He *had* gotten to see more of the hospital. But seeing more walls covered with mirror writing signs wasn't reassuring. Those same signs hadn't been reversed when he visited an old friend from work here six months ago.

He even got a few glimpses of the parking lot and the road that passed the hospital. All of the license plates were reversed and traffic passed blissfully by on the wrong side of the road.

Bob came by during lunch to tell him they were getting closer to figuring out what was wrong with him but wouldn't answer any direct questions or give Sam a clue as to when he could go home. He also told him another doctor would be coming by to see him.

A little after 1:00 PM, Bob returned. Sam was propped up in bed writing in the journal he'd begun. His entries appeared completely normal to him. To everyone else he was writing swiftly and effortlessly in mirror writing. He looked up to see Julie follow Bob into the room.

Julie glanced at the journal and tensed for a moment when she came over to give Sam a hug and a very chaste kiss on the forehead. Before Sam could grab her and embrace her properly, she had moved out of range and taken a seat.

She sat down carefully, as though afraid to make a sound. "Oh, Sam. I'm so sorry to see you like this. How are they treating you here?"

"Sweetheart, why has it taken you so long to come? I've missed you so much. How are the kids?"

"Everyone is fine, Sam. We're all just so worried about you." Sam noticed she looked over at Bob as if for approval.

Bob smiled then turned to Sam. "I can't let Julie stay too long right now. We have a lot more tests to run. We're going to figure out how to make you well, my friend."

Julie smiled at Bob's confident words.

"I promised to let you see Julie and here she is. You see, I do keep my word. But now she needs to go." Bob placed a hand under Julie's elbow, helped her up, and guided her to the door.

"Wait a damn minute here. This is my wife. The mother of my children. I need to talk with her privately. Can't you give us a few minutes alone? Julie, please, come back. I love you, sweetheart."

Julie glanced back briefly. Sam saw tears in her eyes. She bowed her head and shook it slowly from side to side before disappearing through the door.

"Sam, she's having a hard time with all of this. You need to give her some space. Besides, you need to focus on the tests and do your best to help us help you."

"What's going on, Bob? Have I gone crazy or has the world?"

"We're trying to figure that out." His cell phone rang before he could continue. "Sorry, I have to take this."

Chapter Eleven

Saturday, March 16, 1:15 PM

With a sharp rap on the doorframe, Keone entered a room cluttered with boxes and filing cabinets to find himself staring at a man's running shorts, the posterior of which pointed directly up in the air. The man's body balanced precariously on the edge of a wooden crate filled with office supplies.

"Mr. Walden?" Keone asked.

"That's me. Are you from the moving company?" Walden asked without extricating himself.

"No. I'm Sergeant Boyd of the Maui Police Department." Keone pulled out his notebook. He expected to be writing a lot.

Keone heard the resonant bang of Walden's head connecting with the side of the crate, as he scrambled out to face Keone. After studying Keone's credentials, he said, "I'm sorry, Sergeant. What can I do for you? If this is about Sam's accident, I wasn't there."

Already distancing himself.

"I realize that, Mr. Walden. But, as Mr. Loftus's best friend and a family member, I assume you spent a great deal of time with him prior to the accident."

"Why is that relevant?"

This guy really is a lawyer.

"Mr. Loftus was driving on the wrong side of the road at the time of the accident. We don't know if he was drunk, mentally ill, on drugs, distracted, had a heart attack, or just decided to end it all. The more we can discover about his baseline mental and physical state, the easier it will be to determine the cause of the crash."

Walden seemed to relax and ran his fingers through his mane of red hair. He winced when he touched the spot where he'd connected with the packing crate. "Of course it would. Sorry, you caught me off guard. I'd be happy to answer any questions you have. Sam and I have been friends since college."

Not Best Friends.

"Tell me about Sam."

"One thing I can promise you is Sam never messed with drugs. Here." He swept a pile of folders onto the floor, clearing two chairs. "Let's sit down. This will take a while."

Moved the papers to provide himself time to think.

Keone looked forward to the tale Walden was preparing to spin.

"I met Sam at IU when we were both freshmen. Neither of us knew anything about the Midwest. We both wanted to study away from home, and IU offered to pay the full deal. I grew up in the Bay Area and Sam was from Southern California."

"Where in the Bay Area?"

"Palo Alto. We shared a dorm room and hit it off from the start."

"Did you have classes together?"

"A few, but I was a science geek before I saw the financial advantages of being pre-law. And he was always interested in math and business. I knew enough to take a few business courses, for when I had my own practice. But Sam loved numbers. He took higher math classes for fun that had nothing to do with his major. He was even intrigued with astrophysics, which is mostly math. He had a friend from those days who was a physics major, but I can't remember the guy's name."

Always provides more than he's asked. Tries to redirect the interrogation to safe ground. He's been interrogated before.

"That's all right. Did you do things together outside of class?"

"We were both terrified of drowning, so naturally we decided to go white water rafting. There was a wonderful place called the Upper Gauley River in West Virginia where a lot of the Indiana, Ohio, and Kentucky guys liked to go. So we decided to go with them one early fall weekend...."

He's off on another story.

"Did anything special happen during these trips?"

"Well we each had a few out-of-boat experiences, but nothing lethal."

"Lethal, really?"

"The first time we went a guy from another raft fell out next to an undercut boulder."

"What happened?"

"He got sucked under. Whoosh. And thousands of gallons of water pinned him to the base of the boulder."

"I guess that was the only time you went rafting, then."

"No way. We were young, sailing through college, and sure it would never be us that got pulled under. We rafted every year through college and twice a year through graduate school. Hell, Sam still does it. But on the island it's ocean kayaking that floats his boat."

Sam still does it.

"Do you ever go with him?"

"I did once, right after he and Janet moved here. Too boring for me. Not like the adrenaline rush from rafting. Besides, I was too busy building up my practice."

Contradicts Sam's comment from last night. Good old Dave likes an adrenaline rush. I wonder what else he likes.

"Do you enjoy any sports on the island?"

"I took up golf over here.

Golf. Now there's an adrenaline rush.

"The courses over here are so beautiful and you meet so many great people. It can really help you calm down."

What does he need to calm down from?

"About your wives, how did you meet them?"

"The good old Indiana State Fair. A treasure trove of pork butts and other fried things on sticks, smelly livestock, and a fun zone filled with lovely young coeds. We saw them go into the haunted house ride and waited at the exit to accidentally bump into them."

"When was this?"

"The summer before our last year of graduate school, Kelley Business School for Sam and IU Law School for me. Although we lived in Bloomington most of our time in college, we lived in Indianapolis that summer since we were both doing internships there. We shared graduate student housing at Hewey Pewey."

"Where?"

"Indiana University and Purdue University at Indianapolis, IUPUI."

He did it again. What a schmoozer.

"Your wives?" Keone didn't hide his impatience.

"Sure. Sure. We spotted these two hotties and decided to flip a coin for them. People exited the haunted house from two different doors. We made a deal that when the girls emerged from the haunted house, the winner would hit on the girl who came out on the right and the loser the one on the left. Sam won the toss, Janet came out on the right and the rest, as they say, is history."

But if left is right?

"You each ended up marrying a girl based on which side she happened to get off a carnival ride?"

"Yep. It was the best decision we ever made."

"Did you ever date other girls after that or even the other sister?"

"No. It was love at first sight. Or, loves at first sights, I guess."

"And you've all remained friends ever since?"

"More than friends, we're all related. We both took our honeymoons here on Maui. Sam and Janet got married in June and were back in time for Julie and my wedding in July. We're at each other's houses for all the major holidays."

"Tell me about your wife." Keone needed to know if Sam had any reason to believe Julie was, or could become, his.

"She was pre-med when we met, but minored in performance art. She had dreams of being a pediatrician, but also loved to perform. When we got married, she was worried that two demanding professions might make things hard, so she focused on performing, especially in children's theatre."

"Probably a good decision."

They made the choice that was best for him.

"Yes, as it turned out. She was so damn talented that she ended up with a theater group when we moved to Maui. She joined and started writing plays for children. Then she tried her hand at writing children's books."

"Wait a minute. What was your wife's maiden name?"

"Madison."

"Julia Madison. She's the one that wrote the Hawai'i Anna books, right?"

"She sure is. Ten books and three movies later, I closed down my practice to work full-time as her agent."

"What do you know?" Keone said to himself, but Dave heard him.

"Yeah, what do you know? Well, it's been great talking with you. If you have all you need, I'd like to get back to packing up."

"Sure. Just a couple more questions." *That always worked for Columbo.*

"Did Janet ever seem jealous of her sister's success?"

"Are you kidding? They're closer than ever. Besides Janet's as successful a designer as Julie is a writer. I keep telling Sam to quit working. Neither of us needs to work anymore. But Sam..."

"Yes."

"Sam's a worker bee. Always plays by the rules. Rules are important to him. Too important. I think it's the OCD."

I struck a nerve here. Does Dave have trouble following the rules? Did Sam's need to play by the rules affect their friendship?

"What about children? I understand neither of you ever had kids."

For the first time Dave paused. "Well, Julie and I thought about kids at first, but she has all the kids who read her books. She does readings in schools all the time. Every once in a while she...But, no, we're completely happy the way we are. A kid now would just get in the way."

Whose way?

"What about Sam and Janet?"

"They can't have kids, something to do with Janet's plumbing. Janet looked into adoption. It was going to take a long time and would have meant looking overseas. Sam likes things to be in alignment, you know. He just couldn't see himself with foreign kids, especially ones who didn't look like him. He's not a bigot or anything. He's just..."

"A little anal. So I keep hearing."

Wants me to focus on Sam, not him.

"He's not mental or anything, just very precise. Hey, you'd rather have an anal accountant than a sloppy one, right? He's a good guy and a perfect match for Janet."

Doesn't want to be too obvious about throwing Sam under the bus.

"I met Janet last night. She was pretty shaken up by his accident."

"She puts on a good front, but underneath she has emotions. She sure loves Sam. They're very comfortable together, you know. They don't have to talk a lot to communicate. Julie's more outgoing than Janet, but Janet is a Chatty Cathy compared to Sam."

Shyness inconsistent with my impression of Sam.

"Closing your office must be a little sad, after being here so long. I ate at Lahaina Fresheners today and Max told me you were a good customer."

"Max should be a little more circumspect talking with strangers."

A quick glimpse of good old Dave's underside. Despite his short stature, Keone saw in Dave a man who knew how to coil his body for attack.

"Oh hell. I bet you're not strangers. Everybody on this island seems to know each other. Max is a good guy. I love those burritos of his."

Dave's body quickly uncoils. *Trying hard to cover his slip.*

"I'm recovering from one right now."

They both made laughing sounds. But there was no laughter in Dave's eyes.

"Did you or Sam ever take clients there for lunch?"

"No. Sam spends the day at his desk crunching numbers. My clients prefer a little classier atmosphere."

A lie.

"One last question. Whose idea was it to move to Maui?"

"We all fell in love with this place on our honeymoons, but Julie and I moved here first. I had a great job opportunity and she could do her writing and performing here as well as anywhere else.

What job opportunity? You opened a private legal practice

"When Sam's company opened a branch here and needed a CFO, he and Janet jumped at the opportunity. They moved over about two years after we did. They started in Lahaina and we were in Kula. After a year they moved to Pukalani, which brought us closer together."

So close that you only get together on holidays

"Thank you, Mr. Walden. I'll probably need to talk with your wife at some point, but you've given me what I need for now."

"Do you think Sam will snap out of this...uh...delusion he has? He's a good guy. I'd like to see him get back home and back to normal as soon as possible."

Sam's delusion makes him nervous.

"You need to ask his doctor about that. Has he had delusions before?"

"Absolutely not. Sam is more grounded in reality than any person I know. He doesn't even *read* fiction. He spends his free time reading history, science, and a lot of that political crap that passes for non-fiction these days."

Keone had heard enough. "Thank you again, Mr. Walden.

Good luck with your packing."

Walden inserted his short frame back into the box, again losing contact with the floor. Keone saw himself out.

Walden left a bad taste in Keone's mouth. He'd seen too many like him before. What Walden let you see was a role that he was playing. A part he played to appear friendly and non-threatening. But Keone's questions had scratched that surface to reveal something less palatable beneath. Keone decided to learn more about Sam's *best friend*.

Chapter Twelve

Saturday, March 16, 2:30 PM

Mid-afternoon at Maui Memorial Hospital was a slow time on the wards. Sam was finishing another replay of Julie's visit in his mind, when he looked up to see a stranger enter his room. The stranger wore a white coat, so Sam assumed the first of Bob's specialists was here.

"Mr. Loftus, I'm Dr. Field. My specialty is neurology. I'd like to discuss the results of some of your tests with you. Some of what I am going to tell you may be disturbing, but please hear me out before reacting. I believe that I have a pretty good idea what is causing at least some of your symptoms and think it's time you knew as well. Your family doctor is concerned about you and your family and wanted to avoid sharing idle speculation until we had a solid diagnosis."

"Dr. Field, you're the first person I have seen in the past couple days who seems to be willing to level with me. I appreciate that. I'm open to anything you have to tell me."

"Thank you. First, let me assure you that some of your symptoms—possibly all of them—are the direct result of your injury in the car crash. Physical injury to the brain can cause very unsettling symptoms that are often unique for each patient, but a couple of your most pronounced symptoms have been observed, if rarely, in other patients.

"I had a patient a few years ago, a fifty-eight-year-old man, who suddenly developed left-handedness and the ability to read and write in mirror writing. In his case this was the result of encephalitis and some resulting surgical procedures. He also had some other problems, unrelated to yours, but the mirror writing and reading were very similar to yours."

Mirror writing and reading. So my observations have been accurate.

"What do you mean other problems?"

"Well, he was not an educated man such as yourself. He only had four years of elementary education."

"What other problems?"

"Well, he believed George Wallace was President of the United States and Abraham Lincoln his immediate predecessor."

"Great."

"But you are not displaying any of that. Your answers to questions regarding current events, mathematics, and language have all been perfectly normal. As I said, every patient is different."

"All right. Go on."

"Well, the second major problem is your belief that your sister-in-law is your wife and vice-versa."

Sam began to interrupt, but Dr. Field held up his hand. "Mr. Loftus, you have to hear this. I know it will be hard, but we all want you to regain your health and this is the only way to do it."

Sam held his tongue, but fumed inside.

"There is another rare disorder called Capgras, uh, disorder. I have a colleague who's had patients with Capgras. I've asked him to meet with you this afternoon. He can explain this aspect far better than I.

"You see, Sam. I believe the crash caused the left-right problem and I have experience treating such a defect. My colleague has experience treating Capgras. It will take time but I firmly believe that together we can return you to your mental and emotional state before the accident."

Sam was floored. *What a moron.*

Didn't he realize that the left-right thing happened before

the accident? Maybe he didn't. Sam hadn't mentioned passing through the film to Bob Wayne or anyone else except the cop and Lee.

Something weird was going on here. And he needed to find out what but couldn't do that lying in a hospital bed. Maybe their faulty assumption would work in his favor.

"Doctor Field. I can't tell you how relieved I am that you've discovered an underlying physical cause for my condition. Does this mean that I might be able to go home and be treated on, what do you call it...?"

"An outpatient basis. Yes, that is a possibility. But I will need my colleague, Dr. Drayton, to examine you first about the other aspect of your illness. I'm sure together we can start you on a regime of medication, therapy, and exercise that will quickly bring you to a state where you can leave the hospital. We have to make certain there are no hidden issues, but I think it is very likely that with significant progress you could go home in a few weeks."

"Thank you, doctor. What is Dr. Drayton's area of specialization?" Sam was pretty certain he knew the answer to this question, but wanted to put Field on the spot.

"Dr. Drayton is a psychiatrist."

"So you think I'm crazy." Sam clenched his fists under the covers.

"Oh, no. We just need to be sure that the symptoms are completely physical. Dr. Drayton is an outstanding physician. He is in an excellent position to assure both you and your wife that there are no dangerous aspects to your condition. I know you want everyone to be comfortable when you return to your family."

"Of course," Sam said, but he thought, *I'll return to my family all right. To Julie and the kids. And nobody will suspect that I know this is all a load of crap.*

Chapter Thirteen

Saturday, March 16, 3:00 PM

Keone looked at his watch. His conversation with Sam's boss had been singularly uninformative. Sam was a great worker, quiet but friendly, had no close friends at work, and was liked by everyone. Sam had never done anything remotely unusual during his time there, thus his recent behavior was completely out of character. Keone wondered if Sam's boss really even knew Sam.

His next stop was the District Four headquarters of the Maui PD. The grey concrete buildings held police, fire, and other county agencies.

Entering the police station, Keone was welcomed by a number of friends who'd heard about his accident and were glad to see him vertical. He asked the senior man on duty, Roger Walker, about Sam Loftus.

"I honestly don't know the guy. I looked him up on the computer when I heard about the accident, because I couldn't believe I'd never heard of someone who spent so much time over here. His file is nearly empty. Never had a moving violation. Hell, he's never had a parking ticket. Guy must really keep to himself. Nobody here knows him."

"What about Dave Walden?" Keone asked.

"The Great Waldo? Is he involved in this?"

"Yeah, he's Loftus's brother-in-law. Loftus thinks Walden's

wife is his wife."

"I don't blame him. She's a knockout and does a lot for the community, too. My two girls love her books."

"I'm more interested in Walden. He's a lawyer, yeah?"

"Yeah. He has an office in that complex on Dickenson. At least he did until a little while ago. I hear he's moving. We never bump noses professionally. He doesn't touch criminal law or even litigation. Contract law and estate planning keep him busy and more than pay the bills. I know him mostly from the golf tournament he organizes each year for the MPD."

"Oh hell. Why didn't I make the connection? I'm not a golfer, but that tournament makes a lot of money each year for the department's community service efforts. Why do you call him The Great Waldo?"

"He's an amateur magician—and a great putter. He knows all kinds of weird putting tricks. We started calling him The Great Waldo, the magician of the greens, and it kinda stuck. When we first talked about having a charity tournament, he came up with the theme, 'Making Magic for Maui's Moms.' The money all goes to family assistance programs started and sponsored by the MPD.

"He brings a bunch of wealthy friends of his over every year from the mainland and other places. They contribute a lot to play and boost the local economy while they're here. We play every year, right up the road on the Royal Course at Ka'anapali."

Another red flag on Walden. This guy deserves a closer look.

"Does Walden have a rap sheet?"

Roger hesitated. "Look, he's a good friend to the department. He's had some minor infractions, but our guys always give him the benefit of the doubt."

"So he has a sheet."

"I've told you more about him than his file will."

"Can I see his sheet, or do I have to bring it up myself when I get back to the office?"

"No. I'll have somebody print it out for you. Listen, this guy does a lot for us. Don't screw it up, imagining connections that aren't really there."

"Got it. The whole thing's routine anyway. I'll probably close the case in a week."

"Sorry about your new car."

"Me, too."

Keone knew he'd have to be careful. This guy had important friends inside and outside the department. He was already stretching the scope of the crash investigation pretty far. Funny how often he did that on cases.

A detective's job was finding and following leads. There were rules. Good rules. But Keone always considered them more like guidelines. Unfortunately, his superiors considered them rules.

Saturday, March 16, 5:00 PM

On his drive back along the winding cliffside road between Lahaina and Ma'alaea, Keone called to set up a meeting with Mrs. Janet Loftus. Janet answered on the second ring with, "Loftus residence."

"Hello, Mrs. Loftus. This is Sergeant Boyd. We met last night at the hospital."

"Oh, yes, Sergeant. I remember. How can I help you?"

"I need to ask you a few questions as part of my investigation into the crash. I need to schedule a time to get together. I also hoped you could give me your sister's telephone number. I'll need to talk to her, as well. But there's no rush."

"Actually, you couldn't have called at a better time. Julie is on her way over right now. Being together always helps when we have to deal with difficult times. Why don't you come by in a couple of hours, and you can talk with both of us?"

"I don't want to impose on your private time."

"Don't be silly. It'll save you a trip and get this over with sooner."

Professionally, Keone was unsatisfied with this

arrangement. He preferred to interview witnesses separately to avoid even unintentional influence on each other's testimony. Personally, he was looking forward to meeting Mrs. Walden to see why everyone thought she was such a knockout. "Okay. I'll stop by at seven. You live in Pukalani, yeah?"

Janet gave him directions before ending the call. Keone didn't need them. He made it his business to know every inch of this island. But he'd discovered when people provided directions to a police officer they felt less threatened.

Keone was relieved he had time to stop by his condo. He wanted to clean up and change into a freshly pressed uniform. While he showered, his mind tried to reconcile the Sam Loftus he met and the one his friends and coworkers described.

Did that bump on his head give Sam a different personality or just rewrite part of his memory?

He put on his sharpest-looking uniform and told himself this had nothing to do with the fact that the knockout sister was going to be present. He didn't believe himself for a minute.

When Keone first decided he needed to meet one-on-one with each of Sam Loftus's alleged wives, he was not relishing either meeting. Now he was going to see them in the same room at the same time. Yet, somehow he was looking forward to it.

Professional. You're a Professional.

Part III: Visits and Calls

"The first thing in a visit is to say 'How d'ye do?' and shake hands!" And here the two brothers gave each other a hug, and then they held out the two hands that were free, to shake hands with her.

Lewis Carroll, author

RICK LUDWIG

Chapter Fourteen

Saturday, March 16, 5:30 PM

After his meeting with Field, Sam decided to behave as normally as possible, although he wasn't sure what normal was anymore. He began by initiating friendly conversations with each of his nurses when they came in to take his vital signs or take him for another test.

Mrs. Millicent (Millie) Brown, Gwen Tanaka's mid-afternoon replacement, was significantly older than Gwen. She'd been a nurse for her entire adult life, first in her native Ireland, then San Francisco. She had a lilt in her voice and an easy manner that made Sam enjoy her company. He could tell she enjoyed having someone actually listen to her stories.

She moved to Maui from San Francisco at the urging of her husband, a retired commander in the U.S. Navy. He'd fallen in love with the islands when he was stationed at Pearl Harbor. Unfortunately, Commander Brown's retirement was cut short by his sudden death from a cardiac arrest. He was deep-sea fishing at the time, while Mrs. Brown was at work. Millie confided to Sam that she always regretted turning down his offer to go fishing.

Sam assured her that she shouldn't blame herself. She should remember their wonderful times together and enjoy her life for her husband. He tried not to lay it on too thick, but he wanted the staff to know what a caring person he was. He wanted them on his side when the decision whether or not to send him home was made. Sam decided to become everyone at Maui Memorial Hospital's new best friend.

Sam was about to ring for Millie when she entered his room. "Mr. Loftus, you have another visitor if you feel up to it. Dr. Wayne approved the visit."

"Who is it?"

"It's an older gentleman. I believe he is a friend of yours from work. A Mr. Marder."

"Oh, sure. Send Lee in. I need to talk to him. He was my passenger when I had the accident." Sam used the word accident as often as possible to make sure everyone who heard him knew the crash was no one's fault, especially his.

Millie left and Lee came through the door, balancing a potted plant and an oversized card in his hands. "Sammy, how are you?"

"I'm feeling pretty good, considering. I've got a little bump on my head, from the airbag I guess. But all my components are functioning normally. How about you?"

"Pretty much the same. They kept me overnight for observation. But I guess they didn't observe nothin' interesting, so they cut me loose this morning."

"I'm so glad you weren't hurt. I feel so responsible." Sam's tone conveyed how much he meant this. Lee was a good friend, his best on the island next to Dave and, of course, Julie.

"Oh Sammy, I'm just fine. Say, did that cop come and see you? The one we hit."

"Sure did. Yesterday and again this morning. He seems like the suspicious sort. Plus he's still pissed about his car. Can't blame him. I would be, too. It was a brand new Morgan."

"What the hell's a Morgan?"

"A very exclusive British roadster. There's a minimum year-long wait just to start the process of acquiring one. They build each one to order and encourage you to visit their shop while your car's being built. And his was brand new."

"That can't be good."

"He kept himself under control. But I don't think I made a

friend."

"Sammy. I'm worried about you. You were talkin' kind of strange before the crash."

This was exactly what Sam was waiting to hear. He motioned his friend closer to the bed. "Lee, could you tell me exactly what I said?"

"Sure. Right after we passed the turnoff down to the Marina, you know by Buzz's Wharf, a shiver passed through your whole body and you said, 'Did you hear that pop?' When I said no, you said, 'It was like a huge soap bubble. My God, everything's changed. I'm on the wrong side of the road!' Then you swerved onto the wrong side.

"When you saw all those cars lined up, you tried to swerve back, but we started to roll and then it was:

Urch, screech,
Ring the mop,
Don't forget the
Soda pop."

Sam marveled that Lee always seemed to have a little phrase stored away for every occasion. "The airbag must have knocked me out."

"Me, too."

"Have you told anyone about this?"

Lee looked embarrassed. "Well, I might have told that cop. I'm not sure. I was pretty groggy."

"Don't worry about it. I'm just glad you're safe and out of this place." Sam was sure Lee had told the detective everything. But he'd told Boyd a lot that morning, too, before formulating his strategy.

"You'll be out, too, real soon. I know it."

Field and Wayne didn't seem to know the left-right stuff happened before the accident. He'd see about Drayton when he came in. He decided to keep these facts between the two of them for now and hope the cop didn't blab to the doctors. For some reason, he thought the cop would share as little as possible with the doctors. After all, this was an ongoing investigation.

"Lee. You've got to be careful what you say to people until you talk to a lawyer."

"I'll back you up a hundred percent. You know I will."

"I know, Lee. You're a good friend. Let's keep the part about what I said and did before the crash between ourselves from now on, okay?"

"Sure."

"So what have you got in your hands?"

"Oh. I forgot. Here's a card. Everybody at work signed it except Fran, she's on the mainland. And I got these here *Bromy lads* for you, 'cause I know you have 'em in your garden."

"They're perfect, Lee! I don't have this species in my collection yet."

"What's so special about these things? They look kind of deformed to me."

"Bromeliads are exotic and unusual plants. They're grown commercially just above where Julie and I live in Pukalani." Sam noticed that Lee winced when he said Julie, instead of Janet.

"Are they good for anything—other than looking exotic, I mean?"

"There's one that tastes pretty good. It's called a pineapple."

"Well, I'll be damned."

During the pause that followed, Sam decided that Lee could provide him some needed help.

"Lee, how's your energy level?"

"The iron in my veins has turned to lead in my ass, but I'm still kicking."

"Could you do a favor for me?"

"Sure, Sammy, anything."

"My lawyer, Tom Conrad, probably doesn't know what's happened. You should talk with him. I'll pay for the consultation. He can tell you what you should and shouldn't say to folks about the accident. Oh, and be sure to always call it the accident and not the crash."

"Say no more. I know Tom. He does work for the company, too, right?"

"That's right."

"But you don't need to pay for it."

'I want to, Lee. And I want you to do one more thing for me. I'd like you to take him a message."

"I'm happy to do anything for you, Sammy. You know that."

"Call Tom—No. Go see him for me, give him my message, and tell him everything. Even the stuff I want you to keep to yourself for now. Okay?"

"I'll call for an appointment on my way home and go by first thing after work tomorrow."

"That would be perfect. He's usually in the office until about seven each evening. And, Lee, don't tell anyone else that you're doing this for me, okay? Let me write something down. Have you got some paper?"

"Here, use the envelope. I forgot to address it anyway and it's real big."

Sam started to write, then realized the problem. If Tom were like everyone else in this world, he wouldn't be able to read Sam's handwriting. "Lee, my hand's a little shaky, could you write if I dictate?"

"Sure, Sammy. Shoot."

When the message was done, Sam read it, surreptitiously using the mirror in the over-bed table. "Thanks, Lee. I'll never forget this.

"You just get better real quick."

"I will. Mahalo—for everything."

Chapter Fifteen

Saturday, March 16, 7:00 PM

Keone pulled up in front of the Loftus home in Pukalani and took a moment to look around. He saw a neat, simple house, neither new nor terribly old, built in the standard off-the-ground style of most of the houses on Maui. The garden was meticulously tended. Most homes on the island incorporated natural, tropical-style foliage, but the Loftus home rose above a formal English garden. The plant species were native or early transplants, but they were trimmed in ways he had never seen before—and he was born here. Multiple species of Bromeliads were scattered throughout. He always thought these plants looked like ET planted them before flying back home to that place he kept phoning. Not just off-island in origin, but off-planet. He knew they came from South America and loved the variety of colors. But their odd shapes and spiky features took some getting used to.

Janet Loftus greeted him at the door and ushered him into a spotless, if somewhat spartan, living room. Julie Walden sat stiffly in a ladder-backed chair. Keone's first impression was that these sisters didn't share much in the way of a family resemblance. Blonde Janet was short and thin, with the grace of a model. Julie was taller and rounder, with the kind of physique that catches most men's eyes and is rapidly transmitted to lower regions of the anatomy. She also had long, wavy red hair. The kind a man could get lost in. In summary, she was hot. Where Janet was attractive and professional, Julie was cute and sexy, even when uncomfortable and waiting for an unwanted interrogation.

"Mrs. Walden, it is a pleasure to meet you. I'm Keone Boyd from the Maui police department." For some reason, he didn't want to use his formal title with this woman. She seemed vulnerable in a way that made him want to comfort her.

"Hello. I'll be happy to answer any questions you have for me. But I doubt I know anything that could help your investigation." Julie's voice was quieter and slightly lower-pitched than her sister's, but she didn't seem in any way subordinate.

"Sergeant, if it's all right with you, I'll bring us some coffee and biscuits," Janet said. "You must have questions for Julie that I don't need to hear."

Janet Loftus just jumped a notch in Keone's esteem. "That would be fine, Mrs. Loftus."

"Please, we're Jan and Julie. We know you're here to help."

Julie nodded at this and Keone decided to play by their rules, for the moment.

When Jan left the room, Julie seemed to relax a bit. A signal to Keone that he could begin questioning.

"Julie, I want to get to the biggest question first."

"Good. I hate people who beat around the bush. You want to know why Sam says I'm his wife, right?"

"Yes."

"I don't have a clue. Until last night, Sam always seemed to see me as either an extension of Dave or Jan. He and I have very little in common. I write fiction for children and he hates fiction. I love kids. He's uncomfortable around kids. He is very detail oriented and I leave all that to Dave, who leaves it to other people on his payroll."

"How would you describe your interactions with Sam?"

"Friendly. Non-invasive. Sam's a good guy, but he was more Dave's friend than mine. He's a good brother-in-law and has always been a supportive partner for my sister."

Keone noticed she said Sam was more Dave's friend.

"Has Sam ever acted oddly around you?"

"Not until today."

"You've visited Sam?"

"Yes, Dr. Wayne thought it might help snap Sam out of his...illness."

"Did it?"

"No. I was only there for a minute or two, but the man in that bed was nothing like the Sam Loftus I know."

"In what way?"

"When Dr. Wayne told him I had to leave, he blew up. Shouted that I was his wife and the mother of his children." Julie's voice cracked and she closed her eyes, as if to block out the memory.

Keone needed to direct the interview down a less emotional path. "I'm sorry that happened. I take it Sam is normally less offensive."

Julie seemed calmer when she opened her eyes. "He's normally very sweet. He's a little on the quiet side, but not withdrawn or repressed or anything like that. He's actually very thoughtful."

"I've heard he's a bit anal."

"He's very precise in what he says and does. That may be why he's such a good accountant. But he's a very friendly guy. His dry wit complements Dave's broader, bawdier sense of humor. I think that's one of the reasons they were once such good friends. They seemed to shine brighter in each other's presence."

Time to follow up. "You said Sam was once Dave's good friend. I understand they had a falling out after Sam and Janet moved to Maui."

"You sure do your homework, don't you? It was about six months after they moved here to Pukalani. Jan and I were so happy to be close by and so were Sam and Dave—at first. Dave had a business proposition he wanted to get Sam in on and they agreed to discuss it on a two-day, ocean-kayaking excursion. They took off as happy as clams. When they got back, Dave was really moody. He kept calling Sam, 'that straight-arrow, number cruncher,' under his breath. I tried to get him to tell me what was wrong and he said, "Nothing. We're just different that's all. We're not in college anymore."

Jan returned with the coffee service and some classy European cookies—presumably called biscuits in her circle.

"Thank you, Mrs...uh...Janet...Jan. Let me ask you the question I just asked your sister. What caused Sam and Dave to grow apart after you moved to this house?"

"I guess Julie told you about that botched kayaking trip."

Keone nodded.

"Afterward, I asked Sam, 'What is it between you two? You've been friends since college.' He thought for a minute and said, 'I guess we learned different lessons in college. Dave's still Julie's husband and your brother-in-law, but we can never be close friends again.'"

"Do you have any idea what happened during the trip?"

"Julie and I hoped it was some little thing. Like, maybe Sam liked to kayak and David didn't. But it must have been deeper than that."

"I think you're right."

"I just remembered something that might be of interest to you, Sergeant."

Boyd gave in. "Call me Keone."

"Keone. What a lovely name." Jan smiled.

Keone waited.

"Anyway, Dr. Wayne called this afternoon. He asked me when Sam and David had their disagreement and if they'd patched things up. He seemed disappointed when I told him how long ago it was and that they never really reconciled. He mentioned something about not being consistent with short-term memory loss. But I think he was talking to himself."

"Before the crash did Sam ever behave unusually?"

"No. That's just it. Sam never does anything out of the ordinary. He's stable as a rock. I think that's what attracted me to him in the first place."

"He still takes medicine, though, doesn't he?"

"Yeah. You know it's funny what he said to Dr. Wayne last night about not taking any magic pills. He takes medicine for cholesterol and acid reflux. Oh, and that anti-depressant."

"He takes an anti-depressant?"

"Yes. Sam went through a bad patch a few years ago. I always thought it had something to do with his break from David, but he's been fine for years. I think he just takes the medication out of habit. They've never changed the dose from once a week."

Keone sipped his coffee and peered at the two sisters over the rim of his cup. Although Julie seemed the most open of the two, he sensed she was hiding something. The fact that she wore long sleeves and long pants despite the warm Maui weather, coupled with the heavier than necessary makeup around her eyes, raised a red flag.

"Julie, could you tell me a little about you and your husband? I met him today and I understand he's closed his legal practice."

The tension was back in Julie's posture and in her face. He'd hit a nerve.

"David and I are making some changes as a result of the success of my writing. He's a lawyer and has been uncomfortable with some of the agreements I've entered into regarding my work. I didn't ask him to close his practice, that was his idea and—"

"What does this have to do with Sam and the accident?" Jan seemed confused, but not angry.

"Probably nothing. We just try to get a full picture of the subject's environment and I know you two couples spend time together."

"Yes, we do. We've always enjoyed each other's company. My sister and I may be a little unusual in that regard, but we've always been close. Our marriages brought us even closer. I can't imagine being far apart from Julie and David. And I know Sam feels the same way. Or at least he always has."

"Look, do you know if Dr. Wayne or his colleagues are making any progress with Sam? I really want him back. I'm so lonely here without him."

Jan's eyes were starting to tear and Keone realized it was time to stop, for now. "I'm sure they're doing their best. Dr. Wayne has brought in some excellent specialists. He seems confident that together they can help Sam."

"I'm sure they'll do their best."

Keone finished his cookie, then rose to leave. "Thank you for seeing me and for the refreshments." He drew two cards from his wallet and handed one to each sister. "If you think of anything else that might help us in our investigation, call me anytime." He shook hands with Julie Walden before Jan Loftus slipped her arm through his and walked him to the door.

As she opened the door, Jan leaned in and spoke softly to Keone. "Do you think he's going to have any criminal charges from the accident?"

"I can't discuss an ongoing investigation, but there will be no action on that front until your husband's health is completely assessed. I know he wants to find out what happened to cause the crash as much as we do."

With that he left the Loftus home and headed back to his condo. He wasn't comfortable drawing many conclusions, yet. But he knew one thing from today's experiences. Julie Walden and her husband were having marital problems. He'd stake his badge on it. He also couldn't shake the feeling that understanding the causes of the break between Dave and Sam might be relevant to unraveling events. He needed to speak to Julie alone again at some point and not because he found her so attractive. *Well, not just because of that.*

Chapter Sixteen

Sunday, March 17, 8:00 AM

Eyes closed, Sam debated going back to sleep rather than face another day of everything being backwards. He knew there would be more tests and more doctors today and doubted he was any closer to being released.

He sensed something different in his room.

Was that someone breathing next to the bed? Keeping his eyes closed, Sam decided to focus on what his other senses might tell him. From the direction of the breathing, he deduced the person was either a child or an adult sitting in a chair. There was a fragrance, but not a woman's perfume. He decided it was deodorant fighting a losing battle with male sweat. Was one of the doctors observing him as he slept? That would be better than his non-wife, Janet, sitting there staring at him. He supposed he'd should open his eyes.

"Hi, Sammy boy. I was wondering when you'd decide to open those peepers of yours."

Sam pulled himself upright. Sitting by his bed with a huge grin on his face was his best friend. "Dave, am I glad to see you. Everything's crazy in this place."

"It's a place for sick people. What do you expect?"

"I need a reality check, old buddy. Maybe you can bring some sense to my world."

Dave's grin gradually transformed into a sneer as he idly

tapped on the IV tube running into Sam's arm. "Do you know how easy it would be to kill someone hooked up to a tube like this? Just fill a syringe with air and shoot it in. Air embolism. Wouldn't leave a trace. You'd just be dead."

The comment seemed odd, even for Dave, who always liked to turn everything around to get a laugh.

"Big joke. Did they tell you they think I'm crazy? Bob Wayne brought in specialists who think I bumped my head and went whacko. Julie came by for a minute, but she acted like she barely knew me."

Dave rose from the chair.

Looming over Sam with a scowl on his face, he grabbed the front of Sam's gown with his fist, twisting it tight around his neck. "Where in the hell do you get off telling people you're married to my wife? If you so much as look Julie in the eyes again, it'll be the last thing you ever see."

Dave's raspy whisper sent a shiver up Sam's spine.

"I never wanted to hurt you or Julie," Sam croaked. "My memories are just warped. The doctors say someday I'll remember everything the way you do."

Dave released his grasp on Sam's gown. "You mean that crap Julie told me is true? You really are messed up from the crash?"

"That's what they tell me."

Dave sat back down in his chair. "That giant Hawaiian detective came sniffing around my old office yesterday asking all kinds of questions."

"What kinds of questions?"

"Doesn't matter. I don't like anyone sniffing around in my business. You were an idiot to reject the sweet deal I offered you when you first got here. But you promised you'd never tell anyone about it."

"I honestly don't know what you're talking about, Dave. You and I, we're like brothers. I'd never share any of your confidences with anyone, especially the cops."

"Where the hell do you think we are? Back home again in Indiana? We haven't been close since that day on the kayak. I risked everything to let you in on the ground floor. Is this some kind of a sick act?"

Sam couldn't keep his hands from shaking. This man was nothing like his dear friend. He seemed hardened and mean. Dave was always a joker, the life of every party. But this man wasn't joking. He was deadly serious.

"They say my brain got scrambled in the crash, Dave. I didn't believe them. My memories are so vivid of you and Janet and Julie and our kids."

"What kids?"

"Yours and mine?"

"We don't have any kids."

"What about Rain and Mist?"

"What? You're asking about the weather now? What's wrong with you? Maybe your brain really is scrambled."

"I swear, Dave. I know nothing about you that could be of interest to the police. You have to believe me."

"I don't have to do anything, except keep my eye on you. If you keep away from me and mine and keep your trap shut, you might manage to stay alive. But don't test me. Got it?"

"Yes."

Dave switched to a louder, more jovial voice. "That's great, Sammy boy. You just do what the doctors and those pretty little nurses tell you and you'll be good as new. I'll see you soon, old friend."

With that Dave slipped out the door and left Sam dazed and exhausted.

What in God's name was happening?

The Dave he knew would have tried to find some way, any way, to help Sam. Even if he thought he was crazy, Dave would have humored him, not thrown Sam's condition back in his face. This Dave scared him. This Dave was dangerous.

Sam struggled to find some shred of reality in what he'd just experienced. But, before he could order his thoughts, Sergeant Boyd came through the door Dave had so recently closed.

Sunday, March 17, 8:30 AM

The man Keone Boyd saw in the hospital bed was not the confident, if confusing, Sam Loftus he had interviewed the day before. This man was nervous, unsure, and weary.

"Mr. Loftus. Do you remember me from yesterday?"

Sam pulled the sheet up to cover his hospital gown. "Sergeant Boyd. Yes, I remember you. But I'm not sure about much else."

"What do you mean?"

"Since we last spoke. I have been poked, prodded and viewed in many ingenious ways. My visitors think I'm crazy and so do my eminent doctors. I've been told that left is right, my sister-in law is my wife, my wife is married to my best friend, and, just now, my best friend paid me a surprise visit and told me to keep the hell away from his wife—my wife...." Sam threw up his hands helplessly and his eyes glistened with tears.

"Dave Walden was here?"

"You just missed him."

"That is a lot to handle in twenty-four hours," Keone said. "I've spent that time trying to learn more about you, your friends, and your family."

Sam didn't comment.

"Do you want to know what I've found out?"

Sam looked away from Keone and replied, "Not really. I don't think I could handle one more piece of information. Is Dr. Wayne aware that you're here?"

"Yes. He's allowed me another fifteen-minute visit. In strict compliance with the law in cases such as this."

"Cases such as this? Is this a case? What are you talking about? I thought I was in an accident."

"It's my job to confirm that. I believe there's something else involved here. Something you said yesterday caught my interest. You described the crash to me and clearly demonstrated that your confusion began before the accident with the clear bubble that enveloped you."

"The what?" Sam replied.

Keone flipped open his notebook. He knew when he was being conned. "I have it in my notes. You said, and I quote, 'I felt like I passed through a kind of film, like a clear bubble, and heard a loud pop.' Have you forgotten?"

"If I said something as loony as that, I can see why they're keeping me here. I just felt dizzy and thought I was on the wrong side of the road. That's all."

"Has anyone coached you on what to say to the police since we last spoke?"

"No one here has said anything about the police, except Bob, when he told me I needed to talk with you yesterday. I'm sorry if I said anything weird. I was still pretty out of it."

"Did your friend Dave mention that I'd been to see him?"

"I don't think so. Once I explained it was my injuries that made me into a raving lunatic last night, he apologized. He became concerned for me. Asked about my injuries and things."

"He's your best friend."

"Yes. We've been very close since college. Married a pair of sisters, you know."

"Yes, I know. You just think you married a different sister than he does. Sounds like that made him a little, I don't know, pissed off?"

"Dave's a great friend. Once he understood what was really happening, his main focus was how he and Julie could help Janet and me. The doctors tell me I'll get everything straight again if I let them work on me. I really want to get out of here, so I'm going to do exactly as they say."

"Time's up, Sergeant." It was Sam's nurse, Gwen, this time.

"Thank you, Mr. Loftus, you've given me a lot to think about."

When Keone left, he asked the nurse about visitors.

"Dr. Wayne brought a woman yesterday, I think it was Sam's sister, or sister-in-law. Another older man visited in the evening after Dr. Field saw him. I think his name was Lee. Dr.

Wayne authorized that visit as well."

"What about his brother-in-law, Mr. Walden?"

"Dr. Wayne specifically prohibited any unsupervised visits from him or his wife."

"Is there any time he could have slipped in unnoticed?"

"Well, the nurses are all together in the conference room for change of shift report. There are usually some therapists and food service folks around then. I could check."

"Would you please? Has Sam received any calls?"

"Dr. Wayne had the phone in his room removed before Mr. Loftus arrived."

"Thank you, Nurse..."

"Tanaka. Gwen Tanaka."

Keone didn't think Sam imagined Walden's visit. He also knew it had been anything but friendly. Walden had been too careful not to be observed.

Sam Loftus hadn't lawyered up. He'd been threatened. That visit from good old Dave had shaken Sam to his core. Sam and Dave might be playing the parts of best friends, but their wives told a different story. Walden was certainly lying and Sam wasn't telling the whole truth.

Keone Boyd was not a good person to lie to.

Chapter Seventeen

Monday, March 18, 3:00 PM

Sam Loftus had done his homework on Dr. Evan Drayton. According to both Gwen and Millie, Drayton was a fussy man. He liked to dress informally, but would rush home and change if he spilled a drop of anything on his clothing. He loved neatness and order. In this, at least, he shared common cause with Sam Loftus.

As an accountant Sam liked to see everything add up. Unfortunately, Sam's current condition didn't add up at all.

Their first session took place two days after Dr. Field's visit. The intervening hours were filled with multiple batteries of oral and written tests, administered by various mental health technicians with complicated titles. The only allowance they made for Sam's condition was the use of reversed copies of each of the written tests, which he could read perfectly. He assumed they made reversed copies of his answers so they could evaluate them.

Sam was ready for the meticulous Dr. Drayton when he at last made his entrance. The good doctor tried to get him to open up about his experiences. But Sam was too smart for him. He spoke freely for hours without exposing his conviction that his state was not a delusion, but a reality. He did, however, grill Drayton about the disorder Field had mentioned, Capgras.

"Capgras Delusion was first described by a French psychiatrist in 1923," Drayton began.

Oh, so it's a delusion is it? No wonder Field had trouble spitting that out.

"He called it *l'illusion des sosies*, the illusion of doubles. A number of cases have been identified throughout the years. I had a patient with Capgras. I'll call her Barbara. She was thirty years old and believed that a stranger had replaced her husband. She refused to go home from the hospital with him. When sedated and taken to her home, she refused to sleep with her husband, locked herself in a separate bedroom, and pulled a gun on us when we suggested she be returned to the hospital."

"Did she have a head injury, like me?"

"No, she was psychotic, but the disorder has also been observed in patients with head injuries."

So Drayton thought everything was the result of the crash, too. Sam felt both Drayton and Field were stretching to find an acceptable diagnosis. He also knew they were wrong. But, if keeping them satisfied would get him out of here, he would play along.

"Let's assume for a moment that you and Dr. Field are right. Who am I to say, as a layman?"

"A very enlightened approach, Mr. Loftus."

"Thank you. I can see how I could learn to un-transpose left and right through something like occupational therapy. I suppose I could even be trained to read what for me appears to be mirror writing. But how could I ever learn to accept a different woman as my wife?"

"That's an honest and logical question. In the few cases of Capgras where I, or others, have been successful, it has been a long slow process of adaptation. It also requires complete commitment from the patient and his loved ones. But it can work."

"What can work?"

"Rehabituation."

"I'm unfamiliar with that term."

"It's most often used in cases of post-traumatic stress disorder, or PTSD. When a soldier returns from a particularly horrendous experience in combat, you can't just throw him back into civilian life. It requires a gradual re-adaptation to a formerly familiar environment."

"I've heard about this on *Sixty Minutes* and some of the other news programs. But how would it work for me?"

"I haven't finished detailing the entire protocol, but I can give you the basics. You would go through a series of steps to re-acquaint yourself with your former life. You would live in your house and sleep in your bedroom."

"Sleeping with someone I don't believe is my wife?"

Dr. Drayton smiled. "No. She would sleep in a separate bedroom. You would live together like housemates in the first phase as well as the second."

"What happens in the second phase?"

"Once you feel a sense of comfort and security in your own home, we would gradually add external activities. One of the first would be to return to work."

"I would really like that. I miss my job."

"Other external activities would follow. You could entertain or go out for dinner with your wife or to a friend's house."

"I would love to be able to spend time with our friends, again."

"That's wonderful. You could see it as a reward for achieving intermediate goals.

"In the third phase you would take the next step in re-establishing your relationship with your wife as lover and partner. Up to this point you will have re-established your friendship, which is how you first operated in your original courtship. You only take the final step when you and Janet feel you're both ready."

"I see. You can imagine how frightening this all appears to me now."

"Yes. Of course I do. That's why we take it one step at a time. As you are an educated individual, I felt it appropriate to delineate the big picture for you at the outset. I hope you appreciate this."

"Yes, I do doctor." Sam said. *Especially since you just told me how I need to play this to regain my freedom.*

"The first and most important step is that you trust me and agree to accept that you are ill and need help. If you can do this, Dr. Field and Dr. Wayne have agreed to place you under my care and abide by my decisions regarding your rehabilitation."

Bingo. This is the opening I've been waiting for. It'll be a hell of a lot easier to fool one of these morons than all three of them. Besides, I don't know how far I should trust Bob Wayne.

What Sam said was, "Dr. Drayton, you have been totally honest with me, so I will be the same with you. I know I'm screwed up. All of the evidence points to the fault lying in my mind and not in the outside world. I'm frightened of the treatment plan you just described. Still if there's a chance this could restore my ordered life, I'd be a fool not to try. I have to take this at my own pace, though. Some of the things you suggest give me chills at this point. I am a very methodical individual. That's probably why I love mathematics. One proof leads to another in a logical progression until you are able to accept concepts that once seemed impossible."

"Mr. Loftus, I can see we are going to be able to work together to solve your problem. I'll begin by assigning you to Occupational Therapy. When we're able to send you home, you'll be able to read and write in a manner acceptable to society and left and right will have the same meanings for you that they do for the rest of us."

"Thank you, Doctor. God bless you." Sam didn't even have to fake the tears, and letting them out helped him keep from laughing.

Chapter Eighteen

Monday, March 18, 4:00 PM

When Keone Boyd parked his rental car at Maui Police headquarters in Wailuku, he looked forward to spending most of the evening in the tiny cubicle assigned to him. The normally tedious process of transferring the notes from each of his interviews onto the appropriate case file documents on his computer was a welcome respite from the strangeness of the past few days.

From the first two days of his investigation, he had notes from interviews with Dr. Robert Wayne, Dave Walden, Julie Walden, Jan Loftus, Lee Marder, Sam's boss and co-workers, and his two short interludes with Sam. Since then he'd interviewed Dr. Evan Drayton, Dr. John Field, Julie's agent, and publisher, the president of the decorating firm Jan worked for, and six of her clients.

After Julie Walden provided Dave's client list by e-mail, he'd called a cross-section. Each gave Dave glowing reviews, as Keone guessed they would. From the Ka'anapali Golf Course, he obtained a list of the high-rollers involved in the charity golf tournament. This list was more intriguing but, to this point, he had been unable to score a telephone interview with any of them.

Entering every piece of information into the computer, Keone went into the zone.

A detective's job is filled with a series of pieces. Places, people, events, physical evidence, and oral evidence are usually obtained in a somewhat illogical order, based on witness availability, crime scene clearance, lab reports, and even the illogical order in which a detective becomes aware of events. He knew the start of this case wasn't the moment Sam Loftus had his strange sense of passing through a bubble. Everything that happened was the direct or indirect result of something that happened prior to that moment.

Putting all of his findings and speculations down in one continuous session always helped him identify potential causative elements and events. It was a kind of act of faith to do all of this work with the expectation that a path for subsequent investigation would emerge. But he was seldom disappointed.

After more than an hour of reviewing, editing, and entering data into the computer Keone created his cards. Each of these 3" x 5" cards contained key information about the case: people, places, interactions, physical evidence, even hunches. He used these and a corkboard wall in his cubicle to identify potential connections. Single strands of yarn represented individual connections between specific cards, such as the strand between, Dave Walden and Ka'anapali Golf Course.

Once he posted all the cards and mapped all the connections, Keone rarely had to return to the computer files. As new information came in he added it to the computer files, created new cards, and tied these to existing cards via yarn.

He laid the cards, pushpins, and yarn on the narrow table in front of his corkboard wall and was about to stick the Sam Loftus card in the center, when Lieutenant Tony Alcala tapped on the entrance to Keone's cubicle. "Got a minute, Big Guy?"

"Sure, Boss. What can I do for you?"

"First, I'd like to know what the hell you're doing here. Didn't I hear something about a major car crash with one of my detectives pinned in a jumble of scrap metal that used to be a sports car?"

"I was lucky. The medics checked me out."

"And told you to go to the hospital and see a doctor."

"I went to the hospital right after the crash. And I saw a couple of doctors." Keone knew how to spin things his way.

"Was one of them Hiram Lloyd?"

"Yes. I believe I did run into him there."

"But he didn't examine you, did he?"

"No. That was another doctor."

"Was he an ER doctor?"

"You know, I'm not sure." Keone plucked one of his three-by-five cards off the table. "Dr. Wayne was the guy. He was there to examine his own patient, a Mr. Sam Loftus. He spent some time with me after he finished. He didn't suggest I needed to have any further treatment, so I returned to work. I'm sure I can get a note from him if you need one."

"No. I just wondered why Dr. Lloyd said none of his doctors had seen you."

Keone should have known that little prick, Lloyd, couldn't resist complaining to Tony.

Tony glanced at the cards on Keone's table. "What're you working on?"

"Well, I know we're short-handed. So, since I was pretty familiar with the crash, I decided to collect some data for the accident investigation."

"You know that's against department policy. You were a victim of the crash, for Christ's sake."

"You want me to turn it over to somebody else? I'm putting everything into my report."

"No. You're right about us being short-handed. Just wrap it up quickly." Alcala knew Keone could finish the investigation faster than it would take another officer just to get up to speed.

"I'll be done in another day, two days tops. The cause of the crash is clearly related to the mental state of the wrong-way driver. I've already interviewed him, his work colleagues, two close friends, and his wife and sister-in-law."

"Why the sister-in-law?"

"Since the crash Loftus believes she's his wife and that his wife's his sister-in-law. It's sort of confusing."

"Just close the case. Fast. I've got better things for you to work on."

"Sure thing, Boss," Keone said to Alcala's rapidly departing back.

From the next cubicle he heard a snort followed by the squeal of a chair being pushed away from a desk. "Dodged another one, eh, Keone?"

The rotund form of Frank Kulima filled the entrance to Keone's cubicle.

"What?" Keone asked.

"I lost count of how many department policies you violated in just the last twenty-four hours. I wish I knew how you get away with it."

"I consider them more like guidelines."

"Right."

"You're just pissed because I made sergeant before you."

"I am not bothered in the least. I know you'll screw up. I've got my eyes on you."

"I don't like threats, Frank. I'm not in competition with you."

"No threat intended. I'm just a good detective doing his job. Enjoy your afternoon. I've got real detective work to do." Kulima made a sharp about face, almost toppling over from the rapid redistribution of weight, and headed out of the station.

Keone didn't have time for this shit. He needed to analyze his data while it was still fresh in his mind.

After another hour, Keone's corkboard looked like a spider's web, with colorful strands linking key people, places, actions, and miscellaneous other information. He circled certain key contact points that needed to be further examined. In the days to come the spider's web would become more complex and more circled contacts would emerge. But, as he knew when he left the Loftus home, three key contacts to explore were the ones between Julie and Dave Walden, Sam Loftus and Dave Walden, and Dave Walden and the high rollers. Of course he would pursue the Julie-Sam connection and the Jan-Sam connection, but he sensed this wasn't where he would strike gold.

Keone's office phone rang as he stared at the corkboard. Startled, he reached for the receiver. "Maui Police Department, Criminal Investigation Division, this is Sergeant Boyd. How may I help you?"

"Keone this is Julie." She sounded dazed and out of breath. "I...I need to talk to you. I'm in trouble. Could you please come to my house? Now!"

"Yes. Of course."

Julie gave him her address in Kula. As he left his office, he knew he'd circled at least one key connection.

Part IV: Plans and Pains

It didn't sound a comfortable plan, Alice thought, and for a few minutes she walked on in silence, puzzling over the idea, and every now and then stopping to help the poor Knight, who certainly was NOT a good rider.

Whenever the horse stopped (which it did very often), he fell off in front; and whenever it went on again (which it generally did rather suddenly), he fell off behind. Otherwise he kept on pretty well, except that he had a habit of now and then falling off sideways; and as he generally did this on the side on which Alice was walking, she soon found that it was the best plan not to walk QUITE close to the horse.

Lewis Carroll, author

Chapter Nineteen

Monday, March 18, 6:00 PM

Sam knew the psychiatrist and neurologist were completely wrong about him, but he didn't have an alternate explanation for what was happening to him. Either he was crazy or the world was. Neither alternative was acceptable. He just needed to get out of the hospital as soon as possible to start investigating things for himself. He was prepared to do anything to make that happen—even play damaged.

His formidable nurse, a new one, brought a telephone into his room, but it had no dial.

"You are to be permitted incoming calls now." With that pronouncement, she was gone.

Sam had a suspicion who might call him and found he was right moments later when the telephone rang.

He lifted the receiver as though the action alone could free him from captivity. "Hello?"

"Hi, Sam, it's Tom Conrad. I'm glad to see my protests shook somebody up enough to provide you with access to your lawyer."

"Hi, Tom. Damn, it's good to hear your voice. I feel so

isolated here. They think I'm crazy and treat me like I'm in jail."

"I know. Lee gave me your note. As your lawyer, let me advise you that this is the best thing they could possibly think. You must do nothing to disabuse them of their delusion that you're delusional. I'm pretty sure this is just the ticket to get you off the hook for any charges stemming from your traffic accident."

"But I'm not crazy!"

"Sssh. Don't say that too loud. I know you're not crazy. But you could be in a shitload of trouble. I need you to play along until I can sort all this out. Promise me?"

Since Tom was suggesting exactly what he'd planned to do anyway, Sam decided to let him think it was his idea. "Okay, for now. But once I get out of this place, we're gonna talk."

"Sure, sure. I'll try to get you sprung from there as soon as I can. Just be smart, Sam. Bye."

Chapter Twenty

Monday, March 18, 6:15 PM

Keone was filled with conflicting emotions as he drove to the Walden home. He'd only met Julie Walden once, but he already cared about her. As crazy as this case had become, she seemed to be the eye of the storm, while a hurricane swirled around her. Why had he taken an instant dislike to her husband? He'd seemed collegial enough. Why did he initially see Jan as remote and cold? She was obviously concerned about her husband. And what about Sam? He still didn't know what to think about Sam.

The Walden home was as different from the Loftus home as he could imagine. It was an example of an old Maui standard turned into a luxury abode. It had once exhibited the classic two stories with the top floor overhanging an open carport structure common to the hilly parts of Maui. He could see it had been completely reconstructed with steel piers and floor to ceiling windows, instead of the usual concrete blocks and wooden frames. This house would have been at home on Mt. Tantalus in O'ahu, where TV stars rented homes while they worked on the longer-lived series filmed there.

The usual open carport had been replaced with a completely enclosed four-car garage and the landscaping was lush, but elite, with tall metal gates and fences enclosing everything from the sidewalk inward, including the driveway.

Keone parked on the street and walked to the front gate, where he found a button to press.

"Yes?"

"Julie? It's Keone Boyd."

"Just a sec. I'll let you in."

A buzzer alerted him that the gate was now unlocked and he entered the front garden. It was a Japanese garden and included a winding gravel path that led up the hill over a Koi-filled stream to the entrance on the top story. The word pretentious entered his head. But Julie seemed so down to earth that he replaced that word with arty.

He could hear Julie stumble as she approached the front door. When she opened the door, at last, her hair was bathed in blood. She had bruises on her face and shoulders. Her posture and the dark stains on her clothing suggested he would find similar marks on her back and the back of her legs.

"My God, what happened?"

"Hit me. Fell back into glass." She collapsed into his arms.

"Who hit you?"

"Dave," she gasped. Her eyes rolled up and her knees began to buckle.

Keone felt her full weight in his arms. Feeling shards of glass protruding from her legs, back, and shoulders, he adjusted his hold so he wouldn't push them further in. He carried her through the small entry into the debris field that was once a sunken living room. Broken crockery, shards from a cracked picture window, and splintered furniture were scattered across the room. The remnants of a shattered glass-top coffee table crunched under his shoes as he carried Julie to the one couch that appeared free of broken glass.

He gently laid Julie on the couch, checked to make sure she was breathing normally, and made a quick visual inspection to assure himself there were no life-threatening external wounds.

Keone removed his Glock 45 from it's holster and clipped the compact, Surefire flashlight to the bottom of the frame, then began a room-by-room search until he had cleared the whole house. Walden had fled

Keone lifted up a dishtowel Julie had thrown over her bleeding head, brushed a lock of hair from her eyes, and called for an ambulance on his cell. Before calling for a crime scene crew, Keone wanted to make his own visual search of the living room. But he did call an officer that he knew patrolled this area and asked him to make certain the husband didn't return unannounced.

Keone closed his cell and crouched on the floor beside Julie. He lifted her wrist with his right hand so he could monitor her pulse. At the same time, he applied pressure with his left hand to the dishtowel, which he'd moved to the back of Julie's head.

He began his visual circuit of the room at the front door. He noted the molding near the latch was freshly cracked and guessed Dave hadn't closed the door gently when he left. The parquet floor of the entrance alcove was polished to a gloss but the only shoe prints he saw were his own. There were also bloody imprints from Julie's bare feet. He assumed she and Dave, like most Maui residents, left their shoes and slippahs outside the door. Through the still-open door he could see a pair of women's sandals beside the doormat. He suspected an evidence team would find residue from Dave's bare feet on the parquet floor as well, though it appeared Dave had avoided stepping in any of the blood.

The living room was rectangular and two steps below the entrance. He started his assessment of the space beginning at the front door and proceeded first in a clockwise direction. If the entrance was at twelve o'clock from his position by the couch, there was a hallway that led off the entrance alcove at two and ten o'clock. A wall unit containing expensive curios was centered at three o'clock on the living room wall. At nine o'clock on the opposite wall a china cabinet had once stood. It was now a mass of expensive broken Royal Dalton, splintered wood, and pieces from the glass front. Keone noted there was no blood on these.

The couch where Julie lay was at right angles to the left edge of the picture window that dominated the far wall, opposite the entrance. A large end table separated this couch from a longer, narrower couch under the window.

He found the largest concentration of blood here. The window had a cracked circular area just above the center of the couch. There was a little blood there but a large pool stained the seat of the couch and another covered the pieces of the shattered glass-top table that had fronted the couch.

His entire circuit of the room had taken less than a minute. Still, Keone turned back to Julie with a clearer picture of what had happened. In that short time, Julie's breathing had become labored, her color ashen, and her pulse thready.

I'm losing her. She must be bleeding somewhere else.

He dropped her arm, ran to the kitchen, and grabbed two handfuls of dishtowels hanging by the sink. He sopped the blood off her scalp and examined it for a wound. He located every area on her body that was bleeding and either tied or laid a towel there to absorb and, hopefully, help control the bleeding.

Where's that damn ambulance?

His thoughts were immediately followed by the sound of sirens. When he heard them stop in front of the house, he ran out the front door and waved them up, shouting, "Up here. Serious head, back, and leg bleeds. Unconscious." He noticed a patrol unit and an ambulance pull up behind the EMTs.

He rushed back to Julie's side and applied pressure to a serious bleeder soaking the towel on her inner thigh. The head wound was now just oozing. She was still breathing, if erratically, but her pulse was even threadier than before.

The ambulance attendants and EMTs moved Keone away, applied an oxygen mask, and started replacing lost fluids. He pointed to the wound in her thigh and an EMT said, "I see it. Eldon, you've got some sewing to do."

Keone was elated to see his friend start to work on Julie's wound. He had already assessed the other wounds and decided this one was most critical. With Eldon on the job, Keone could finally take time to call the crime scene team.

By the time he'd finished on the phone, Eldon and his team

had Julie stabilized. Julie opened her eyes once, briefly, when the ambulance crew lifted her onto a collapsible rolling stretcher.

Eldon flashed a smile at Keone. Julie would make it.

While they secured Julie on the stretcher, Keone looked at her battered face and arms.

She's even lovely bruised, cut, and unconscious.

He forced himself to look away from Julie's face and concentrate on helping the attendants wheel her down the winding path to the street level. Julie's eyes flickered open as they reached the door to the ambulance.

"Julie?"

She turned her head toward Keone's voice and reached for his arm.

"Keone, I've never seen him like that. I thought I could break it to him gently. I thought he knew our marriage was over."

"Has he ever hit you before?"

"Yes. Occasionally. But he always used an open palm, before. This time he punched me in the chin with his fist. I flew over the coffee table...banged my head on the window. When I came down, I hit the coffee table...I passed out for a few minutes, before I called you...It hurts so much. Keone...I'm scared." Her eyes began to defocus.

"Just rest. These guys will take good care of you. I'll see you at the hospital."

The ambulance door slammed closed and they sped off, leaving Keone with the uniforms, watching the EMTs pack up and depart the scene.

"What do you need us to do, Sarge?"

"It would really help if you could canvas the neighborhood. See if anybody saw anything. "

And stay away from the house so I can do some detective work.

"Oh, and keep a lookout for Dave Walden, too."

"The golf tournament guy? Is this his house?"

"Yeah. He beat the crap out of his wife."

"You want us to put out an APB?"

"That's a good idea. We need to catch this bastard."

"You got it, Sarge."

"Mahalo. I secured the scene, but I'll hang around until the evidence guys get here."

As the officers rushed off to do as he'd requested, Keone retraced his steps to the entrance and began his search of the remainder of the house.

Julie confirmed what my visual circuit of the living room told me. But I need to look around the rest of this place more carefully before the crime scene team arrives.

The living room opened directly off the entrance, but the two hallways that led away from the entrance area caught Keone's attention. He followed the left hallway first assuming it would lead to the master bedroom. He was right and wrong. After passing a laundry room on the right, he found Julie's workroom on the left and a large bedroom at the end of the hall. The latter was decorated in an open friendly style. It was very feminine but not girlish. He noted the door had double locks. Keone felt an unusual sense of intruding, standing in what was clearly Julie's bedroom. Besides Julie wasn't the suspect here.

Returning to the entrance, Keone proceeded down the other hall. After passing the kitchen on the left, where he'd grabbed the dishtowels, he found a large den on the right with the hall ending at a second master bedroom. He wasn't surprised to find this room very manly in style. The closets held Dave Walden's extensive wardrobe and the bathroom his cosmetics.

So, the Walden's don't share a bedroom. I wonder what else they don't share?

Keone returned to the den and again sensed the aura of the man of the house. He also noticed double locks on the currently open door. Toward the front of the house, Dave's massive oak desk was centered under a window. The walls were paneled with rich dark wood, maybe Koa and the flooring was the same, although covered almost to the walls with a lush, colorful Persian rug. The bright rug and wooden floor were inconsistent with the pale wall-to-wall carpeting in all the other rooms.

The kitchen was clearly one of Julie's rooms. It was country casual in style and smelled like a bakery. The lattice-crusted, cherry and apple pies cooling on a rack on the kitchen's center island were still slightly warm and smelled delicious.

As he walked back toward the entrance a question troubled him. How did they enter the house from the garages below? Surely, they had steps inside so they wouldn't have to walk around.

When he reached the entrance he noticed two doors facing each other across the entrance area. The one on his right held coats, but the one opposite opened onto a stairway to the lower level.

He flipped on the light switch by the stairs. *What the...?*

There was only a two-car garage. Each side with its own door and opening apparatus. But he'd seen four garage doors when he arrived.

Expecting the crime scene team at any moment, Keone ran outside and down the walkway to the fence enclosing the driveway. Since he'd left the light on he could see thin streams of light spilling from the seams around the two garage doors on the left side, but nothing from the two on the right. He climbed the fence to get closer. When he examined the right side garage doors up close, it became clear they were false fronts attached to a cinderblock cube that abutted the house. He climbed back over the fence and examined the position of the faux garages in relation to the layout of the rest of the house.

Of course.

The mysterious enclosed space lay directly beneath Dave's study.

"Anybody here?" A voice called. Keone spun around to see the crime scene team advancing up the front walk. He pointed to the front door and said, "There's blood and a lot of debris in the living room. I left the door open when I went in. The medics treated the victim on site and transported her to the hospital."

Keone turned to leave. But, before he reached his car, one of the crime scene team asked, "Did you touch anything?"

"I carried the victim to the living room and laid her on the couch that's at a right angle to the picture window. I also ran down the hall to find something to stop the bleeding. I ended up using dishtowels from the kitchen. I know enough not to disturb the scene."

"I'm sure you do, Sergeant. But, you know I have to ask."

"Sure. Since you guys are securing the area, I'll get out of your way. You need anything else?"

"We're good."

Keone nodded and slipped behind the wheel of his car. He headed for the hospital sorting through what had just happened.

Dave Walden beat up his wife. Julie said he'd done it before, but without fists. Could Julie be having an affair with Sam? Is that why Julie's divorcing Dave? But why would that translate into a long-term marriage and kids in Sam's mind? And what was in Dave's secret room?

He doubted the crime scene guys would find the hidden entrance that he was sure existed from Dave's study to the secret room. Besides, it was well outside the scope of their investigation.

Keone knew from experience that finding things that didn't add up was often the key to breaking a case wide open. He knew he was on the right track.

Chapter Twenty-one

Monday, March 25, 2:00 PM

Sam's first formal session with Dr. Drayton went so well he could feel his freedom coming closer. He knew he'd have to work hard at reading mirror writing and convince them all that he was beginning to accept their definitions of left and right. It was an interesting mental challenge to learn their way without losing track of the real left and right. He had a lot of things to keep straight to make this work but was confident he could do it. He maintained his journal in his normal handwriting, but kept it hidden.

The next two weeks he rarely saw Dr. Field or Bob Wayne. He spent most of his time in Occupational Therapy learning to do what for him was mirror math, mirror reading, and mirror writing. He was surprised how difficult it was. He thought the math part would be a piece of cake. Especially since the computer programs were identical to those he'd used at work for years. Rows and columns were still rows and columns. Spreadsheets were still spreadsheets, but inverting the order of numbers and columns annoyed him so much, that he struggled. At the end of two weeks, Sam's boss came in and couldn't hide his disappointment. The OT specialist assured him that the worst was over. He predicted Sam's rate of improvement during the next two weeks would be exponential.

Conversely, Sam mastered reading backwards rapidly once

he began recognizing inverted words instead of inverted letters. Flashcards were the secret here. He made a game out of trying to read them faster than his therapist. Everything he saw in this new world—magazines, newspapers, even television shows—were an opportunity to practice. It was like the Hawaiian language immersion program he took a few years back.

Learning to type backwards was harder than reading backwards, yet vastly easier than learning to write backwards in cursive. After many days struggling to write with his left hand (which the therapists called his right), the OT tech suggested he try using his left hand (which Sam called his right). Sam experimented with a number of styles, but finally discovered he did best writing backhand with his right hand. Although he wrote much slower than normal, his penmanship was actually easier to read. He only used his normal handwriting for his journal.

His sessions with Dr. Drayton were his greatest challenge. The man was a good psychiatrist and worked diligently to address Sam's delusions. Even though he tried to appear receptive, Sam couldn't make himself consider the possibility that his children were figments of his imagination. He did let Drayton believe he was willing to consider Janet, and not Julie, was really his wife. Sam confided that the idea of showing affection to Janet still made him uncomfortable. This must have jibed well with some theory of Drayton's, because he was preparing to send Sam home on a trial basis in just a few weeks.

"At first, just think of Janet as a close friend who is sharing a house with you. Did you have dorm mates in college?" Drayton asked.

"Sure. Dave and I even shared a house with both men and women when we were in graduate school."

"How are your visits with Janet going?"

"They're still pretty formal, but I no longer dread them. I can envision her becoming my friend." Sam could say this with conviction because he actually believed it to be true.

"That's all we need you to do, in addition to passing your

final OT exams, to release you to go home. Habituation is not an instant process. It's gradual like real life. Learning to love someone is a process. It takes time."

"You mean like dating?" Sam enjoyed playing a bit dense for Drayton.

"Yes. You need to get to first base, before you try to go farther."

Sam suppressed a shiver. "I'll just focus on the friend thing for now, okay?

"Sure. Sure. You're making good progress."

I'm making progress all right, you dumbass. My home run is just a little different than what you think it is.

Monday, March 25, 3:00 PM

Back in his room, Sam rang the call bell. Nurse Tanaka was there in a flash.

"How can I help you, Mr. Loftus?"

"Please. You promised."

"Okay. What do you need, Sam?"

"That's so much better. After all this time, I know we can be friends."

"What do you want, Sam?"

"I'd like to take a little stroll around the hospital. You asked me to tell you each time before I left."

"Sure, Sam. I trust you to stay within the walls of Maui Memorial. After those first couple rough days, you turned into my most compliant and considerate patient."

Sam climbed out of bed and headed for the door.

"Just let me know when you get back. And keep it under an hour this time."

"Your wish is my command, my lovely angel of mercy."

"Stop that. You know that stuff doesn't work on me."

But of course it did.

Sam made a complete circuit of his floor before taking the stairwell to the second floor and a particularly well-concealed space where he kept his journal and a burner cell phone that his lawyer smuggled in to him.

Tom Conrad answered on the first ring. "I have good news, Sam. The affidavits from all of the doctors have been filed with the county court and Maui PD. My discussion with Chief Watanabe confirmed that, if everything is in order, no criminal charges will be issued. The case will be officially closed."

"That's great. Now I just have to keep up my end of the bargain."

"I know what a pain it is to pretend they're winning. But, if you keep giving them what they want, you'll be out of there by the end of the month."

"You know, Tom, you might just be right."

Chapter Twenty-two

Tuesday, March 26, 9:00 AM

Julie ached inside and out. No matter how they adjusted her hospital bed, some portion of her body felt twisted. To be honest, her whole life felt twisted. She knew Dave had a temper, but he had never left marks like this before. Or had she just convinced herself that the frequent face slaps and shoves into the wall weren't that bad? Having the man you believed loved you lose control so completely and hit you with such force was something she never expected. Dave was secretive and often angry at things outside their home life that he didn't share with her. But she had never seen Dave with such uncontrollable rage. She felt like a stranger had inhabited her husband's body. Julie realized she didn't know who Dave Walden was—inside.

A light knock on her door ended her reflections. "Come in."

The first thing to appear around the doorframe was a plush doll version of her character, Hawai'i Anna. The doll's hands held a diminutive bouquet of orchids and baby's breath. She was pleased when the person holding the doll showed himself. It was Keone Boyd.

"Do you bring flowers to all the women you rescue from their violent husbands?"

"No. But I didn't really rescue you. Your husband was gone

when I arrived."

"Thank you very much, Sergeant Boyd."

"Keone."

"Keone. I used to know what that meant in Hawaiian."

"It means *sand* or *homeland*, which is pretty much the same for me since I was born on Maui."

"Have you found Dave?"

"No, but we're looking. What he did to you is a crime."

"I knew we'd grown apart, but I thought he did, too. He seemed so surprised when I told him I wanted a divorce."

"Men can fool themselves sometimes. Also, I believe he had a number of other concerns that evening."

"Like what?"

"I'll tell you when I know more. For now, just know he's been doing some illegal things."

"I knew he had desires I couldn't—wouldn't—satisfy for him. He's had mistresses since we moved to Maui. But we got along. He could get abrupt at times, but most of the time he was charming. He used to make me laugh all the time.

"He would never talk about it, but I knew he used drugs. He did even in Grad school, but then it was mostly pot. Hell, everybody smoked pot. He won't tell me what he takes now, but I know he needs it."

"Julie, he does more than visit prostitutes and take drugs. Illegal drugs are his main business."

Julie's entire body began to shake. It took a full minute before she could control herself enough to speak. "You probably think I should have guessed, but I didn't. He made friends of so many important people here on Maui and all over the place. He was especially nice to me when we went out. I felt like his prize possession."

"No one should ever feel like another person's possession. Especially not you."

Julie decided to change the subject. "They say I can go home today. I'd better call Jan and ask her to pick me up."

"I think Jan has enough on her plate with Sam, don't you? I would be honored to drive you home."

"Thank you. I guess I'm a little nervous that Dave will come back."

"I have some paperwork here that should help with that. The first is the formal assault charge against Dave. All you need to do is sign it."

Julie didn't hesitate before she signed.

"I also have a request for a restraining order. An attorney friend of mine put it together for you."

This time Julie hesitated. "Will I have to appear in court?"

"He said probably not. But you'll have to let him take a deposition. You can do that at home, though."

Julie gazed at the document for a few seconds. Then her face took on a confident look and she signed.

"Do you think he'll come back?"

"I doubt it, with the charges he's facing. We can arrest him if he shows his face almost anywhere."

"But he still has a key?"

"All your locks have been changed."

"What if he's hiding in our house?"

"I'll check out every room and the neighborhood before I leave. The fellow who patrols your neighborhood has been alerted to keep a special look out. And I know you have my number in your phone. I'd recommend you put it on speed dial."

"Why are you so concerned about me?"

"First, you are part of my ongoing investigation. Second, your husband has a lot to answer for and not just what he did that night. Finally, I like you. You're very special person, Julie. Hawai'i Anna told me so and made me promise to look after you."

She picked up the doll and looked into her button eyes. "Did you really? You seem to have better taste in men than me, Anna." She made the doll nod its head.

A nurse came in with Julie's release form. "I'll help you get dressed and ready to leave the hospital. I know you're still pretty stiff."

Turning to Keone, the nurse said, "Come back in about

thirty minutes." It wasn't a question. She ushered Keone out the door and shut it behind him.

Tuesday, March 26, 9:30 AM

Keone wandered over to the other wing of the hospital and took the elevator to the floor where Sam Loftus currently resided. Sam was sitting up in bed and trying to read a newspaper when Keone entered the room.

"Hello, Sergeant Boyd. How are you this lovely day?"

"I'm fine, Mr. Loftus. How are you?"

"A little better each day. I'm starting to enjoy reading the paper. Though it still takes forever to finish, my OT guy says it's great exercise for my addled brain."

"I stopped by to let you know that the district attorney has decided to file no criminal charges against you for the accident. You'll still have insurance responsibilities and such, but your record will remain clean."

"Thank you. I've heard from my insurance company and instructed them to pay all claims, especially yours."

"I guess it must be the largest, huh?"

"It is. But that beautiful car of yours was worth it. Are you going to use the money to buy another Morgan?"

"I don't know. It's really a younger man's car. I have to be realistic about the future. I'm Hawaiian, you know. We always have large families."

"Sounds like maybe you've found someone who's got you thinking about the future."

"Too early to tell." Keone did not want to have this conversation, especially with Sam. "*Aloha*, Mr. Loftus."

"Aloha and mahalo, Sergeant Boyd."

Keone was not done with his interest in Sam Loftus and his recovery. He had no illusions that Sam was over Julie. He planned to keep both of her alleged husbands as far away from her as possible.

Tuesday, March 26, 10:15 AM

When Keone returned to Julie's room, she was dressed and getting into a wheelchair for her ride out of the hospital. Keone had used the valet to park his rental car and went down in the elevator with Julie and her nurse.

He could tell that she was still sore and tired. But he also knew she wanted to get out of the hospital more than anything. He thought part of this was because she felt more in control in her own home, despite Dave's actions. She needed to write and she could only do that in her workroom at home.

When Keone first visited her, right after the beating, she talked about creating a story with Hawai'i Anna being in the hospital for some minor surgery. Keone had even taken her by wheelchair down to the pediatrics ward so she could make character sketches based on some of the kids there. But she'd tired quickly, and he never saw her write anything.

When the valet brought the car around, Keone lifted Julie into the passenger seat and fastened her seatbelt. Before he drove off, he saw movement by the hospital entrance. Frank Kulima was just inside the door, watching them. He wondered how long Kulima had been observing his visits with Julie. He'd only visited her twice before today but hadn't been particularly careful not to be seen. He could learn to hate that son of a bitch.

As they drove away from the hospital he glanced over to see that Julie was smiling. "Once again you're rescuing me from somewhere I don't want to be. I hope this gets to be a habit."

Keone smiled, too. But his mind was quickly occupied with other thoughts as they made their way to Kula.

Has Frank told Alcala about my visits to Julie? Did he see my gift? Is he reading something into me taking her home from the hospital?

Keone decided there was nothing he could do. *To hell with Frank Kulima.*

But, as he carried Julie to the front door, he found himself looking around for Kulima's car. He didn't see it, but that didn't prove anything.

He set Julie down so she could walk through the door on her own. He hoped she was pleased to find that the living room she entered looked exactly as it had before Dave bashed it—and her—up.

"Oh my God! What have you done?"

"Is something wrong?"

"Of course not. How did you get everything repaired so fast? How did you know where to put everything?"

"Your decorator was very helpful."

"Jan. I'll have to thank her—and pay her."

Jan entered the living room from the kitchen and threw her arms around her sister. "That won't be necessary. My services are always free to you. And Keone took care of repairing the broken door and window. He said he owed it to you for being so slow in getting over here."

"You dirty birds. How am I ever going to thank you for this?"

"How about dinner in a week or so when you're up and around?" Jan said and Keone nodded

"Deal."

"There are a couple of new items in your house as well." Keone pointed to the door. "These locks are the best in the business. Always use both bolts on each exterior door and on your bedroom door. Jan will explain to you how the new alarm system works."

"It's really pretty easy. He put the same system in our house, too." Jan said.

Reaching into his pocket, Keone removed a tiny remote with a single button. "This is for emergencies. One push of this button and every exterior door is locked and an alarm sent to the security company." *And me.*

"You know, a person with your expertise could really come in handy," Julie said.

"I certainly hope so. Now I've got a house and grounds to search. Say, do you have a key to the other two garages?"

"What?" Jan and Julie asked at the same time.

"Four garage doors and two garages. Didn't you ever notice?"

"Dave said the rest of the space was just a cinder block cube that we could use for storage someday. There's no key. I assumed he'd just have a door added when the time came."

"Makes sense." Keone said before he went off to make sure the house was secure. This time he spent much more time in Dave's bedroom and man-cave. As he'd suspected, he could feel a depressed square under the carpet in the den. Most of it was hidden by the plush chair pushed into the kneehole under Dave's desk. He suspected the square was a small access panel attached to a folding, drop-down stairway into the secret room. Keone's grandmother had a pull down from her attic that was basically the same kind of device.

He didn't want to tear up the house he'd just repaired for Julie, but after she settled in he would ask her permission to have the room entered and searched by the authorities. He was still collecting a trail of evidence against Dave Walden and needed a lot more to justify a search warrant request. It could wait.

When he finished his search of the outside of the house, Keone returned to find the Madison sisters sitting on the couch. Jan was giving Julie an optimistic report on Sam's progress, while Julie struggled to keep her eyes open.

"I know how tired you must be, but I have a favor to ask." Keone turned to Jan. "As you know, I'm looking into Dave's extra-curricular activities. I saw a number of boxes in the study marked 'files and correspondence.' After you get Julie settled, if it's all right with you, Julie, I'd like to send a messenger over from the department to collect those boxes so I can look through them for clues."

"I'd like his crap out of here anyway," Julie said. "You don't mind helping out, do you, Sis?"

"Of course not. Send your man over tomorrow morning after nine. I'm spending the night," Jan replied and gave Keone a look.

"Enough for now," Keone said, lifting Julie up and carrying her into the bedroom.

"I believe this is a bit forward of you, Sergeant. Are you planning to dress me for bed as well?" Julie feigned shocked surprise.

Keone actually blushed as he carried her towards her dressing table, but his dark skin made it hard for others to see. "I expect your sister can handle that phase of your return home. But I know you need some rest."

Jan, who'd followed behind, went to the dresser to collect nightclothes for her sister.

After being gently deposited on the padded chair in front of the dressing table, Julie kept her arms around Keone's massive neck. When he started to pull away she pulled herself up and kissed him on the mouth. "I'll see you later," she said.

Jan smiled at Keone and said, "Get lost, buddy, she needs her rest."

"I'll try to stop by tomorrow to check on you. Aloha, ladies."

At his car, Keone stopped to gaze at false doors covering a cinderblock cube. The combination reminded him of Dave Walden. He needed to find out what Walden did in that space and prayed Julie was safe from what lay inside.

Keone's cell phone interrupted his thoughts with a tune that identified the caller as someone from the department. He looked to see if it was Kulima but it wasn't. The call was from Lieutenant Tony Alcala. He had the answer to one of the questions he'd asked himself on the drive over here. Kulima had spread his gossip to Keone's boss.

Chapter Twenty-three

Wednesday, March 27, 8:15 AM

Keone hated cooling his heels outside Alcala's office. He glanced at his watch. Fifteen minutes. Alcala must really be pissed this time. He'd never made him wait more than five minutes before.

Another ten minutes crept by before Alcala's assistant, Karen, told Keone he could go in. She wasn't smiling.

Alcala didn't look up from the reports on his desk as he told Keone, "Take a seat, Sergeant."

He let Keone stew another five minutes before he looked up. Keone knew enough to keep his mouth shut until the lieutenant spoke.

"It is my understanding that the accident investigation is now closed. Is that correct?"

"Yes, sir."

"You led me to believe that your interactions with..." Alcala looked down at a sheet of paper before continuing, "...Mrs. Julia Walden, were related to that investigation. Is that correct?"

"Yes, sir, they were. But—"

Alcala cut him off. "No buts. Why were you still visiting her yesterday?"

"She is a material witness in another, unrelated, investigation."

"What investigation would that be?"

"The investigation into the criminal activities of her husband, Mr. David Walden, who nearly beat his wife to death nine days ago."

"Why am I unaware of this investigation?"

"Because it was a fortuitous offshoot of the crash investigation. I believe Walden is up to his neck in illicit drug operations on this island with connections back to some major players on the mainland. That's why I felt it was good idea to pay continued attention to his wife." Keone wasn't lying exactly. He just wasn't telling the whole truth. But his personal interest was separate from his professional interest and he intended to keep it that way.

"You better have information to justify that statement, Sergeant. You're walking a fine line here. First, simple drug enforcement and domestic violence are outside your focus. Second, Dave Walden has a lot of friends in this department. Third, I've heard about this knock-out wife of his."

Keone hesitated before looking Tony in the eye and saying, "The only one of those that worries me is the second. I hope I know you as well as I believe I do." With that he set a folder on the lieutenant's desk with all of the data he'd accumulated about Dave Walden and his high-roller friends.

Alcala read the entire file as Keone sat motionless. The lieutenant said nothing, but his occasional nods gave Keone hope that the information he'd gathered was enough.

"All right. You can nail this son of a bitch, but you need to work with the narcs inside the department as well as the DEA." Alcala scribbled some names and numbers on a sheet of paper.

"Thank you, Tony."

"Keone, I've known you a long time and I respect you as a detective. But you screw this up and I won't be able to protect you. Do you honestly believe the Walden woman has anything to do with the criminal activity?"

"No, sir."

"Then stay the hell away from her."

"Is there anything else, sir?"
"No. Get outta here."

Chapter Twenty-four

Thursday, April 10, 1:00 PM

Keone Boyd was mad.

As he left his condo this morning, he'd stopped by the mailbox to find a letter from the Morgan Motor Company smiling up at him. He knew his insurance company had contacted the company that built his now deceased sports car to determine the cost of a replacement and wondered why they were contacting him. Opening the envelope, he found a typed message from the owner of the Morgan Motor Company:

My dear Mr. Boyd,

My colleagues and I were extremely distressed to hear of the terrible accident that destroyed the new vehicle you purchased from our organization. We all wish you a swift and total recovery from any injuries that you sustained.

In response to a request from your insurance company, we provided the full cost to replace your vehicle including anticipated inflationary impact upon the purchase price of a new roadster. We felt it appropriate to remind you of the very long waiting list for such a vehicle and are willing to use the date we were contacted by the insurance company as your request date. This would mean your wait time for delivery in Maui, Hawai'i would be only twenty-five months. We cannot hold this date very long and would appreciate it if you would respond by return mail, confirming that you wish us to build a new Morgan Roadster for you. We will of course require the same deposit you sent when you first ordered the vehicle...

Keone had read enough. It would be months before he'd get anything from the insurance company. Even the deposit was out of reach at present. He'd already decided to use the money for something else. But he didn't appreciate this reminder that his one-time passion was now out of reach. By the time he could receive some form of payment from the insurance company, send a request with the deposit, and get his name back on the list, he was looking at three more years before he would be able to drive a new Morgan.

He'd had just enough money in his savings account to purchase a typical Maui beater. He got into the worn-out Toyota and began the drive to Lahaina to visit an old *friend*, who spent a lot of time in parking lots.

His anger over the letter and his enforced separation from Julie Walden could be helpful in his planned encounter with Scooter. He'd busted Scooter, whose real name was Manuel Morales, multiple times before he became a detective. They'd grown up together in Makawao. Scooter had always been one fine schmoozer and started dealing *pakalolo* in high school. After school he'd graduated from marijuana to prescription drugs. Now he provided *batu* to the moderately well-to-do.

It had taken Keone two weeks to go through every piece of paper in Dave Walden's vast collection. Jan had supplemented the boxes he'd seen in the house with files Dave had put in storage under Julie's name. Yesterday, he found one scrap with the name Scooter, a time, and an address in Kahana scrawled in Dave's handwriting in that stored set of files.

Pakalolo could be obtained many places on Maui, when the weather cooperated. Fields were hidden everywhere in the wilder parts of the island. But batu required processing. Known on the mainland as ice or crystal meth, batu is the drug of choice in Hawai'i. Hawai'i has the highest per capita ice usage in the U.S. Marijuana can be obtained from people without vehicles or whose vehicles haven't moved in years, but crystal meth dealers are generally motorized. Motorcycles and scooters are the most popular forms of transit for those in the business. Vans are too obvious and unnecessary. A great advantage of batu, which means rock or stone in *Tagalog*, is the small mass and volume of a typical sale.

Tourists always think the resident hippie town of Pa'ia is the hotbed for drug sales, but Keone knew the smart sellers were in Lahaina and Kihei—Kihei due to the average age of the population and Lahaina due to the average income. Scooter hung out in Lahaina.

Although most tourists think of Lahaina as the cute little village along Front Street, it's actually the largest consensus designated place (CDP) in West Maui. Lahaina includes the entire coastal area from the tunnel on Route 30 below Olowalu all the way up to Napili in the north. This was Scooter's domain—or at least every parking lot, large or small, in this region was.

Keone's beater, a mostly rusted Corolla, drew little or no attention as he checked every lot. This represented a significant advantage, as no patrol car, marked or unmarked, would ever catch Scooter off guard. Extending his route past Napili into the posh environs of Kapalua, Keone finally struck gold. Scooter was holding court in the lot behind the Kapalua General Store. Scooter's chosen ride for the day was a powder blue vehicle with which he shared a name. Keone drove past without slowing down, then worked his way along the road that went by the former site of the Village golf course, before sliding into the parking lot at just the proper angle to block Scooter's egress. Scooter still hadn't spotted him when he placed a very large, very strong hand on the tiny man's shoulder.

"You're slowing down Scooter. You were much harder to catch in the old days."

Scooter stiffened, until he recognized Keone's voice, then

shifted into pure schmoozer mode. "Howzit, mistah defective. To what do I owe this unexpected visit? You didn't get demoted, did you?"

"No, Scoot man. I'm working on a much bigger crime than your pitiful shit. But I would like to have a little talk." Keone tightened his grasp on Scooter's shoulder.

"You know I'd love to talk story with you. But time is money in my business circles. I think I could fit you in next week, Wednesday?"

Keone squeezed hard enough to pinch a nerve.

"Or, now. Now would be good Detective Sergeant Boyd, sir."

Still squeezing Scooter's shoulder, Keone placed Scooter in the Corolla's passenger seat with a look that said, "You move and you *will* be hurting."

They drove well past Kapalua on the narrow road that circled the north side of the island. Keone didn't say a word until they reached an unmarked path that led down to a hidden blowhole.

Scooter knew this place and what MPD officers occasionally used it for. "We don't need to go down there, Keone. That shit's worse than waterboarding."

"I don't know what you're talking about, Scoot. It's a beautiful spot and very few tourists ever come here. We'll have it to ourselves."

"I know the drill. You hold my head facedown over the hole and I hear the roar of the water for minutes before it finally bursts out and gags me. Just ask your damn questions."

"Okay. It's simple, really. Only one question—Dave Walden?"

"Who?"

Keone grabbed Scooter's shoulder again with enormous force and started Scooter down the hill.

"Please, Keone. You and me, we go school to-gedah. That guy's *lolo*. He'll kill me."

"And I won't?" Keone asked in his gentlest voice.

"All right. But I don't know a lot. He's a converter. He gets the powder from important friends on the mainland and cooks it himself."

"Where?"

"He doesn't tell me. I'm small potatoes. Two guys between him and me."

"I need names."

"Shit. You're killing me. If I roll on them where do I get my stuff?"

"Elsewhere."

"Look. I'll give you the guy next to Walden, but not my direct supplier. You gotta give me that much."

"You know, I was really angry when I came out here. I've had a shitty month. But this lovely scenery must be getting to me. Okay, give me the middle guy. But he'd better check out or we might get to take another pleasant drive together."

"Riley. His name's Riley."

"You know I'm just guessing, but I bet Mr. Riley has a first name."

"Damn it. Okay, Eugene. He goes by Gene, but his real name's Yevgenie or some Slavic shit like that."

"Yevgenie Riley? Really?"

"Okay Riley's not his real last name. His real last name is Russian or Ukrainian. It's something like Riastokov."

"I won't ask you for the patronymic. You did okay, Scoot. I guess I'll let you walk down to the blowhole alone. Enjoy."

With that Keone returned to his car, spun a quick U-turn, and headed back to his office in Wailuku. In the rearview he saw Scooter's lips moving and feet stamping but didn't really care.

Chapter Twenty-five

Monday, April 18, 4:00 PM

Janet Loftus was finally preparing to take her husband home, after exactly one month of Occupational Therapy and daily sessions with Dr. Drayton. The rules were simple. She and Sam would occupy separate bedrooms. Sam would have no contact with Julie, unless she visited Jan and Sam together. Sam would not drive until he took and passed a defensive driving course and a state driving test. Sam could return to work in another month if he passed a test devised by his employer.

Jan entered the room with a suitcase. "Hi, Sam. It looks like we're finally getting you out of this place. I'm proud of how hard you've worked to make this possible."

"Janet, I couldn't have done it without your encouragement and patience with me."

Jan believed Sam actually meant this. A month ago it wouldn't have seemed possible. "You go ahead and pack your things and I'll make sure Dr. Drayton has signed all the paperwork."

Jan found Drayton at the nurse's station signing all of the necessary release forms. Tom Conrad was there, too, with other forms for him to sign for the court.

Drayton saw Jan and held up a finger as he signed the last form. "Janet, I have a couple more things to go over with you before you take Sam home."

"I know, I'm not to expect too much."

"Yes. But there's more. In our sessions I've told Sam what I'm going to tell you. Sam may look like the man who was your husband before the accident, but he isn't. He's dealt with a number of severe challenges and done well. Your support had a lot to do with that."

"I like to think so," Jan said with a slight smile.

"No, you really have made a difference. Sam has grown to like you and trust you, but that isn't the same as love."

"I know that."

"You know it in your head, but not in your heart. As I told Sam, when you go home together, I want you to imagine you're friends who have decided to rent a house together. You have your own rooms, your own activities, and your own lives. Gradually you will rediscover some common interests. You can help this by occasionally suggesting some activity you used to do together. A game you played together, a television program you watched together, even reading together in the same room can re-establish feelings. I'm not talking about memories exactly, just comfortable feelings."

"We used to love playing Scrabble and *Mah Jong.*"

"That's exactly the type of thing I'm talking about. Scrabble can also help Sam with his reading comprehension. After a month or so you might consider a first date, something non-threatening like dinner or a movie. It took a while for you two to fall in love the first time. It won't be any different this time. Sam will have highs and lows, and so will you. But you need to be his rock, his firm foundation. You may want to scream sometimes, but don't. Call me. Here is my cell number. Call any time, day or night."

"I will. Thanks for all you've done for Sam and for the advice. I will follow it. And we will make this work. No matter how long it takes."

"I believe you have a real chance to succeed. I'll see Sam for an hour three times a week. After he goes back to work, we'll try to cut back to two. My secretary will work it all out with you."

Nurse Gwen wheeled Sam to the nurses' station in the required wheelchair. Noting Conrad and Drayton at the counter around the nurses' station, Sam waved and said, "I'm grateful to all of you, especially my good buddy, Dr. Drayton, and the lovely Gwen. I hope you won't think it rude of me to want to get the hell out of this place."

Everyone chuckled at this. Jan leaned into Drayton's ear and whispered, "I like this Sam's sense of humor better than the old one's."

Drayton smiled and patted her shoulder. "Onward then, Loftuses. Enjoy your first night back in your home."

Thursday, April 18, 4:30 PM

Sam had smiled as they left the nurses' station, but inside he struggled with his emotions. He was ecstatic to be leaving the hospital after so long but realized the home they were returning to would be unfamiliar to him. Janet would be looking for sparks of recognition, but he doubted he could fake them adequately.

As Janet drove them to Pukalani, he wondered if they would even live in the same house. The address on his, now voided, driver's license was the same as he remembered, but the house itself...

"I bet you're glad to see some familiar sights outside the hospital, eh, Sam?"

"Well, the Queen K Shopping Center looks the same, but I wish everybody wouldn't insist on driving on the wrong damn side of the road."

"Now, Sam."

"Just kidding. Besides, I've driven in England, you know."

As they travelled past the airport on the Hana Highway, everything did look familiar. He could even read the street signs now, without difficulty. They turned onto Haleakala Highway and entered Pukalani, at last. Sam held his breath as they approached the house, but it looked just the same as it had when he left for work a long, long time ago. His Bromeliads were all right where they should be and the yard was green and lovely, if an inch longer than he used to keep it.

Entering the house, he didn't have to fake sparks of recognition. They were real. About half of the furnishings were familiar, and their locations were as remembered in about three-quarters of the cases. The windows and doors were all where they were supposed to be.

I wonder.

While Janet took the suitcase to his bedroom, Sam decided to take a look in the kids' rooms. He gasped. "Cindy, my little munchkin, where have you gone?"

Cindy's room was now Janet's workroom/office. In his mind he saw it as it was before. The bed with its fluffy pink comforter and lace-tipped pink canopy. The white dresser with her special treasures neatly lined up for display. Her rocking chair with that ridiculous blue bear she called Bluey filling the entire seat. He'd won it for her at the fair.

Across the hallway, Timmy's room was now an office for him. He recognized the furniture and knick-knacks from his actual office. These should have been in the guest room, where Janet would be sleeping.

Again he saw the room as it was in his memories. Instead of the neat desk and filing cabinets, toys were strewn across the floor. Legos predominated, but trucks and cars and a variety of rubber balls of various sizes were there too. Timmy's racecar bed filled one wall and his simple wooden dresser the other. The top of his dresser, unlike Cindy's, was invisible under a complex pile of rubbish

"Timmy, I can't lose you, too."

Tears dripped from his eyes and he couldn't hide them from Janet.

"You knew this would be hard and so did I. Don't be ashamed to cry. Your life has been turned inside out, literally. Why don't you head to the bedroom and lie down while I fix some lunch?" Janet said this with a gentleness in her voice that Sam needed and appreciated.

"Thank you, Janet. I think I will."

With that he went to the bedroom, also fifty percent familiar, and flopped on the mattress. The feel of the Posturepedic was one hundred percent familiar. He hadn't realized how exhausting this would be. He fell asleep as soon as he closed his eyes.

Chapter Twenty-six

Thursday, April 25, 5:00 PM

The wait outside Alcala's office was very brief this time and Karen smiled as she said, "Go on in. He's waiting for you."

Alcala walked around his desk as Keone entered and shook his hand. "Great work on Riastokov. Finding him on the mainland and liaising with those cops in New York to bring him back here was excellent police work."

"It wasn't too hard once they found out they were bringing him to Maui."

"I hate it when you try to be modest. It was good work. You'll take the compliment and like it. I'm still working to erase Frank's bullshit from your file and this will help."

Keone knew enough to keep quiet.

"This testimony you got from Riastokov is golden. What are your next steps?"

"Now that we got Dave's direct contact to roll on him and describe the conversion lab in the house, I want to get an evidence team and hazardous waste disposal team in there ASAP. The wife is in danger given the nature of the chemicals used in the conversion process. A number of these operations have blown up."

"You'll have a warrant by tomorrow morning. Better send someone by to get the wife out of the place."

Keone nodded.

"What about Walden? We've got that bastard dead to rights. Now we just need to find him. Do you think he left the island?"

"I sincerely doubt it, but I'd like to float the possibility with his mainland partners. DEA is sending me detailed files on all of them. I should have stuff to review by the weekend."

"What's the point?"

"I don't want them searching where I'm searching."

"Okay, but work closely with DEA at every step."

"Will do."

Alcala sat behind his desk for another moment before speaking. "Keone, I know I was hard on you about the Walden woman, but I hope you realize it was for your own good."

"I do. And I haven't seen her once since your warning."

"I know. Pissed the shit out of Kulima, too." For the first time in a long time Tony smiled like in the old days.

"Thanks, Boss. I'm glad you've got my back."

"Get outta here and don't make me regret it."

Keone would send someone over to get the Walden woman out of the house, as Tony suggested. He just wouldn't tell Tony who.

Thursday, April 25, 10:00 PM

When Julie opened the front door her eyes were red. Keone assumed she'd been crying. On the phone, when he told her he needed to stop by, the conversation had been stiff and cold. He wanted to be face to face when he explained why he hadn't so much as called since the day he brought her home.

She led him to the couch and sat a good foot farther down. "What is so urgent, Sergeant Boyd?"

"I'll get to that in a minute. First, I have to try to convince you that I'm not the son of a bitch you think I am. Don't say anything, please. I have to tell you why a man who is as crazy about you as I am stayed away from you for nearly a month."

Julie obeyed his request, but her eyes weren't kind.

"Another detective accused me of taking advantage of your vulnerability after Dave's beating and lobbied my lieutenant to take me off the case. The only way I could make sure we nailed Dave was to agree to stop any contact with you. It's been killing me. I don't care what the consequences may be. Once we have Dave behind bars I will see you as much as you'll let me. But if you never want to see me again I understand." Keone waited for Julie to respond.

After a full minute, Julie asked, " May I speak now, Sergeant?"

"Yes."

"You really pissed me off, you know. You could have called. I wouldn't have told anybody."

"But I would have known."

"You really are a good cop, aren't you? No matter how hard you try to hide it. Well, I'll consider forgiving you when this mess is all over. Are you close to finding Dave?"

"I'm sure he hasn't left the islands and I have leads. But, honestly, I'm still looking."

"Is that the urgent thing you had to tell me?"

"No."

"Well?"

"Julie, I have reason to believe that empty space beneath this house is not empty."

"What is Dave messed up in? You need to tell me."

"I interrogated a drug dealer this afternoon. He told me Dave is running a crystal methamphetamine conversion lab. The most logical place for that is the cinderblock cube beneath this house." There was no need to mention Scooter or Riastokov by name.

"But there's no way in."

"Let me show you something." Keone led Julie into Dave's study, still unlocked since their fight put Julie in the hospital. He rolled away the desk chair and said, "Feel the edge of the carpet under Dave's desk."

Julie knelt down and felt what Keone had discovered the

day she returned from the hospital during his cursory examination of the house. "You think this is a trap door, don't you?"

"Yes."

"Why don't we move the desk, fold back the carpet and see?"

"I don't have a search warrant."

"I'll let you."

"I appreciate that. But, if what I suspect is in that room, I need to have a tight chain of evidence and a Hazmat Team. I want your permission to get a search warrant and bring an evidence gathering team in to search the entire house."

"You don't need my permission to get a search warrant, do you? Why are you asking for it?"

"Because you're not just the wife of a suspect to me." Keone's broad Polynesian face wasn't quite dark enough to hide the blush he felt rising on his cheeks.

"Okay, but give me until noon tomorrow to collect my things and arrange for a hotel."

"I really don't think that's a good idea. Meth conversion labs are notoriously dangerous. Most of the solvents they use can become unstable. Labs like this one can and have blown up on Maui."

"I've lived here for many years since Dave remodeled this place. I don't see that one more night makes much difference."

"I do."

"Look, I believe what you're saying about Dave. I had no idea he made or even sold drugs. But I know he used them. As I told you before, all of us experimented with pot in college, but Dave went deeper after we married and moved here. It's one of the reasons our marriage wasn't working."

"So throw some essentials into an overnight case and leave now. You can always come back and retrieve things after we've finished. As a policeman, I shouldn't even let you pack anything before we complete our search."

"To paraphrase what you said a minute ago, I think of you as more than a policeman. I need the next twelve hours in a familiar place to get my head around all of this. I'm begging you, Keone. I know you trust me."

"Of course I trust you. But I don't like this one bit."

Julie wrapped her arms around his neck, unconsciously recreating the scene from the night of her beating. This time she pulled him tight to her and kissed him. She kissed him deep and long. A kiss that communicated more than words ever could. And he kissed back.

After a while they held each other at arm's length and explored each other's eyes. Keone knew then that he would eventually give in.

Part V: Adaptation

"Contrariwise," continued Tweedledee, "if it was so, it might be; and if it were so, it would be; but as it isn't, it ain't. That's logic."

Lewis Carroll, author

RICK LUDWIG

Chapter Twenty-seven

Friday, April 26, 7:00 AM

Sitting at the breakfast table Sam realized he'd been living with Janet for eight days and it had been nice. His days had been full between Janet driving him to his driving lessons, sessions with Dr. Drayton, and studying like mad to get recertified to do his old job. Strangely, the driving had progressed faster than anything. He guessed that's why Brits can learn to drive in the US and vice versa. Once he set his mind to it, he amazed his instructor. Today he'd see if he could pass the Hawai'i state driver's examination.

Janet was as excited as he was. She couldn't wait to drive him to Kahului for the test. He knew she saw this as a first step on the road back to a normal life for the two of them. He also knew she didn't suspect that Sam was still convinced the doctors were wrong. He couldn't help feeling guilty for misleading this nice woman.

As he finished the island-style eggs Benedict, with seared *ahi* tuna in place of Canadian bacon, he marveled at Janet's skill as a cook. If she hadn't gone into decorating, he was sure she could have made a career as a chef. One reason he was anxious to get his license was to allow her to go back to work. He could tell she missed it. That was something they had in common. He couldn't wait to get back to work, either.

Seeing her check the little book that she used for scheduling and addresses, reminded Sam of a series of little books he'd kept since college. Collectively they represented a detailed account of the thoughts and actions of Sam Loftus. He'd continued keeping that record in multiple new journals all his life.

Is it possible my journals are here in this house?

Although decorated somewhat differently, the skeleton of the house hadn't changed.

"Janet, thank you for another wonderful meal."

"I have to make sure you have all the energy you need to pass that test today. I know you can do it."

"I look forward to being able to send you off to work, for a change," Sam replied with an honest smile. He found that he really liked Janet. She was more formal than Julie, with a polished surface that reminded him of a porcelain doll face. Beneath that he felt a real warmth that she reserved for very few people. And he was one of them.

He knew she loved her Sam deeply and wished he could give her the happiness she deserved. But he had no memory of loving her, just liking her. Maybe finding his journals could help resolve matters.

Returning to his bedroom, once their bedroom, he closed and locked the door. He doubted Janet would ever come in unannounced, but he didn't want her to see him searching for his journals. Going to the left side of the bed, he moved the bedside table away from the wall and felt along the baseboard for a tiny tab of tin. His disappointment when it wasn't there was like a rock on his heart. He slid the table back and slumped on the bed.

Gazing up into the image in the mirror over the dresser, he had an idea. Moving to the right side of the bed, he slid the other bedside table out to find the little tin tab just where it should have been on the other side.

"Left is right, dumbass," he muttered to himself.

There behind the baseboard were all of his journals, beginning with the one from his freshman year in college. Aside from being written in mirror writing, which he could now read fluently, it even looked a little like his handwriting. Opening the first journal and beginning to read, he was overjoyed to recognize every word. His description of arriving in Bloomington and being assigned to the dorms was exactly as he remembered. The second paragraph especially brought pleasant memories.

> *When I reached my assigned room, the door was already open and I came face-to-face with my roommate. He said his name was Dave and asked where I was from. When I told him Newport Beach, he said, "A fellow Californian, how wonderful. I'm from Palo Alto. We'll teach these damn Hoosiers how to enjoy college and still get better grades."*
>
> *I liked him at once. He was a chemistry major and I was math and business, but at this stage that was far less relevant than that he had cased the town and found the best place to get pizza. I threw down my gear and joined Dave on a walk down the hill, through the gates, and into the town of Bloomington, Indiana in search of pizza.*

Sam had tears in his eyes when he finished reading this section. He had discovered a new focus for his attention—the study of Sam Loftus's life. He wondered if the journals would all match his memories or if they would diverge at a certain point, describing the life everyone here seemed to think he lived and not the one he remembered. He could just open the last journal and start reading, but he wasn't ready to find out. He'd work his way up to it.

Janet knocked softly on the door. "Are you ready to leave, Sam? You said you wanted to be at DMV by 10:00 AM."

Sam replaced the first journal and closed the door in the baseboard before walking to the bedroom door. "Thanks for reminding me, Janet. I'm as ready as I'll ever be."

During the drive to the DMV, Sam asked Janet what she'd been working on when his return home took her away from her job.

"Well, Ms. Opal is redecorating some of the guest rooms at her ranch and wants a casual elegant look. Try making that combination sometime."

"If memory serves, Ms. Opal is your code word for an immensely wealthy, former TV talk show host, who owns a good chunk of our island. Am I right?"

Janet smiled and said, "My lips are sealed."

From the day after he came home with Janet, they fell easily into this kind of comfortable banter. No matter how different the Dave he met here was, Janet was as warm and friendly as he remembered her.

Janet parked outside the DMV and walked in with Sam for his appointment. She put her arm through his, but it was an expression of friendship and Sam appreciated it. He hadn't realized how nervous he was at taking this damn test. He signed in and waited the usual Maui hour before his number was called. After passing the written exam he went back to waiting until the driving examiner was ready for him.

Janet waited for a half hour while Sam disappeared to take the driving test. When Sam returned, she could tell from the look on his face he'd passed. They rushed together and hugged in honest celebration of Sam's accomplishment.

As it was close to lunchtime, Sam invited Janet to lunch at Koho's, a small local restaurant attached to the Queen Ka'ahumanu Center that had good food and even better prices. Sam had a plate lunch special of baked chicken smothered in their creamy white Koho sauce with rice and mac salad. Janet had the teriyaki version of the chicken with the same sides.

"Sam, this was a great idea. I love this place."

"Me, too." He knew she was thinking about times they'd been here together before, but had refrained from mentioning it to avoid hurting Sam's feelings. For the hundredth time Sam noted what a thoughtful person Janet was.

She displayed that thoughtfulness in her very next sentence. "Sam, after we eat, why don't you drop me at home and drive on over to Dr. Drayton's office."

His smile was broad once more. "Oh, you are one of a kind. I was hoping you'd suggest that. Something about driving gives a man a sense of restored freedom that's hard to match. I promise I'll be very careful of your car."

"It's our car, Sam," she said and quickly added, "Housemates often share cars."

"Yeah. Dave and I shared a beautiful old wreck in grad school."

"Did you think I could forget the snail? Who painted those swirls on the side of your old Vee-dub, anyway?"

"A very clingy art major Dave once dated. She really annoyed him, but he put up with her until she finished painting the car. Then he hooked her up with another budding lawyer that he didn't like very much. When they got married he said the pairing saved two other people from horrible spouses."

"I'm sorry you two grew apart over here. I never really understood it, but I guess people change in different ways. I'm glad we still get together for family things. So is Julie."

Sam saw Janet realized what she'd said the second it came out of her mouth and prepared to apologize. He jumped in. "Maybe we'll start doing that again when I'm better."

It was the nicest thing he could have said to her, and he felt good about it. Although he still defined better as being back with Julie and their kids.

After lunch they wandered around the mall a bit and picked up a few things they needed to maintain their separate bedroom lifestyle. When they got home it was still too early for him to go directly to Drayton's office.

Janet again read his mind. "You go on. Explore the island a little before going to see Dr. Drayton. It'll do you good."

Sam liked this woman.

Chapter Twenty-eight

Friday, April 26, 12:00 PM

As Keone drove to Kula, an evidence team equipped with everything necessary to gain entry to the secret room under the Walden house followed directly behind. But Julie Walden's safety dominated Keone's thoughts.

Why didn't I make her leave last night?

Why had he let her stay? Because he was falling in love with her and cared what she thought of him. Because he was thinking like a lover and not a detective. A good detective would be asking himself different questions.

How do I really know she isn't part of this? Do I even have proof it was Dave that beat her up?

He had to get himself together or they could both be in serious danger.

His concerns were partially dispelled when he turned onto Julie's street and saw her sitting on the curb, well away from the main part of the house with three suitcases, packed and ready to go.

"You see, I do listen to you," she said. "I've been out here for a half hour. All of the doors and windows are locked. Here are the keys."

Keone turned to the evidence team leader and gave him the keys before turning back to Julie. "Smart girl. I still think you put yourself in unnecessary danger. I should never—"

The explosion was tremendous, throwing Keone and Julie five feet in the air. Keone grabbed Julie and rolled, softening her return to earth. Once he thumped onto the ground, he rolled them again so he was on top, protecting Julie from the debris he knew would pummel them next. A piece of the front door struck his head and glass from the window penetrated his suede jacket to pierce his back in three places. But it could have been much worse.

Keone made certain Julie was unharmed, then ran to what had recently been the front of the Walden house. The explosion had blown two members of the evidence team from the steps they were ascending. The team leader lay on the sidewalk, unmoving. Keone noted that he was still breathing and lifted the man's wrist to check his pulse. He was relieved to find it strong, though rapid.

The team member that had been just behind his supervisor on the stairs, lurched over, bruised but alert. The other members of the evidence team called in the explosion before rushing to their comrade's side.

Keone returned to Julie.

"Oh my God, Keone. I'm so sorry I didn't do what you said. I've ruined everything. You won't get any evidence out of that." She pointed vaguely at the crater, engulfed in searing blue flames, that was once the front of her house.

Keone noticed that the area where the real and fake garages once stood was completely gone.

The remnants of what Julie's suitcases had contained were scattered everywhere. Keone saw a black lace bra hanging from the singed branch of a tree and a thong dangling from the antenna of his unmarked police car. One of the evidence men scurried around them, collecting what he could. Keone wondered if the man's bright red face was just from the explosion. Everything he managed to collect fit into a small kitchen garbage bag.

Emergency vehicles arrived with sirens shrieking. But Keone could barely hear them over the ringing in his ears. One EMT went directly to the leader of the evidence team, who had begun to writhe and moan. The other came over to him and Julie.

"You again," Eldon Miranda said, looking at Keone.

"Look—" Keone started.

"I know. Patch you up quick and let you go."

After examining Keone and Julie and giving them both a couple of shots for pain, Eldon told Keone, "I know you'll run right over to the hospital from here. But I've got to stitch up those slices in your back before I let you go. You and your girlfriend were lucky. Please go home and get some sleep."

Keone was surprised how much he liked hearing Eldon call Julie his girlfriend. He would follow his advice and get Julie to bed immediately after they left the scene, but he would write up his report before he crashed on the couch.

After receiving his stitches Keone walked over to Julie. She sat on the tailgate of the EMT wagon shivering, despite the heavy blankets wrapped around her. Her hand shook as she sipped coffee from a Styrofoam cup.

She turned at Keone's approach. He watched a tear slide down her wet cheek.

"Thank you. I know you took the brunt of the blast for me."

"I'm built to take a beating. I'm Hawaiian."

"Can you call a cab to take me and all my worldly goods to the hotel?" She held up the small white trash bag.

"No."

"What?"

"To hell with the hotel. I want you where I can keep an eye on you. You're coming home with me."

Julie smiled through her tears as Keone lifted her in his arms and carried her to his car.

"This is getting to be a habit," she said.

Now Keone smiled, but only for a minute.

Dave Walden's still out there. If I'd caught him this wouldn't have happened.

Chapter Twenty-nine

Friday, April 26, 4:00 PM

"How goes it, Sam?" Drayton always started their session with some form of this question.

"Still kicking." Sam's replies were also predictable.

"Tell me about the house."

"It's a nice house and has some things in it that I remember. I do feel at home there for the most part."

"That's good. As for the items in the house that you remember, do you also remember buying them?"

"Yes. But my memories are of buying them with Julie."

"I see."

"I passed my driving test today. Janet let me drive myself over here solo."

"Remember what I've said about returning to normal activities. How did it feel?"

"Very good, Doc. Very good. I felt a sense of freedom."

Now came one of Drayton's patented conversation gaps. At the beginning Sam took them as challenges and never spoke until Drayton was forced to. This time though, Sam had something on his mind and wasn't going to play. "I found something else at home today. Something I remembered very clearly."

"What was that?"

"A collection of journals I've kept since college. I started reading the first one and remembered everything I'd written word-for-word."

"That's very interesting." Drayton seemed to stiffen briefly, before resuming his normal relaxed attitude.

Sam couldn't tell if he'd made a mistake telling Drayton about the journals, but decided to push on. "I want to read through them in chronological order. I think they could help me get my memory back. My real memory." This was a game Sam knew how to play.

"I agree. Would you be willing to share them with me?"

Sam had to be careful here. "Sure. But, you know, I'd like to finish each book before I hand it over. I trust you, but I'd like to know if I got a little racy anywhere. I know you're a doctor and I won't censor anything. Do you know what I'm saying?"

"Certainly, Sam. I'll read them as you pass them on to me. I'll never discuss anything in them with anyone but you."

"Thanks. I'm not ready to share these with Janet. I kept them private for a reason."

"No problem. Let's talk about how your studies are going...."

Friday, April 26, 5:30 PM

When Sam arrived home he noticed for the first time what excellent care Janet had given his bromeliad garden while he was in the hospital. Whatever his feelings for her, he had no doubt this woman truly loved her husband. When he opened the door he could tell by the fragrant aromas coming from the kitchen that Janet had another mouth-watering dinner waiting. After dinner they played Mah Jong and Sam enjoyed the game. In his mind Janet taught it to him a few days ago. He knew that in Janet's memories they'd played for years, both two-person and occasionally four-person with other couples. After the game Sam said, "That's really a lot of fun, but you're still beating the pants off me."

"You'll improve."

Watching Janet return the pieces to their case, Sam saw a grace in her movements that he hadn't noted before. Her slender fingers seemed to float in the air as she reached for the tiles and carefully placed them into the case without making a sound. Gentleness defined this woman. He honestly enjoyed their time together. "It's been a very exciting day for me. I think I'll turn in and read a while. Goodnight."

"Goodnight, Sam. Sleep tight."

Locking the bedroom door, Sam retrieved the first of his journals and continued reading. When his eyes closed a half-hour later, he was calmed by the fact that everything he read was familiar and unchanged from his memories. He'd assumed this would be the case, but was reassured when it was. Journal number four was the one he dreaded reading the most. It described a certain state fair and meeting two lovely sisters.

Chapter Thirty

Saturday, April 27, 11:00 AM

The first thought Keone had when he woke on Saturday: *This couch was not made for a six-foot-seven, two hundred and seventy-five pound Hawaiian to sleep on.*

The second: *What smells so good?*

He followed his nose into the kitchen to find a table filled with luscious fruits, pancakes, thick bacon, Portuguese sausage, and, of course, Spam.

Julie sat at the table sipping coffee and playing with her plate of fruit.

"How did you do this?" He was amazed.

"Don't get your hopes up, Big Guy. Jan got the cooking genes. I can do a basic breakfast, but it stops there. I'm pretty good with dessert, too."

I know. I remember those two delicious pies you'd made the night Dave went ballistic.

"Actually, that's a good thing. I love to cook dinner, but hate to cook breakfast. I also love to eat desserts but can't produce anything more complicated than fruit salad. Besides, this dinky kitchen can't accommodate more than one cook at a time."

Keone glanced at the clock. He'd slept until eleven. Not surprising. He didn't finish his report until 3:00 AM, then spent an hour on the phone catching up with the desk sergeant on what happened after he and Julie left the scene.

"Did he do it?" Julie asked with no preamble.

"Looks like it."

"How? I never saw him and all the doors were locked when I went outside."

"He had it wired for just such a contingency. He had to be within five hundred yards to set it off remotely, or so the team that arrived after we left seemed to think. They spent the afternoon and evening canvassing the area. Three people saw Dave, wearing a full beard and a hoodie, within ten minutes of the explosion. But it won't be official until they complete their report."

"Sorry about your evidence."

"I didn't really need it. But I wanted to make sure that crap never got on the street. Dave took care of that for me. We have two witnesses, one of whom has been in the lab. We also have a case for him setting off the explosion."

"How's that evidence guy? The one with the concussion."

"He spent the night in the hospital, but the docs think he should be good to go home tomorrow for one week of recovery."

"I'm sorry I caused all this trouble for everyone. I should have gone to the hotel when you asked me to."

"I need to ask—"

Julie tensed. "Why was I so adamant? Why didn't I take your advice?"

Keone nodded.

"I've spent twelve years with Dave controlling every aspect of my life. Always telling me what I should do and punishing me whenever I questioned him. I saw you as the kind of man I wish he was. Then, when you started telling me what I should do—"

"It made you wonder. Plus, I'd just spent a month ignoring you. I don't need any more explanation. I understand.

"I hope you understand I'm nothing like Dave. I trust your judgment and will never tell you what to do. Whenever I suggest you do something, it's just that, a suggestion. I hope someday you'll come to know how much I care what happens to you. I don't want to dominate you and never will."

He watched the tension in Julie's body melt away

"How's your back?" she asked, deftly changing the subject and confirming that they were good.

"The couch was fine."

"I meant those places where you had glass poking into and out of you."

"Must be okay. They don't hurt at all."

"You're a shitty liar. Eat up. I'm going to take a long bath, then a shower, and put on one of my enchanting collections of mismatched tops and bottoms. Unless of course you want to use the bathroom first."

"You may not have noticed, but this place has two. My workout room has its own. It was originally a bedroom. Just let me retrieve a few necessities from the one attached to your room."

Julie looked a bit uncomfortable. "About that. How long do expect to keep me here, Sergeant?"

"At least until Dave's behind bars. I promise to respect your space. I have a reputation as an excellent roommate. You can use the workout room if you feel constricted. There's a great video I watch while I'm using the treadmill. I filmed it myself. It takes you all the way up Haleakala and on the road to Hana. Plus, I'm off today and tomorrow so you can go anywhere you want—as long as it's with me."

While Julie soaked in the tub, Keone called the station and formalized his protective custody assignment. He strategically avoided disclosing which safe house he had her in and which officers he'd assigned to keep an eye on the location, citing the need for absolute secrecy given Walden's previous close association with the department. He also confirmed that the APB on Dave had been extended to all forms of transportation off or between all of the islands, beginning immediately after the explosion. The files from the DEA had been delayed in O'ahu, but would arrive on Monday.

After Keone ended his call to the station, Jan called on

Julie's cell. When Keone answered Jan didn't seem surprised.

"Julie called while you were asleep on the couch and told me she was safe and in your protective custody. Don't worry, she didn't tell me where."

Keone was pleased to see evidence that Julie's smarts extended beyond writing. But he already knew that. "How's Sam doing?"

"You know he's surprising me. He's already driving himself and studying up a storm to get cleared to return to work. Best of all, Dr. Drayton says he's making good progress toward regaining his lost memories."

"I'm pleased for both of you." Keone wished he could shake his continuing suspicion of Sam's recovery. It just seemed too convenient.

"So can I talk to Julie?"

"She's relaxing in the bathtub, but I'll have her call you as soon as she emerges."

"Keone, thank you for looking after my sister. I'd be there in a flash if I didn't have so much to accomplish with Sam right now. You're a Godsend."

"I'll keep her safe. Aloha, Jan, and good luck with Sam."

"Mahalo."

Saturday, April 27, 5:00 PM

Shopping with Julie in the Shops at Wailea Saturday afternoon was less painful than Keone expected. Julie shopped the way he analyzed cases, quickly separating the wheat from the chaff. They arrived at the Shops at three and had completely reconstructed her wardrobe by five. Keone busied himself keeping an eye out for Dave or anyone else who might pose a threat, including the ever-nosy Frank Kulima. In the process, he identified and recorded five drug sales, four new high-priced call girls working the Wailea circuit, and some interesting transactions at one of the art galleries that he would have the fraud division look into. Julie didn't ignore him, though, asking his impressions of a few outfits and listening carefully to his honest responses.

When the last item was loaded into the trunk of Keone's beater, he asked if she'd like something to eat.

"I was hoping you'd ask. Let's hit Cheeseburger's."

"Hell, yeah." Keone was surprised and pleased that she selected a place he liked and not one of the posh restaurants prevalent in Wailea.

Two women started the original Cheeseburger in Paradise restaurant on Front Street in Lahaina and eventually planted a few elsewhere on Maui and O'ahu. The farthest removed was in Las Vegas, a preferred destination for tourists from the islands

When the waitress came by for their orders, Keone deferred to Julie. "We would like one of your monster plates of cheese fries." She looked at Keone.

"With lots of ranch dressing on the side."

"Two original Cheeseburgers in Paradise." Again she glanced at Keone.

"I never mess with perfection."

"And two draught Longboard Lagers?"

Keone looked at the waitress. "You know, I'm really starting to like this woman."

When the waitress went away. Julie looked into Keone's eyes. "It's mutual, buddy."

Keone couldn't hide a grin. "Do you mind telling me about your life before Dave? This is not an interrogation. I promise. I'd just like to know."

"Only if you agree to reciprocate sometime soon."

"Deal."

"Jan and I were born on a hog farm in north central Indiana. Keep the jokes to yourself. The nearest town was Wabash. It's about midway between Fort Wayne and West Lafayette, where Purdue University is. We're fraternal twins and were always close."

"Those are the kind that aren't identical, right?"

"Yep. During my pre-med days I learned that fraternal

twins happen when two separate eggs are fertilized at the same time. Identical twins result from one fertilization event."

"You are a bundle of information, aren't you. Consider me educated. But, I'm more interested in what you two were like when you were growing up."

"We invented imaginary play lands all over the farm. A residual stump became a table in a grand palace represented by surrounding trees. The little creek that ran through our folks' land was certain to lead all the way to a major river and then to the sea. We made little boats and imagined the adventures they'd encounter floating down that little creek.

"As we got older we built our own sets and gave performances to the farm animals. Talk about a tough audience. Eventually we became confident enough to entertain our friends and family. I had primary responsibility for the script and Jan for the sets. We alternated playing the lead part, but both of us loved playing multiple characters. I preferred the funny ones and Jan the more prim and proper."

"What about work around the farm?" Keone asked.

"We could do everything our big brothers could do. As they grew up and went away, we took more and more responsibility for the farm. But Momma and Daddy made sure we both had good educations, all the way through college at IUPUI. She studied design and I divided my time between theater and biology. I always made sure I had the proper credits to apply to medical school after graduation."

"What branch of medicine were you interested in?"

"Pediatrics. I loved kids. I was the most successful babysitter in Clinton County. I also helped write and produce little gospel plays for our church. When we went away to Indianapolis for college, I helped pay my way working with various small children's and community theaters in Marion County. That's where Indianapolis is. Anyway, when I met Dave, I knew one of us would have to choose, as we could never manage both a legal and a medical practice. Dave didn't really have any other potential vocation and I did, so I spent more and more time writing and performing in the Children's

Theater of Indianapolis."

"Do you ever regret your decision?"

"Which one?"

"Not going to medical school."

"Yes. Sometimes. But I love my writing and working with children's theater here on Maui."

"What other decisions do you regret?"

"You think I'm going to say marrying Dave, but that didn't happen until we'd been on Maui for a while. He was a good partner back in Indiana, very affectionate and fun."

"What decision do you regret?"

"Not having children of my own. At first I bought the argument Dave made about not having enough time to provide a newborn the attention it deserved. But later, after we became financially comfortable, there was a different reason."

"Dave."

"I knew he shouldn't be around young children. He couldn't bend enough. And his temper..."

"What do you do for fun?"

"I walk, hike really, all over this lovely island. It clears my head from too much writing and gets the blood circulating. Do you ever hike?"

"All my life. I've walked entirely around Maui in a single excursion, but I like day hikes best. Since I'm Hawaiian I can go places other people might not be welcome. I'd love to show you some of them."

Chapter Thirty-one

Sunday, April 28, 10:00 AM

"Where are we going?" Julie asked, as Keone started up the highway in a borrowed jeep.

"Up country."

"That covers a lot of ground. Anywhere in particular?"

"Makawao."

"Why?"

"I was born there."

"Are you a *paniolo*?" You couldn't spend much time on Maui without hearing about the famous Hawaiian cowboys.

"Third generation. My grandfather's family established the ranch and my mother's family provided most of the great riders."

"I know you're Hawaiian, but what other bloodlines are hiding under that lovely, koa wood surface of yours?"

"My grandfather, who built the ranch, was Scottish, from the highlands. He'd raised cattle west of Glasgow before taking to the sea. He married a local woman when he started the ranch. She was Portuguese-Hawaiian and a local doctor in Makawao. She continued her practice after they were married."

"Tell me about your mother's family."

"My mother's father grew up on Ni'ihau. When he was a small boy, a Japanese pilot crashed there after Pearl Harbor. The islanders eventually killed the pilot when he tried to take control of the island.

"Hokulele Kalama loved riding horses and decided to give paniolo life a chance on my other grandfather's ranch. He became the best roper there and won multiple titles at the Makawao Rodeo every Fourth of July. His sons and daughters were great riders, too. The Kalama family takes ribbons at the rodeo every year."

"How about taking me this year?"

"We'll see," Keone said.

"Kalama was your mother's maiden name. Doesn't that mean 'care for'?"

"No that's *malama*. *Kalama* means 'torch.'"

"What's your full name?"

"Keone Ka'imi Boyd."

"Does it have a meaning?"

"I already told you keone means sand or homeland. *Ka'imi* means seeker."

"A perfect name for a detective."

"*Boyd* is Scottish and people argue about what it means. Some say it's from the Gaelic word for an island in the Firth of Clyde. Others say it came from another Gaelic word *buide*, meaning 'fair' or 'yellow-haired.' It's easier for me to accept the first story for obvious reasons." He gave his black hair a tug with his dark brown hand.

"Here we are." Keone pulled through a gate with the name Boyd-Kalama Ranch formed in letters carved into an arch of dark, veined wood.

"This is beautiful. How could you bear to leave all this to become a cop? No offense."

"None taken."

Like a lot of Hawaiian plantation-style houses, a large veranda surrounded the main house, but Hawaiians would call it a *lanai*. Keone led Julie around the right side of the lanai to the back where a huge lawn was filled with barbeque spits over well-tended kiawe wood fires. Aromas of fragrant wood, searing beef, and piquant barbeque sauces mingled to create a banquet for the nose.

Keone had called this a family barbeque. If he was telling the truth, his family was huge.

"Hey, Mahealani," Keone called to a woman in her early twenties.

She ran over to Keone. They pressed their noses against each other and seemed to sniff before giving each other a warm kiss on each cheek. Keone also squished her in his embrace.

"Take it easy, big bruddah. Ooh, you brought a girl with you. I'm Keone's little sister Mahealani." With that she gave Julie a hug and kisses on each cheek.

"Aloha. I'm Julie."

"You go help the guys with the barbeque, Keone. I want to talk with this lolo girl, who hangs 'round with one *kanaka* like you."

Keone hesitated before joining the men drinking beer, talking story, and pretending to tend the barbeque.

"You like that big clunk?" Mahealani said with no preliminaries.

"He saved my life Friday when my house exploded." Julie decided not to dissemble. She liked Keone's sister.

"I read about that. You lived in Kula, yeah?"

"Yeah."

"I'm so sorry about your home. Do you have a place to stay?"

"Yes. I'm all set for now."

"How well do you know Keone?"

"I met him about a month ago when he was working on my brother-in-law's car crash."

"He told me about that. He said he was worried about you. He thought your husband was mixed up in something."

"He was right. My husband tried to kill me."

"I'm sorry. I talk too much. You're here to have fun. Can I get you something to drink?"

"Iced tea would be great."

"Mango, okay?"

"Perfect."

Mahealani returned with two over-sized, plastic tumblers of iced tea, dripping with condensation. Julie took this opportunity to learn a little more about Keone.

"Did Keone work on the ranch?"

"Sure. He was a good roper, too. Won a couple times at the rodeo. But he wanted to see the mainland. The day he graduated from high school he left for California. He went to college at UC Irvine."

"Did you miss him?"

"Yeah. We were always close, even though he was a lot older. When Dad died he kind of took special care of me. We're both grown up now, but we're still close."

"How do you spend your time?"

"Oh, I take classes at UH Maui College and dance at the Old Lahaina Luau."

"You must be good. We always bring visitors to that luau. It's not commercial like a lot of them."

"We try to be more traditional and help people see what life was like on the islands. Come on, you've got to meet the rest of the family."

About an hour later, Julie's brain was bursting with the names and faces she'd met and the stories she'd heard about Keone and the Boyd family. She was relieved when Keone grabbed her arm and led her to the low table where they sat on tatami mats and watched as a group of Keone's brothers and cousins carried the perfectly prepared sides of beef past each of the diners before laying them on a huge granite table for carving.

"Are you enjoying yourself?" Keone asked.

"Absolutely. You have a great family and Mahealani is a gem. She told me you went to college in California."

"I studied in the Department of Criminology, Law, and Society in the School of Social Ecology at UCI."

"How did the guys on the Maui PD deal with a college boy?"

"Well, I didn't come right back home. I graduated in 2002 and took a job with the Santa Ana Police Department. I speak

Portuguese and Spanish and that helped me with the Hispanic population. When I transferred to the LAPD in 2004, I took a Masters in CLS online from Irvine. That and my performance helped me become a detective in 2008."

"Wow."

"You asked. Anyway, a job opened up in Maui a little while after my promotion. So I came back home. They don't accept lateral transfers from mainland police forces. So I spent my first year in the outside districts before they rotated me through Lahaina, Kihei, and eventually Wailuku. I became a detective sergeant last year, focused on major crimes in the Criminal Investigation Division."

Mahealani rushed over to them and dragged them to the massive array of delicacies spread over multiple picnic tables. "Around here you snooze, you lose. We've got a big family in more ways than one." Julie had noticed the impressive stature of the men of the Boyd and Kalama clans. The older women were also ample, but the younger ones had those strong wiry figures common to hula dancers.

Keone noticed that Julie heaped almost as much food on her long wooden trough of a plate as he did. He knew there was a reason he liked this girl.

Sitting cross-legged around their table, Julie tried to continue the conversation from earlier. "So a new detective sergeant, trained on the mainland. How did that go over with your fellow officers?"

"I felt a little friction from a few old-timers, but a lot of the younger guys knew me, or somebody from my family, which made me easier to accept. I picked up some street smarts from Santa Ana and LA, which helped the older guys trust me."

"You are exceptionally easy to trust. I'm really glad you brought me here today. I needed this."

Music interrupted their conversation, so they focused on eating and watching every male and female member of the family take turns doing the hula. Looking a little embarrassed, Keone joined in. When he motioned for Julie to join him, she didn't hesitate. Her hula was very good for an amateur, bringing a big smile to Keone's and Mahealani's faces and applause and shouts from the crowd.

After everyone was completely stuffed and nearly exhausted, Julie helped clear the tables with the other women in the family. They all made her feel welcome and shared more gossip about Keone. When she was finished cleaning up, Julie wandered onto the lanai to find an older woman sitting in a rocking chair playing the ukulele. The song she played was gentle and soft like the breeze that ruffled her pure white hair. Julie quietly occupied a rocking chair next to the woman and rocked to the tempo of her song.

Keone climbed the stairs and kissed the woman in the rocking chair on the cheek. When the woman finished her song, Keone took Julie's hand and she rose to face the older woman. Keone spoke in Hawaiian until the woman rose, grabbed both of Julie's hands and leaned toward her as if to kiss her. Like Mahealani, she pressed her nose against Julie's and seemed to inhale Julie's fragrance. Julie did the same in return. Then the woman leaned back and smiled at Julie. Without a word she placed Julie's left hand in Keone's and squeezed them together. "Aloha," was all she said, before she went into the house.

Keone picked up the ukulele she left behind. He didn't sing, but his fingers brought a song from the ukulele that went right to Julie's heart. "She told me to play this for you. She likes you."

"That sweet woman is your grandmother, isn't she?" Julie said.

Keone kept playing as he nodded.

Chapter Thirty-two

Monday, April 29, 7:30 AM

Keone didn't notice the discomfort of the couch as much when he woke to his alarm Monday morning. He was pleased with how well Julie fit in with his family at the barbeque. During her time on Maui, she'd learned the critical lesson of how to respect and enjoy Hawaiian culture. Her hula demonstrated that she'd studied at one time or another with a good teacher at a traditional *halau*. He'd have to ask her about that.

Most important, she'd impressed his *tutu*. Although she never said anything, Keone knew his grandmother had always hoped he'd marry a Hawaiian girl. His mother's parents were pure Hawaiian, an increasingly rare thing in modern Hawai'i.

When they spoke in Hawaiian she'd asked Keone, "Does this one make you happy?"

Keone, always completely open and honest with his tutu, answered, "She brings my life joy."

Then his grandmother gave Julie the *honi*. This most traditional Polynesian greeting represents the exchange of the breath of life and spiritual power between two people. Someday he would tell Julie what this meant, when they were both ready.

Anxious to begin his first workday since bringing Julie home, Keone silently slipped out of the house and began his drive across the island. The night before, he'd laid out the rules to assure Julie's security.

"Julie, if I'm going to find Dave, I have to be certain you're being here remains a secret to everyone who might be linked to Dave or his activities," he'd begun.

"I understand completely."

"You cannot leave the condo without me. You cannot answer the door. You cannot tell anyone, including your sister, where you are. Do you think you can manage that."

"Yes. But for how long?"

"Until we catch Dave."

She was silent.

"I know it will be hard, but the only way for you to be truly safe is for me to put Dave behind bars. I promise you I can do this, but I won't try to kid you. It could take weeks or months. The only thing in our favor is that he will not be able to leave the islands."

"I trust you Detective Sergeant Keone Boyd. Go get him."

He saw fire in her eyes when she said this. Then she turned, entered her room, and closed the door. He knew he had her complete trust, and she had his.

The in-box on Keone's desk contained requests to call from a number of the high-rollers who had previously ignored his calls to them. The remainder of his desk was covered with files on Dave and all of his contacts from the DEA, FBI, and Interpol. Now he understood the delay. His contact at DEA was doing a comprehensive job.

Keone was pleased to note that the evidence team had completed their analysis of the explosion that leveled the Walden house, as well. He would start with the analysis, then skim the files, and finally dig deeply into the nefarious activities of Dave and his golf pals. From that he planned to select one or more of Dave's good friends on the mainland, Australia, Asia, or Europe to engage in a nice chat.

The evidence team had identified the site of the explosion as the cinder-block, secret room. That was no surprise. But how they managed to discover evidence that the explosion was intentionally triggered and not the result of unstable chemicals or improper storage conditions was beyond him. They strongly suspected the explosion was triggered remotely from outside the house. They also suspected that the bomber had visual sighting on the house given the timing of the blast just prior to their planned entry. Interviews with neighbors provided the most important piece of evidence in Keone's opinion. Three neighbors, from two different homes, identified David Walden almost a block away from the explosion with a small device that "looked like a garage door opener" in his hand moments before the explosion.

That son of a bitch. He could have killed us all.

After skimming the files on Dave's golf buddies, he concentrated on Dave's file from the DEA. Keone discovered he'd been right all along. Dave had been close to prosecution multiple times, but was as slippery as an eel. He couldn't wait to dive into the files on the men he now knew were Dave's suppliers and bosses.

The phone on Keone's desk rang. "Maui Police Department, Criminal Investigation Division, this is Sergeant Boyd. How may I help you?"

"Morning, Sergeant. This is Agent Freeman with the DEA, O'ahu office. I just wanted to make sure you received the files I sent over."

"Morning, Agent Freeman. Thank you. This stuff is great. I'm glad you waited and sent the FBI and Interpol files along with the stuff from your guys. Our Dave has been a very naughty boy."

"We've nailed a number of his middlemen but could never make anything stick on Walden or prove a direct link to Walden's bosses," Freeman told Keone over the phone.

"I just looked over the lab report from the Walden home. There is absolutely no doubt that he was running a conversion lab in his secret room. The physical evidence along with the testimony of one of his highest middlemen, Riastokov aka Riley, provides enough to send him up for a long time."

"I've seen Riastokov's testimony. Would you send me a

copy of the lab report?"

"Already on its way. From your reports and those from Interpol and the FBI, it's clear his good friends, who sponsored the police charity golf tournament, were the next level up in his organizational chart. They're all very anxious to talk with me, now. You don't suppose they might want to know where to find good old Dave, do you?"

The agent hesitated a moment before commenting. "Sergeant, this could be the chance we've been waiting for. Walden is hiding out from you, but he's even more afraid that his bosses will locate him. We would be extremely grateful for any information you have or might obtain about his whereabouts. If you talk to any of his bosses, be very careful."

"Agent Freeman, I would love to find this guy for you. We're currently scouring Maui and know he hasn't left the state. I think he might be hiding out on another island or in the wilderness areas of the West Maui Mountains. Give me a few days to follow up on some leads. If I get anything hopeful I'll call. You're in Honolulu, yeah?"

"Yes. I can be there in half an hour. I'll look forward to your call."

Based on his review of all of the files, Keone selected one of the high-rollers on his list to call. This gentleman, headquartered in New York City, had ties to all of the others on his list. Before he could pick up the phone, Lieutenant Alcala stopped by for an update. Keone wished he'd waited a half-hour more, but he wasn't about to complain.

"What have you got on the explosion, Keone?"

"I just read the full report from the evidence team and the lab. Here's a copy for you."

"Bottom line?"

"The explosion was deliberately set off remotely and we have Dave Walden a block away with a remote in his hand."

"How many witnesses?"

"Three, from two different houses."

"Good. What else?"

Keone spread his arms to indicate all the files on his desk.

"DEA, FBI, and Interpol files on Walden and his golf buddies. He's in this up to his neck and we've got him cold. I just talked to Agent Freeman at DEA. He'd like to be in on the collar, when we find Walden."

"Make sure that happens. Did he suggest anything else?"

"No, but he agreed with my plan to reply to at least one of these calls from the bosses. I plan to send them on the wild goose chase we discussed earlier to keep them from finding Dave first."

"How many are you planning to call?"

"Just one. There's a guy named Victor Pavin with ties to both Walden and Riastokov. He's very high up in the New York chapter of the Russian mob. I think he's the guy to spread the word."

"Good work, Keone. I heard Mrs. Walden got banged up a little in the explosion but you shielded her from any serious injury with your body."

"Just doing my job 'to preserve and protect.' "

"I understand you put her in a safe house and arranged for coverage."

"That's right. I don't think Walden means to kill her. But he's so scared now, his actions are impossible to predict."

"I agree. Just make sure you stay as far away from her as possible."

"I will," Keone replied. Although he was pretty sure sleeping on the couch and not entering his own bedroom were probably not the precautions the captain had in mind.

As soon as Alcala left he took a deep breath and dialed his phone.

"Can I speak to Mr. Pavin, please? This is Sergeant Boyd from the Maui Police Department returning his call." The wait was short.

"Sergeant Boyd? This is Vic Pavin. Did I meet you when I was out there playing in your charity tournament?" Pavin was Mr. Congeniality so far.

"No. I'm afraid I don't play golf."

"Too bad. It's a great game and those courses on Maui are

to die for."

Keone waited.

"Uh, I heard you tried to contact me the other day. I'm sorry I missed your call. Called back on Friday, but you must have been out."

"Yes. I was dealing with an emergency."

"Really. I hope no one was hurt."

"Not seriously, but a structure was destroyed."

"I'm sorry to hear that."

"The structure belonged to a friend of yours, I believe—David Walden."

Now it was Pavin's turn to pause.

"You do know Mr. Walden, don't you, the Volunteer Chairman of the Maui Police Department's 'Making Magic for Maui's Moms' Tournament?"

"Oh sure. He's a nice guy. A bit of a schmoozer. Is he okay?"

"Well, I don't know. He wasn't in his home at the time of the explosion and now he seems to be hiding from us. Do you know any reason why Mr. Walden might do that?"

"Hide from the police? No. I thought he was a big supporter of law enforcement, like my colleagues and me. Do you have any idea where he might be?"

The question I was waiting for.

"Mr. Pavin, I was hoping you might know the answer to that question. He doesn't happen to be in New York, does he?"

"No. He's not anywhere in the northeast."

"How do you happen to know that?"

"I don't know it. There's just no reason for him to be here. What is this? Am I under suspicion for something? Who do you think you're talking to, anyway. Do you know who I am?"

"I do now."

"What do you mean by that crack? I'm a well-respected businessman.

"Oh, I'm sure you are. I'm sorry you took my questions the wrong way. I thought he had clients there, such as yourself."

"I'm not Walden's client. I just know him from the tournament."

"I must have misunderstood your relationship."

"Yeah, well, nice talking with you, Sergeant. Sorry I couldn't be more help."

"You have been a great help. Thank you for your time. Aloha."

The call accomplished exactly what Keone intended. Pavin would tell his colleagues the hick Maui PD hadn't found Walden and thought he might be on the mainland. They would run around in circles trying to find him there, providing Keone enough time to find him in the islands, without any interference. He sent an email to Agent Freeman with a transcript from the call.

Now, he had only one mystery to solve. *Where the hell was Dave Walden?*

Chapter Thirty-three

Monday, April 29, 9:00 AM

Over the weekend, Sam read a great deal in his journals each night before falling asleep. But, with Janet back at work today, Sam planned to spend the entire morning and most of the afternoon reading.

Sunday evening he'd reached the section about the Indiana State Fair and his fears were validated. From that point on the journal diverged from his memories. He could hear his own voice in the writing. In a mirror he could see it was even his own handwriting. It wasn't a forgery. But it described events he'd never experienced. Or had he? Were the doctors right, after all? Were his memories a delusion? For the first time he considered the possibility and its consequences.

He realized that being Janet's husband had many advantages. He really liked this woman and she obviously adored him. They had a lovely home and enjoyed their jobs. Was it really so horrible? Julie didn't seem to care about him at all.

What about Cindy and Timmy? This thought represented an unbreachable barrier to acceptance.

His problem was, he had no other possible explanations for his experiences. He'd scoured the library, the web, and the media. Sam was, if anything, a logical man. He had to find a logical way out of this nightmare he was living. Oh, yes, he had actual nightmares, too, every night. The worst was one where he woke up one morning and remembered his life exactly the way everyone else did. He realized he had no children and went to work as though everything was just fine. His screams on waking had brought Janet to the door to see if he was all right.

"Just a dream," he'd said.

But what if last night was more than just a dream? What if his subconscious mind was trying to make sense of things? What if, some day during a session with Drayton, or dinner with Janet, or back at work, his mind just reassembled his memories into a pattern that fit his current life? Would that be a miraculous cure or a heartless punishment? He saw the danger, but couldn't stop reading the journals.

He immersed himself in reading about a life he didn't remember, not even stopping for lunch. He was shocked when the alarm told him it was time to leave for his session with Dr. Drayton. He grabbed the first four journals off his bed and took them with him. The sixth journal, which described the end of his friendship with Dave Walden, he sealed back in the baseboard with all the rest.

Monday, April 29, 4:00 PM

Sam always felt calmer when he entered Dr. Drayton's office. Everything was orderly and balanced. Drayton represented the same traits in his person, as he sat behind his desk waiting for Sam.

"Hiya, Doc." Sam decided to pre-empt Drayton's usual question about how he was doing.

"Hello, Sam. You seem to have something on your mind."

Sam recognized one of Drayton's skills was knowing when to let his patient take the lead.

"I brought the first four journals in for you to read."

"I appreciate your trust in me, Sam. I will not abuse it."

"I know you won't."

"Tell me about what you read."

Sam decided to be completely open, for the first time. "The first two books, about college, describe events precisely as I remember them and are recorded just as I remember recording them. The third book, about graduate school, is the same. The fourth book is the same until the last few pages."

Drayton busily took notes. "Tell me about those last few pages."

"They describe our day at the Indiana State Fair. I still won the coin toss with Dave and still picked the girl on the right, but the girl on the right was Janet, not Julie."

"I see."

"The rest of that journal describes our early courtship and all of the reasons I fell in love with Janet. I almost wished I'd been there."

"Go on."

"The fifth journal, which I've not quite finished, describes our marriage and honeymoon and the close relationship we had with Dave and Julie before they moved to Maui. It also covers the next two years we lived in Indianapolis before we moved here."

"Was it similar to what you remembered?"

"Some of it was. The trip to Maui, the description of my work at the main office, my friends there, the letters between Julie and Janet, were very familiar. But the differences made them bizarre. I would say something that I remembered saying to Julie, but I was saying it to Janet. The friendships we developed outside of work were very different and with people I don't even know. Before they left for Maui, Dave was different, too. He seemed to be high a lot and not on pot. This was completely wrong. Once he and Janet married, he never touched drugs again. He knew he'd lose her if he did, and he really loved her."

"But in the journals, he married Julie. Wasn't she more of a free spirit than Janet?"

"Not so much in my memories. In my memories we spent more years in Indianapolis, while she finished medical school.

But in the journal she decided on performing rather than pediatrics and that environment can be...well...freeing, I guess."

"I told you in the hospital that you struck me as an educated and logical individual. Do you remember?"

"Yes, it was one of the reasons I liked you."

"You know we believe you are suffering delusions."

"Yes." Sam tried to hide his disgust at the term.

"Something you may not know is that I believe intelligent, logical individuals have intelligent, logical delusions."

"Huh?"

"When a creative person has a delusion it can be extremely unrealistic. But someone like you couldn't accept such a thing. Your delusions must make sense to you at some level. They must be internally consistent. It's one of the things that made me think of Capgras. People with Capgras are known for the internal consistency of their delusions."

"What makes you think my *delusional* memories are logical?"

"Your Left-Right Transposition explains the differences in your memories. You remember Julie coming out of the right door, but for you the right door is the left. We need to pursue this. Assume for one instant that you were unhappy with your life and felt that everything would have been better if you'd chosen the other girl. If left were right, you would have. Then everything you believe happened would have been perfectly consistent with logic."

"That sounds frighteningly plausible. But Janet said she and I were perfectly happy."

"Maybe she was and believed you were, too. But only you knew if you were happy. And you have a way to find out what you knew."

"The journals."

"Yes. I encourage you to keep on reading."

"I will."

Chapter Thirty-four

Monday, May 13, 3:00 PM

Two weeks and no Dave Walden. Keone was certain Walden was not on Maui or O'ahu. Police in Kaua'i had also come up empty. That left Moloka'i, Lana'i, and the Big Island. There was absolutely no way Dave could have hidden himself on Ni'ihau. Only Hawaiians were allowed there and a *haole* like Dave would be spotted and ejected in less than twenty-four hours.

Parking his car in the carport, Keone slowly climbed the stairs to the condo. Julie was in the kitchen.

"What are you doing in there?" he asked.

"Don't worry. I didn't cook. Jan brought this over."

After the first week Keone relented and allowed Jan to visit. He picked her up the first time and brought her over from her work. He impressed upon her the real danger if anyone discovered where Julie was. He forbade her from discussing this with Sam, writing down the address, or even calling Julie. Julie would call her when she wanted to set up a visit.

Smelling the wonderful aromas from the kitchen, Keone saw the value in his decision.

"What are you doing home so early? Rough day?"

"You could say that. Not only did I fail to find your husband, who I know is still in the islands, but my good friend and boss, Tony Alcala, gave me a formal reprimand."

"For not finding Dave? That seems a bit harsh."

"No. He knows we're following every lead. I was reprimanded for two other things. The first was not closing some of my other cases fast enough."

"What was the second?

"Strangely enough, I was chewed out for finding someone."

"Who?"

"You."

"Oh, shit. Kulima?"

"He must have seen us shopping at the market last week. Luckily, we didn't go directly home."

"That was the day you went by Jan's work and picked her up."

"He followed us to Jan's work, but no farther. Frank told Tony he got another call. I'm still trying to keep the safe house story viable, thanks to a couple of friends staking out one that's unoccupied."

"So what did you tell Alcala?"

"I told him you were lonesome and wanted to see your sister. I also told him I didn't trust anyone else to take you to her. I explained that the trip to the market was just for show, so no one would see us go from the safe house to Jan's work."

"Did he buy that?"

"On the surface, yes. But he made me admit I had feelings for you and that I planned to act on them if and when you were ever free of Dave."

"So he doesn't know I'm living here."

"It's just a matter of time. I'm sure Kulima won't settle for the reprimand. He's gonna keep on digging."

"Let's go ahead and eat. Since you're early I won't have to re-heat what Jan brought." She put her arm as far around Keone's waist as she could and led him into the kitchen.

Keone ate the food with relish, but Julie could tell something was still wrong and had a pretty good idea what it was. "So, no Dave, huh?"

"No. I know a lot of places he isn't, but not where he is."

"Maybe I could help. I lived with the bastard for twelve

years."

Keone thought about this. He'd avoided discussing Dave with Julie since the explosion, focusing more on, well, becoming closer to her. But he knew she was right. Besides, there was a new urgency, Alcala might remove him from the case at any moment. "Okay. Is there anyplace I wouldn't know about where he might go? I've checked every piece of real estate he owns, every friend or employee he has, and every contact of his in the islands."

"You're sure he's in the islands?"

"Yes, but not Maui, Kaua'i, or O'ahu."

"You can forget the Big Island, too. With his asthma he avoids the place like the plague. He can't tolerate vog."

Even Keone had respiratory issues with vog, the volcanic version of smog prevalent in the vicinity of Kilauea's continuing eruption. "Okay, what about Lana'i or Moloka'i?"

"There's something about Moloka'i. What is it? It was right after we moved here. I wish I could remember."

"Just relax. Close your eyes and take a deep breath."

Julie did as she was told.

"Did you visit there for some reason?"

"Yes. But not as tourists. He needed to check something out. Some property. That's it." Julie opened her eyes.

"He said a client of his wanted to pay him with some undeveloped land on Moloka'i. We went and looked at it. Undeveloped was an understatement. It was just jungle, from what I saw, and well away from any roads. We had to drive for miles down dirt paths to get close enough to see it from the top of a cliff."

"Why didn't it show up on his real estate records?"

"He put it in his uncle's name for tax reasons. He said it was because he thought his uncle might decide to come over some time and hunt. What a load of crap. His uncle could barely walk by then. The only building there was a tumbled-down shack. I doubt if it's still standing."

But what if it was?

Keone needed to check this out. The ferry left from

Lahaina for Moloka'i at 7:15 AM tomorrow morning and he'd be on it.

Monday, May 13, 3:15 PM

It had felt good to finish a day's work, leave the office, and walk down the stairway to his car. This initial day back represented the first time Sam had felt absolutely normal since the crash. Even the mirror numbers didn't bother him. He'd become truly indifferent to whether the columns were left to right or right to left. The reversed QWERTY keyboard was normal to him now, as was the numerical keyboard.

Sam worked nine to three these days so he could get to his appointments with Dr. Drayton on time. The sessions had become more and more interesting as he worked his way through his journals. Last night he'd finished reading the final set and was anxious to share some critical aspects with Drayton.

Sam now knew the truth about Dave Walden. He also understood why they could no longer be friends. He knew, too, how close he'd been to Janet right before the crash, and why she cared so much about him. He no longer feigned anything around her or Drayton. He saw Drayton as a friend and mentor.

His usual space was available outside the medical clinic. There were advantages to being the last appointment of the day. The receptionist was happy to see him, and he enjoyed talking with her a little before each visit.

"Hello, Maria. How is every little thing with you?"

"Pretty good, Sam. And the doctor is in a pretty good mood, too. He just had a journal article accepted. Don't worry, though. It wasn't about you."

"No, he's saving that one for JAMA. I'm one of a kind."

"I think you're just a very nice man."

"Thank you, Maria. I really try to be."

Evan Drayton came out to usher Sam into his office.

"Hello, my friend. I'm looking forward to our session today. Your E-mail mentioned you finished reading the last set of journals." He closed the door behind them.

Sam moved to the table where they had begun spending their sessions so he could point out things in the journals as they talked. "They told me many things about myself and about my brother-in-law."

"In the journals I read, you discovered he was involved in illegal activities when he tried to get you involved. That was during a kayaking trip, right?"

"That's right. I took him ocean kayaking. I thought we would enjoy tackling a new version of an activity we once shared. He went, but only to tell me what a jerk I was to play by the rules. He was strung out on some drug the whole trip. I had to dive in and save him three times, before I gave up and rowed us to shore. It had only been two years since we were as close as brothers, and now he disgusted me."

"He begged you to tell no one about the deal he offered you, so you didn't share that portion of the journal with me. Are you comfortable telling me about it now?"

"Yes. He'd met a bunch of wealthy, high-level criminals vacationing here and they invited him to a meeting in New York. He knew before he went they were probably drug kingpins, but that only increased his interest."

"He was different from the Dave you remembered. Do you have any idea why he was not a user in your memories?"

"In my memories, he married Janet, who was totally grounded. She weaned him off of pot and party drugs before they ever left Indiana. But here in the real world, he discovered Maui was a great place to indulge all his baser interests."

Sam noticed Drayton smile at his use of the term *real world* to refer to the world described in his journals.

"So what was the deal he offered you during the kayaking trip?"

"A full partnership in the most extensive ice ring on Maui. He'd been working for the mainland bosses for a year when we arrived. He said he did something called *conversion* in a lab he'd rented and wanted to keep it going while he built a new lab somewhere more secure. He had another chemist, but he needed someone to manage the business."

"You refused him."

"I lost my temper. Told him he was an idiot to get into something like this and he needed to get out. He tried to punch me in the face, but his aim was off. I told him our friendship was over. He begged me not to tell anyone, especially Julie and Janet. I agreed to keep up an appearance of congeniality but told him that would be limited to major holidays—and it was."

"Thanks for filling in that gap for me. Let's move on to what you've just finished reading."

Sam paused before moving forward. "Evan, I started our relationship by lying to you and under-rating your talent as a psychiatrist."

"We're past all that now."

"I know, but I want you to know how much I appreciate this second chance you've given me. I'm committed to using it wisely. I may not be able to remember loving Janet, but I do love her now. All of these journals have shown me how much I loved her before the accident and why, but these last two touched me more deeply than anything I'd read before." Sam's voice faltered on the last two words.

"I see."

"Not really, but you will when you've read them. I want to focus on something from the very last entry, the night before the crash."

"The last entry would have been on March fourteenth, right?"

"Yes. It was Janet and Julie's birthday and we got together at Dave and Julie's for dinner and presents. The evening moved slowly to a conclusion, but the girls seemed happy with their presents. The catered dinner was fabulous. But I suspected Dave was just showing off.

"Julie had a little more champagne than usual. She was only a little tipsy, but started talking about Dave closing his practice to work full time as her agent. Dave immediately tried to change the subject, but she kept on, saying Dave should just retire and play golf and leave managing her career to her longtime agent Fred.

"Dave said it was time for bed and ushered Janet and me out of the house as quickly as possible. We agreed that Janet, who'd had no alcohol as usual, would drive us home. As we drove off, I glanced back and saw Dave yelling at Julie through the small window beside the door. As we turned the corner, I saw him draw his arm back to slap Julie across the face."

"Did you actually see him strike her?"

"No. That's why I didn't have Janet turn the car around or mention anything about it to her. I had a suspicion, but no proof."

"Is that where this stood, when you had the crash?"

"Not quite. When we got home I called a friend who still socialized with Dave and Julie. I laid it all out for him and asked what he knew. He hesitated, but eventually told me about my brother-in-law. Dave had become a player with multiple mistresses. The friend had seen Dave slap Julie across the mouth more than once. Dave always waited until they were outside or in their car. But the friend had seen him make contact with her face."

"Did you tell Janet?"

"I decided to wait until the next evening." He opened the top journal to the last page. "I wanted to check the story with a few other people when I was at work, but I say in the journal:"

> *I now know that Dave is hurting Julie. We need to help her get out of this situation. At dinner tomorrow, I'll tell Jan and get her to take Julie to a lawyer friend we know. We have to protect her. I have to protect her.*

"When I read that, I had an idea why my mind might have done this thing to me."

"To save Julie from an abusive relationship. Sam, I think you're on to something."

"Remember that earlier session when we talked about how the left-right transposition might account for why I thought Julie was my wife?"

"Yes, it made the coin toss connect you with Julie instead of Janet."

"But I think we're looking at this backwards. What if I really had amnesia, but retained the desire to save Julie from Dave?"

"And your mind changed one small fact to make it possible for you to save Julie without restoring your entire memory. If she were your wife, Dave couldn't hurt her anymore. He could never have hurt her at all."

"That's what I've been thinking. But, what do I do now?"

"Exactly what you planned to do before the crash. Tell Janet."

"I will. Maybe that will give my memory a jolt and get me back on track."

"Maybe, but don't expect anything to happen too fast. I believe this is a critical step on the road to your complete recovery, but that road may still be a little longer than you'd like."

"I understand, Doc. But I can't wait to take Janet out to dinner tonight. We're having our first date night."

Chapter Thirty-five

Monday, May 13, 7:00 PM

Sam and Janet arrived at the Kula Lodge and were led to their table next to one of the floor-to-ceiling windows. From here they enjoyed a breathtaking view of the Valley Isle, from the bright lights of Kahului in the east to those of Kihei in the west. The darkness of the cane fields contrasted with the inverted bouquets of lights that narrowed as they stretched up the many canyons of the West Maui Mountains. The restaurant was a feast for the eyes, as well. From the enclosed space where they sat they saw tables spilling down the hillside on stone-tiled plateaus surrounded by luscious gardens. A huge cairn dominated the center of this lovely outdoor seating area. Although there were a variety of niches in the stone structure, one larger opening provided access to a wood-fired, pizza oven.

They both had memories of eating here as a couple, but the couples each remembered were different. Over a steaming bowl of French onion soup made, of course, with sweet Maui onions, they reminisced about how they met.

"I know you thought you guys spotted us at the fair that day, but we'd caught multiple glimpses of you two cruising the midway before we got on that haunted house ride."

"Were we that obvious?"

"Oh, yes. When Julie and I exited the haunted house, we

weren't surprised in the slightest to find you there. Remember how that moving wall made sure alternating guests exited on different sides of the ride? Julie came out first on one side and I came out on the other to find you waiting."

In his memories Sam waited outside the left door (his right) and met Julie. But he had read the journal and knew the other scenario so well he could recite it to Janet. "I believe you were wearing a yellow polka-dot sun dress."

"That's right. I'm surprised you remember what I was wearing."

"You looked very lovely, as you do tonight." He was glad he'd read the journal to confirm that she'd worn the same dress there as in his memories. This was the point where the journal and his memory diverged, but at least this piece was the same.

"You were wearing light grey slacks and a short-sleeve blue dress shirt—unlike your scruffy colleague in tank-top and shorts."

"I was always a little self-conscious about bare legs, unlike Dave."

When the main course of two gourmet wood-fired pizzas arrived, Sam served one slice of each to Janet.

"I'm glad to see you also remember we like to share. These last few weeks with you have been very nice for me, Sam. I hope they've been like that for you."

"They have, Jan. I hope you don't mind if I call you that. I know I used to."

"Of course I don't mind."

"Every moment I've spent with you since I came home has brought me joy. We fit well together."

Jan took a bite of pizza. Sam guessed she was afraid to say anything that would dispel the mood.

"Drayton and I had a valuable session today. I know I don't usually share things from our sessions, but tonight I want to, if it's all right with you."

"I'd be honored." Jan looked up at him with hope in her eyes.

171

"First, I need to give you a little background. The day after I came home from the hospital, I found something hidden in the bedroom that only I knew about, my personal journals. I started keeping these when I entered college and never stopped. As you can imagine, these were written in mirror writing for me, but when I looked at them in a mirror, I recognized my own handwriting. Thanks to my rehab at the hospital, I didn't need a mirror to read them. I read one or two each day until I reached the present."

"Did they bring back memories?"

"I wish they had, but they did provide important information. All of the writing in the journals until the moment we met at the fair was exactly as I'd remembered entering it."

"Then they diverged." The hope in her eyes faded.

"Yes, but don't lose hope, Jan. As I read through the remaining journals I discovered what Dr. Drayton and I think may be the cause of my delusions."

Jan's hands began to shake. Sam had never admitted to having delusions until this moment.

"Up until today, Dr. Drayton was operating on the assumption that I had some suppressed desire for Julie that caused the delusions."

"And you didn't?"

Sam could tell Jan had the same suspicion as Drayton. "According to the journals, I discovered Dave was abusing Julie and that I wanted desperately to protect her. But I had no romantic feelings for her. Before the crash, I had decided to ask you to confront Julie and see if you could convince her to leave Dave."

Jan's smile suggested some irony regarding what Sam was telling her, but Sam continued. "Drayton feels that the trauma of the accident pushed my mind down an alternative path to save Julie from pain. If I were her husband she would be instantly freed from Dave's abuse."

"That makes perfect sense. But why left and right?"

"Before you and Julie came out of the haunted house, Dave and I flipped a coin. I picked the right side to wait for my new girlfriend."

"So. I came out on the right."

"You came out on the right for you, but Julie came out on the right for me, if left and right were switched."

"Whoa. Your mind came up with this whole mirror world thing just to create a logical reason why Julie was your wife?"

"That's what Drayton thinks. He's seen similar things before. I'm still not able to suppress those memories, but he feels my recognition of what is going on is a major step forward."

"It is. I'm so happy for you."

"I'm happy, too. Neither he nor I can guarantee what will happen now, but maybe this can provide you with a glimmer of hope."

"It does, Sam. It does."

"By the way, you really should talk to Julie about Dave."

For the first time since Sam's accident Jan broke into a hearty laugh."

Sam was caught off-guard, but Jan quickly explained.

"Oh, my poor Sam, Julie knows. Let me catch you up on a little story that has been unfolding while you've been healing. Drayton wouldn't let me tell you about it before, but I'm sure it's okay now."

"Please do."

"Where to begin? Well, the afternoon after your accident Sergeant Boyd interviewed Julie and me at our house...."

Monday, May 13, 10:00 PM

On the way home from the Kula Lodge, Jan felt comfortable enough to risk one last question about Sam's session with Drayton.

"Sam, you've made me very happy tonight. You've always been a thoughtful man and the kindness you showed me tonight was very special. I know you still have conflicting memories to deal with and promise not to push you. But I wondered if Dr. Drayton had any thoughts about your memory of the crash."

"It's fine, Jan. I don't mind talking about it. I've concealed part of my memories from him and from you. You see, I remember passing through a film, like a soap bubble, before I discovered we were on what I believed was wrong side of the road and swerved into the wrong lane. I still remember left being right before the accident."

"Before the accident. No wonder you doubted your doctors' diagnoses."

"Today I came clean with Evan. I told him what I just told you. But he made a valid point. These are still memories. If my memories of the distant past can be disrupted by the delusion, why couldn't those of the moments before the crash?"

"I guess that's true."

"I'm not able to remember the way life really was, yet. But I am willing to accept the possibility, probability, that the other memories are part of a delusion. There really isn't any other logical explanation. And, as you know..."

"You're a very logical man. And a very special one."

When they walked up to their front door, Jan felt like a high school girl after a date.

"Thank you for a wonderful evening," Jan said, as she searched her purse for her keys.

"Thank you, Miss Madison. Would you like to do this again sometime?" Sam smiled.

"I would like that very much, Mr. Loftus."

Sam gently grasped her arm and turned her to face him. Their eyes locked for the first time since the accident. He hesitated then pulled her closer until their lips brushed. Suppressed emotion surged to the surface. They kissed, sharing their passion, locked in each other's arms. Sensation overwhelmed conscious thought. Finally, breathless, they ended the kiss. They gazed at each other with tentative smiles. Jan turned and entered the house.

Without a word they went to their separate bedrooms and closed the doors. They had taken an important first step. But

Jan understood a long difficult journey lay ahead.

For the first time since the accident, Jan dreamed of her days together with Sam before the calamity of the crash. For the first time, she allowed herself to believe those days would come again.

Part VI: What if Right's not Right, Either?

Alice laughed. "There's no use trying," she said: "one CAN'T believe impossible things."

"I daresay you haven't had much practice," said the Queen. "When I was your age, I always did it for half-an-hour a day. Why, sometimes I've believed as many as six impossible things before breakfast...."

Lewis Carroll, author

RICK LUDWIG

Chapter Thirty-six

Tuesday, May 14

Timmy stared at the sand. He seemed to be working something out in his mind before proceeding with the construction of his castle. Sam appreciated that about Tim. He never rushed into things. He always had a plan in his mind and stuck to it. He reminded Sam of, well, Sam.

Cindy was off in the waves with her trusty Boogie board in hand. She was a risk taker, who never hesitated to try anything. That's why he and Julie had to keep a sharp eye on her at all times.

Julie was riding alongside their daughter on her own Boogie board. Smiling as the surf splashed her eyes and the trade winds tossed her hair. She was an object of fascination to him. In her work as a pediatrician, she had to help parents deal with terrible tragedy. Her empathy was deep and honest. After all, she had two young children of her own. Her patients appreciated that.

But when she came home to them each evening, she brought none of this with her. She loved her work and her family, but kept them absolutely separate. The kids knew she was a doctor who helped kids get well, but no work visits were ever allowed. She also refused to treat her own children. Sam was responsible for all bandaging and boo-boo kissing at home—a task he loved.

Cindy ran up from the shore break and threw her wet arms around her daddy's neck before planting a saltwater kiss on his lips. Julie stopped to admire Timmy's sand castle before joining the rest of the family. After toweling off, she spread out the blanket and lay beside Sam on her stomach with Cindy beside her in the same orientation.

Soon Timmy ran up and grabbed his father's hand. "Come see my fortress of solitude, Daddy. It's totally tremendous."

Sam stood with effort and followed his son down to see his newest creation. The smooth lines of the humped structure reminded Sam of a prehistoric mud hut, but he complimented Timmy on his craftsmanship. "It is a truly stable structure in harmony with its environment, yet has a somewhat dreamlike lightness to it as well."

"But we're real, Daddy, not dreams. Cindy and Mommy and me are real. Don't let them make you forget us. We love you. We love you so, so much."

Now Cindy and Julie were standing by Timmy. "We're real. You can't forget us or we'll die."

As they cried these words, first Julie, then Cindy, then Timmy gradually started to lose their color. Soon they were all grey and then they were gone.

Tuesday, May 14, 9:00 AM

Sam woke sobbing. Tears streamed down his cheeks. He'd assumed that once he understood his delusion, his subconscious mind would stop torturing him with dreams of the family he could never have.

He could accept the truth, why couldn't his wayward mind? His mind had been betraying him and torturing him ever since the accident. Hadn't he suffered enough? If he couldn't get past this he really would go mad. He would have to take things more slowly. He would have to control his impatience to return to normal.

Normal was always important to Sam. He remembered

when he was very young his father would make fun of his mother for her eccentric tastes. "Can't you just be normal?" he would say with a pretend scowl on his face. Sam's dad never had to say that to him. He loved normal. Normal was clean and neat and orderly. Normal was the way things should be.

The jingle of their home telephone interrupted his thoughts. Glancing at the clock on his bedside stand he realized he'd slept in. Jan had already left for work without disturbing him. He scrambled to answer the phone. "Hello."

"Hello. Is this Sam Loftus?" a male voice said.

"Yes." Sam didn't recognize the voice.

"Do you remember a nerdy guy you used to know at IU, who had the entire original *Cosmos* series on VHS?"

"Brad? Brad Carvell? How the hell are you? Where the hell are you? What possessed you to call me after all these years?"

"Still full of questions, eh, Sam? First, I'm fine. I did become an astrophysicist as planned and love my work. Second, I'm on Maui. Third, I wanted to catch up with an old friend after too many years apart."

"You here on vacation?"

"No, my wife and I moved here a few months ago. I work at the observatory on Haleakala."

"Wow. How did you find me?"

"I read about your accident and asked each of our friends on the island and my colleagues at the observatory if they knew you. I struck out for weeks until one of the security guys heard I was asking and told me he knew someone who knew you, your receptionist Kimmey. I called her yesterday afternoon and she gave me your phone number. I hear you're back at work."

"Just back. Yesterday was my first day."

"I don't want to make you late for work, but I would like to see you. How would you like a personal tour of the observatory?"

"You know I'd love it. I've always been an amateur astronomer."

"Kimmey said you were working some half days this week. Could you make it up here one of those?"

"Actually, tomorrow would be really good. I get off at noon and I don't have a doctor's appointment. Would that work for you?"

"It would be perfect. Do you know how to get up here?"

"I sure do. At least I know how to get to that big scary gate."

"I'll let them know you're coming. That's just the first gate, by the way. It's kind of hyper-secure up here. Just roll with it, okay? How about 2 PM?"

"Great. I'll let you know if I run into any problems." Sam was thinking, *I hope neither Jan nor Evan have a problem with this.*

"And, Sam, I'm going to show you things up here that will blow your mind. See you tomorrow."

After Brad hung up, Sam thought to himself, *This is the first time I've ever been glad that Kimmey is such a flake. No reasonable receptionist would give out an employee's phone number to a total stranger. Welcome to Maui.*

Then Sam reflected on the last thing Brad had said, "...I'm going to show you things up here that will blow your mind..."

Hasn't my mind been blown enough?

Tuesday, May 14, 10:30 AM

The nickname *Vomit Ferry* was bestowed by numerous tourists upon the shuttle that runs between Lahaina Harbor, Maui and Kaunakakai Harbor, Moloka'i. But for Keone, the trip through the Kalohi Channel, which separates Lana'i and Moloka'i, is a thrilling Hawaiian roller coaster ride. Although known for strong winds and choppy seas, the ferry takes this channel because it's smooth compared to the rougher Pailolo Channel, which lies between Maui and Moloka'i. *Pailolo* in Hawaiian means "crazy fisherman," referring to any fisherman who would be crazy enough to try to navigate this tough channel. The only time Keone suffered from seasickness was when one of his friends got their fishing boat too close to the Pailolo Channel.

Once ashore in Kaunakakai, Keone picked up the rental car he'd reserved and drove two hours to his favorite spot on the island, Uncle Kimo's. Hawaiians often refer to any older male as uncle, but Kimo was Keone's actual uncle, his mother's brother. Kimo Kalama left Maui twenty years ago because, he said, "It got too. Too many, too much, too fast, too loud, and too haole."

Uncle Kimo was not a bigot. He liked people of all races, as long as they stayed off his island. There were many like Kimo on Moloka'i. The dichotomy was that tourism brought necessary income to the island. Kimo accepted this only so much. The lovely hand-carved plaque above his front door expressed his level of acceptance succinctly. "*E Komo Mai o Moloka'i.* Now go the hell home."

Keone wiped his shoes on Kimo's front doormat. *Kimo would never call it a welcome mat.*

"Aloha. You deah, Uncle?"

"Keone? Why you not tell me you come?"

"Let's see. You have no phone, no mailbox, and hate visitors."

"Ah, you no visitor, you family. Get inside."

Keone needed Kimo's help with his search for Dave Walden, but he knew better than to ask. Things were done a certain way with his uncle.

"How you family on that haole island ovah deah?"

"Everyone is fine. We had a big luau a couple weeks ago and everybody came to the ranch." Keone knew better than to say barbeque.

After a full hour catching up on family activities, Kimo asked the two questions that allowed Keone to request his help. "Why you here? How I help you?"

There was absolutely nothing that happened on Moloka'i that Kimo didn't know about. His work with a group dedicated to the restoration of the legal Hawaiian government and his status as *Ali'i* gave him a position of great importance on this island. He knew about the haole hiding in the backcountry. He knew about the plot of land he owned with its decrepit shack.

He knew the man called Dave was completely strung out on batu. But he needed to know why Keone was looking for him before he would agree to help.

"Dave Walden is a bad man who's taking money from Hawaiians and sending it off-island. He beat his wife savagely and blew up their house with her right outside. I saved her life."

"And?"

Keone couldn't fool his uncle. "And I'm falling in love with her."

"Let's go. I take you to him."

"There is one other thing. I have to call in another guy to help me with the arrest."

"Is this other guy Hawaiian?"

"I doubt it. But he lives on O'ahu."

"Hell. You call that damn place Hawaiian?"

Keone decided to say no more. He certainly wasn't going to mention that his friend was a federal agent.

"I don't have to talk to him, do I?"

"No, just lead us to the place Dave is hiding out, then you can take off and we'll take it from there."

"Okay. Call dat S.O.B."

Keone stepped outside to call Agent Freeman while Uncle Kimo gathered up a few items and put them in his battered jeep.

"Freeman."

"Hello, this is Boyd, from Maui, about Dave Walden."

"Yes, Sergeant, what have you got?"

"I believe Walden is hiding out on an undeveloped plot of land on Moloka'i."

"I can be there in thirty-five minutes."

"Great. It will take us a little longer. Let's meet at the Moloka'i Airport at 2:00 PM. There's just one thing."

"What?"

"What's your first name?"

"Tom."

"Mine's Keone. The local who is taking us to Walden needs

to think you're just a friend of mine. You can't mention your affiliation."

"I'll have to identify myself to Walden when we take him."

"That's fine. Uncle Kimo will be long gone by then."

"You wouldn't be talking about Kimo Kalama, would you?"

"You haven't met, have you?"

"No. No. It's just his name comes up a lot here in the Federal Building in Honolulu. I bet you want me to talk to you and not to him, right?"

"Right. I owe you one."

"I'll find a way to collect sometime."

Chapter Thirty-seven

Tuesday, May 14, 11:00 AM

"Are you ready?" Jan asked as she picked up her sister in the parking lot outside Keone's condo.

"I hope so. We have to be back before Keone gets back from Moloka'i."

"No problem. Our appointment is at eleven-thirty. You kind of like that Hawaiian of yours, don't you?"

"I'd do anything for him. That's why I don't want him to know I broke his rules and went out without him. You're certain this lawyer is not affiliated with Dave or his friends in any way?"

"Julie, he does work for my design firm. George knows who David is but has never met him. And he's disgusted by how David supplements his legal income. His sister died of a drug overdose when she was only sixteen."

"I know that I need to do this. But I hate actually filing for divorce. Let's talk about something else."

"I'm bursting to tell you something, but I don't want to jinx it."

Julie seemed surprised to see her normally controlled sister so excited. "Is it about Sam?"

"Yes. He kissed me last night after our first date." Jan sounded like she did when they were teenagers, talking about their first crushes.

"Was it a peck or the whole enchilada?"

"With sour cream, guacamole, and salsa."

"I'm so happy for you, but don't get ahead of yourself."

"No. I won't. But the kiss wasn't the biggest thing. He accepts the fact that he's having delusions. He and Drayton believe his mind created all of this to protect you from David."

"What?"

"Sam read a bunch of personal journals he kept and discovered that he knew David was abusing you. He was going to ask me to tell you to leave David before the accident damaged his memories. He and Drayton both believe he has a much better chance of recovery now that they know the source of the delusions."

"That's wonderful news."

"Keep your fingers crossed. I know I am. Did you say Keone's on Moloka'i?"

"Yeah. He's following up on a clue I gave him." Julie smiled broadly.

"You gave a clue to a detective?"

"I remembered that Dave owns some undeveloped land on Moloka'i that isn't recorded as belonging to him. Keone thinks he might be hiding out there."

"I hope he finds him, locks him up, and throws away the key." David Walden had never been high on Jan's list of friends and family. Now she truly hated him.

Pulling into the parking lot by George Frick's office, Jan glanced at Julie to see her hands were trembling. "I'll be with you every second, honey. You're doing the right thing."

Jan watched as Julie steeled herself, threw open the car door, and said, "Let's do this."

Tuesday, May 14, 2:00 PM

The road up Haleakala, despite all the switchbacks, was fun for Sam. He loved the sense of freedom he felt being this high and seeing so far. Up here he felt free from stress, noise, and painful memories. He looked forward to the day he could look back on his delusions as just that. He knew he was making progress and felt this visit to an old friend could only help.

He was wrong.

Turning off the main road that led to the visitor center for the National Park, Sam approached the first gate onto the observatory proper. An armed guard approached his window to see if he had legitimate business at the observatory.

"I'm Samuel Loftus," he said, handing over his driver's license. "I'm here to visit Dr. Bradley Carvell."

The guard took Sam's license with him back to his shelter and disappeared for ten minutes. When the guard returned, he said, "You are cleared to proceed beyond this gate, Mr. Loftus. Dr. Carvell will meet you at the next gate and transfer you to the observatory in his vehicle."

Sam was pleased to see Brad waiting for him at the next gate. A guard here directed him to a small parking lot outside this second fence. When Sam reached the gate the guard again took his driver's license as Sam passed through the gate, but did not offer to return it. Brad immediately grabbed Sam's hand and shook it vigorously.

"Welcome, old friend. I can't wait to tell you about my recent discoveries, but there will be fewer questions if I give you the tour first. They have quite a facility up here."

Sam glanced back toward the gate to find the guard had returned to his shelter.

"You'll get your license back when you leave. The security gets even stricter from here on in. Here, put this on."

Brad gave Sam an exotic badge attached to a lanyard, which Sam slipped over his head.

"The lettering on the badge is time sensitive. In four hours, your name and visitor status will fade away to be replaced by the word 'void' in bright red. My name, as your host, will remain visible so they know who to blame for your unauthorized presence."

They passed through two more gates, both equipped with

metal detectors, before arriving at the facility scattered across the very top of the crater's rim.

As they exited the vehicle, Brad winked and began an obviously canned lecture about the facility. "Haleakala Observatory is one of the most valuable sites in the world. Above the tropical inversion layer and blessed with clear skies in the night and evening hours, it is an excellent spot to observe the universe. The University of Hawai'i Institute for Astronomy manages this site today, as it has for over forty years. Much of the work done here could not be conducted anywhere else on Earth. Scientists from NASA, the NSF, the Space Telescope Institute, the Pan-STARRS consortium, the Air Force, and many other prestigious institutions work here." His second wink came as he said the Air Force.

There were a large number of structures here, many with the familiar spherical shape of observatories. Brad specifically pointed out the Mees Observatory, the two Pan-STARRS (PS-1 and PS-2, prototypes for a larger telescope to be built on Mauna Kea on the Big Island), the LCO Faulkes Observatory, and the Zodiacal Light Observatory. Less conventional structures included the TLRS Laser Ranging System, the Maui Space Surveillance Site, the Advanced Electro-Optical System [AEOS], and the facility they were about to enter, which he referred to as home.

"There is a name for this facility. But if I told you I'd have to shoot you."

"That secret, huh?"

"No. That stupid. It's the Southwestern Center for Regional Extreme Electro-magnetic Wave Detection."

"S-C-R-E-E-W-D?"

"And guess how it's pronounced?"

Sam couldn't suppress his laughter. He noticed Brad waited to open the door until he'd brought himself back under control.

Inside the door another round of security checking took place before they could enter the rather spacious, but bleak, cinderblock structure.

"We entered on the top floor, which is at ground level. This is where all of the offices reside surrounding that huge square chasm in front of you. All of the equipment is down there, well below our line of site," Brad explained.

"Hello, Brad. Nice to see your friend arrived." A very dignified grey-haired gentleman approached, wearing a less dignified set of cargo shorts and an aloha shirt.

"Sam Loftus, I'd like to introduce you to my boss, Dr. Martin Hassellbach. Dr. Hassellbach oversees all work here at the top of the world for the UH Institute of Astronomy."

"Pleasure to meet you, sir."

"The pleasure is ours. We have rather few non-scientist visitors here at the observatory. I hope you enjoyed your tour."

So that was the tour. Pointing at a bunch of domes and square buildings. Sam was pretty disappointed. But he was really here to see Brad, so what the hell. "You have a very extensive facility. Brad told me this is the only place in the world where most of the work done here could be effectively carried out."

Hassellbach smiled. Sam guessed it was because he quoted directly from the script Brad followed, to the letter. "I'll let you two old friends catch up on old times in your office, right, Brad?"

"Yes, sir. That's where we'll be."

Sam suspected Brad's words confirmed for Hassellbach that they would not venture beyond this non-classified space.

When they entered Brad's crowded work area, he closed and locked the door. "Sam, I apologize for rushing through the tour, but I have something much more important to discuss with you. Your supposed delusions. Please sit down. This will take a while."

Tuesday, May 14, 2:00 PM

Keone and Kimo took different vehicles to the little airport on Moloka'i. Tom Freeman's unmarked helicopter arrived just as they did. Keone went out to meet Tom and reinforced the need to maintain the façade that they were old friends. Tom played along perfectly, giving Keone a bear hug and kept his arm around Keone's shoulder as they walked back to the cars.

Before they got into the rental, Keone waved an arm towards the beat up, mud-encrusted Nissan pick-up and said, "That's my uncle. He's going to lead the way."

This was the only acknowledgement that Uncle Kimo was even there. Kimo stared straight ahead at the helicopter. Once Tom and Keone were in their seats and the engine was running, Kimo tore out of the little parking lot, daring Keone to keep up.

"Can you tell me a little more about how you found Walden?" Freeman asked.

"His wife, Julie, remembered some property he bought in his maternal uncle's name, which hadn't shown up in our searches. She didn't know its location, except that it was on Moloka'i. Uncle Kimo knows everything that goes on here, but can only be reached in person. Until he confirmed that Walden was here and that he knew where, I really had nothing solid. That's when I called you."

"Got it. This is your collar for the abuse and arson, but I'll need to charge him with the drug stuff at the same time to justify our use of the helicopter to extract him."

"I understand. He's probably going to be in pretty shitty shape. He brought a lot of product with him. So, we may have to take him directly to Maui Memorial."

"Let's not get ahead of ourselves. Could he be armed?"

"We have to assume he is, but my instincts tell me he isn't. This guy is a schmoozer and beats up women. I bet we'll either have to wake him or scrape him off the walls of the shack to arrest him."

After two hours of spine-cracking travel bouncing down dirt tracks, Kimo pulled over and got out of his car. Keone stopped right behind and got out. Freeman trailed him by a good ten steps. Keone was developing a strong respect for the agent. This guy knew his stuff.

"Okay, Keone. Down deah." Kimo pointed down a steep cliff to a level area overgrown with every type of Hawaiian flora.

"The shack's between da two Kiawe and dat Monkeypod. You see?"

At first Keone didn't but, eventually, he made out about one board width of the cabin through the trees. "*Mahalo nui loa*, Uncle. I owe you big time."

"I know. Aloha." His farewell did not include Agent Freeman. He was in his pick-up and out of sight before Freeman caught up to where Keone stood pondering their best path down the cliff face.

"See the two kiawe at about ten o'clock?"

Freeman had brought binoculars from the car and used them now. "I would never have spotted that piece of the cabin with my naked eyes. You guys are good."

"We're Hawaiian." Keone smiled.

"I've got rope and climbing gloves in my pack. We better get started. I'm not sure if we'll get reception down there. I'll call my pilot and give him the coordinates."

"Don't let him take off until we're actually at the cabin. I don't want to spook Walden. Our journey will take a hell of a lot longer than your pilot's. It's 4 PM now. Tell him to pick us up in two hours. If we're not there by then, we're screwed."

Chapter Thirty-eight

Tuesday, May 14, 4:00 PM

"What the hell are you talking about, Brad?" Sam was in no mood to have his world turned inside out again.

"I guess not everyone knows your diagnosis, huh?"

"That's right." *Who's been shooting their mouth off?* he thought. It didn't take long to figure it out. "It was Kimmey, wasn't it?"

"Don't fire her, okay? I laid it on pretty thick about how we were close friends and how worried I was about you. Besides, when you hear what I have to say, you might kiss her."

Sam sincerely doubted that.

"This is going to take some time to explain in detail, but what you've experienced is a perfectly logical physical phenomenon."

"Really. Confusing left and right, forgetting who your wife is, and having detailed memories about a life that didn't happen is perfectly logical." *How have you been feeling lately, Brad?*

But the fact that they were in Brad's office at a major research facility suggested Sam should at least listen to what the man had to say.

"Just listen, hear me out. Even scientists have difficulty understanding some of this stuff, but I remember what a quick study you were in college."

Sam crossed his arms. He'd decided to listen but wasn't going to be easily sold. He was just starting to get his life with

Jan back on track.

"Sam did you watch that new *Cosmos* show when it was on, with Neil Degrasse Tyson?"

"Of course. I loved it."

"Do you remember him talking about the multiverse?"

"Yes. He said there could be an infinite number of parallel universes displaced from each other in time. They would be invisible to each other."

"You were always a good student. What he described is a popular theory in modern physics that many people are studying, including me. It's why I'm here on Maui."

"Why Maui?"

"I learned about the presence of this facility through a colleague and it offered me the perfect tools to study a theory I have about contact points between parallel universes."

"Contact points."

"Yes. I won't bore you with all the math, though I think you'd find it fascinating. If these separate universes occasionally bumped into each other, just for a moment, it could be possible for something or someone to travel between them. However, it would have to be a two-way transfer or it would violate the law of conservation of mass and energy."

"If what you're suggesting was even possible, which I doubt, wouldn't it be measurable in some way?"

"Yes. It would and it has."

"You've measured it?"

"Yes. I've been measuring these rare contacts for years. I discovered that the Hawaiian archipelago represents a uniquely active contact point, but my measurements were extremely inaccurate until I arrived here."

"At the eye of the storm."

"In a way. Anyway, the strongest single measurement to date was at 16:48:30 hours on March 15 of this year. It was located on the Honoapi'ilani highway near Ma'alaea Harbor."

Sam was speechless. He'd passed through the bubble at precisely this time and place.

Could I really be in another world, another universe? No, it's all too neat.

"How different from each other would these parallel universes be?"

"Theoretically the differences could be anything from unnoticeable to massive. The idea is that every possible decision could be made in any possible way. If I flip a coin, it could land either heads or tails, right?"

This sounded way too familiar to Sam. "Yes."

"In one of the major theories, if a coin lands heads in this universe, there is another parallel universe where it lands tails. That simple change results in a series of events which is different between the two universes."

"You mean like in one universe left could be left and in another left could be right?"

"Precisely. Those words are just symbols for physical realities. Such symbols are arbitrary and could have developed differently in different universes. Many terms are based on established conventions. For example, up and down are based on action in a gravitational field. There is no up or down in space."

"Could someone from one universe adapt to such a dramatic difference?"

"Absolutely. I remember watching a movie in physics class in high school. It was really old. This scientist wears glasses that reverse up and down. At first he's a mess. He can't catch a ball or read or anything. After a few months, he sees everything normally. They explained that the image the brain receives from the optic nerve is actually upside-down and the brain reverses it. When he took off the special glasses he became completely uncoordinated again until his brain could flip everything back."

"From what you say, my situation is different from the guy with the weird glasses. I see everything the same way you do. I just name things differently. Yes, the writing is backwards for me and I can now read it, but I can still read writing that isn't backwards, too."

"You're right. I was just illustrating the adaptability of

humans to change. "What are North/South, East/West, Left/Right, and Up/Down? These are all conventions. The sun comes up in the same place, and the earth spins in the same direction in both your universe and mine. In your world Australia is still in the Southern Hemisphere, what we call east you call east, what we call up you call up. In both worlds people write from different directions in English and Hebrew. Drive on the different sides of the road in America and the UK. Only the meaning of left and right are switched and everything that depends on this."

"I don't know. I'm not sure there isn't a flaw in your argument. You don't know everything I've experienced since the crash."

"Too bad you haven't recorded everything."

"I did. I keep a journal. I mean, I've always kept a journal, but I've continued to since the crash."

"Would you mind sharing it with me?"

"Sure. But you won't be able to read it."

"Mirror writing. I have an imaging program that converts, it's helpful with some of my measurements. If you lend me your journal, I'll make a transposed copy and return the original to you."

"I have it in my car. I'll give it to you when you take me back."

"That'll work." Carvell looked thoughtful for a moment. "I'll just head home from there."

"Brad, I understand what you're telling me and why, but...I just reached a better place recently and I'm not sure I want to leave it."

"They've started to convince you. I got in touch with you just in time. Look, I understand your concerns, but look at this from my point of view. You're an integral component of the data that prove my theory."

"I'm also very skeptical. I know I'll find a thousand holes in this once I've had a chance to think about it for a while."

"Good. I want you to. Hit me with everything you've got. I'm confident you'll be as convinced of this as I am once all your concerns are addressed."

"Can we meet again?" Sam suggested.

"Sure. How about at my house? Here, I'll give you the address. You went right past it on your way up here. Can we meet...say...June fifth to continue our discussions? I'm free in the morning, early."

"Seven?"

"That works for me. I'll have your journal transposed and read before we meet. If I find any contradictions, I'll highlight them for you. And I expect you to read up on the multiverse and be ready with a battery of reasons why I'm full of it."

"Okay. Just remember, it's not personal." *Not for you, anyway*, Sam thought.

Tuesday, May 14, 4:30 PM

After a thirty-minute descent down the sheer cliff face, punctuated at multiple points by razor-sharp, horizontal projections, Keone and Agent Freeman were still far above the floor of the depression. Keone was an expert rock-climber and Freeman was handling himself pretty well until he unknowingly caught his line over one of the projections.

Before Keone could warn him to ease off on the line, the edge wore through the line and Freeman started to plummet. Keone braced himself for what was to come, but Freeman was unaware that before they began their descent Keone had clipped an extra line onto Freeman's carabineer. When the line halted Freeman's descent with a jerk, the agent looked around for some explanation of his miraculous reprieve from death.

When Freeman's eyes finally landed on Keone bracing against the cliff face with all his might, Keone just smiled.

"When did you hook that on?" Freeman asked.

"At the top."

"What if you'd fallen? Wouldn't that have taken me with you?"

"I didn't plan on falling."

Freeman scrambled back up to the ledge above Keone and then held the line so Keone could join him.

As they rested, Keone attached a new line to what remained of Freeman's main line and tested it.

"Okay, now that you've saved my ass, I think it's time we went from Agent Freeman and Sergeant Boyd to Tom and Keone."

"Well, I was gonna wait until you saved my ass, but this works. Let's get going, Tom."

Keone let Tom lead the rest of the descent. They reached the bottom safely but exhausted after another half hour of tough climbing. The cabin was still almost a mile away through dense tropical growth and they decided to rest a few minutes before pulling out machetes to hack their way through.

"I sure hope this guy's in bad shape when we get there or he's liable to beat the crap out of both of us," Tom said, handing a plastic water bottle to Keone.

"If his future ex-wife is right, he's probably OD'd on ice. We may just need to bag him."

Tom wasn't convinced and neither was Keone. If Dave was just highly medicated and not over-dosed, he could be extremely violent.

The other thing that troubled Keone was just how Dave had managed to reach the cabin. "Tom, how do you suppose he got in here? He's no rock climber and Uncle Kimo told me there was no easier trail in."

"Chopper. I'm sure he has an on-island contact who could fly him in here and pick him up whenever things cooled down."

"Your probably right. I checked all the licensed charters, but there are a lot of pakalolo farmers here who need to get their goods to market."

"And they have their own *air force*."

From this point, they continued through the brush deliberately and quietly.

Chapter Thirty-nine

Tuesday, May 14, 5:30 PM

Keone and Tom had hacked their way across three-quarters of the depression that held Dave Walden's cabin, when they were able to put away the machetes. They quietly worked their way through the slightly less dense growth until they were within one hundred yards of the cabin. Here the sparseness of the foliage provided a real possibility of being seen.

"We should separate," Keone whispered.

"You take the front and I'll take the back. I doubt there's a back door, but I'm sure I can find a window or something I can enter through," Tom replied in a similar low tone.

"When you hear me kick in the front door, come in through the back."

Two, near-simultaneous crashes roused Walden to his knees. But he was in no condition to resist arrest.

Shaking violently in the corner, Dave slowly rolled his eyes towards Keone. "Boyd? Damn, you're good. I didn't think anybody could find me out here."

"Just be glad it's us and not Pavin and his friends," Keone replied.

"You know about Pavin? I'm really screwed."

Keone put on the cuffs and shoved Dave over to Freeman "This gentleman will read you your rights and tell you a few of the things we're arresting you for. Personally, I'm arresting you for spousal abuse and arson."

"I wasn't trying to hurt Julie. I waited until she was outside. I was going to wait until you drove away, but those evidence guys were heading for the door."

"Stop. Not another word until he reads you your rights."

Tom began, "I am Agent Thomas Freeman of the Drug Enforcement Agency of the United States of America and I am arresting you for the illegal production and distribution of controlled substances. You have the right to remain silent...."

Keone left the fetid cabin with Tom trailing behind, half-carrying the fragile Walden. Keone checked his watch—5:50 PM. "We'll have a little wait before—"

As if on cue, he was interrupted by the roar of a helicopter advancing towards them. He was glad they wouldn't have to wait for their ride.

"Get down. Now," Tom shouted and fired at the chopper.

Keone hit the ground, grabbed his own weapon and rolled into firing position. Machine gun shells were tearing up the ground around Tom Freeman and Walden. But the shooter seemed to be ignoring Keone.

Taking aim, Keone put two rounds into the helicopter's rear stabilizer. The pilot tried to pull up, but crashed into the Kiawe trees beside the cabin. Keone hoped they were low enough and moving slowly enough to avoid an explosion.

They weren't.

Curling into a ball and covering his head for protection, Keone hoped the others had time to do the same.

The explosion rocked him, but the shrapnel from the devastated helicopter flew over him and into the jungle.

"Are you all right," he yelled as he ran to Freeman and Walden's location.

"Walden's hit, but he'll live. I got my bell rung protecting our suspect."

"That shout to get down saved my ass."

"Just wanted to even the scales."

"Consider us square and probably good friends for life. But

how could you tell that wasn't your chopper? When you yelled I couldn't even see it."

"Neither could I. It was the sound. Then I caught a glimpse of that M60 poking out of the open door and figured they weren't here to make friends.

"That pile of debris," Tom said, indicating the rubble that was recently a chopper, "hadn't been serviced properly in months if not years. We take excellent care of our helicopters. They're our most valuable asset for catching growers, processers, and dealers on the islands. I knew it wasn't our chopper the second I heard it."

Keone helped Tom drag Walden over to where they'd stashed their packs before rushing the cabin. He pulled out the first aid kit and let Tom get on with bandaging Dave. While the other two were occupied, Keone headed to the site of the helicopter's remains. He found one head in fairly good condition but no other identifiable body parts. He photographed the face and returned to find another helicopter heading toward them. The smile on Tom Freeman's face told him this was a friendly.

"Have you got a plastic bag in your pack?" he asked, holding up the remains by its wavy blonde hair.

Tuesday, May 14, 8:00 PM

When Julie pulled up to the entrance to Maui Memorial Hospital, Keone was happy to see she was driving the beater. She must've picked it up from Lahaina, where he'd left it. He was even happier when he saw she'd also picked up Panda Express. He was starving.

"Who beat the crap out of you? Not Dave?" Julie asked, as Keone slumped into the passenger seat.

"No. He was pretty out of it by the time we found him. Most of this is courtesy of the island of Moloka'i, although a helicopter sent by Dave's former good friends helped a bit."

"Tell me."

"As I said on the phone, we caught Dave hiding just where you suspected, but it was a hell of a hike in to catch him. He didn't put up any fight, as he was fairly well iced, but some unexpected visitors in a helicopter tried to put an end to him. A fantastic DEA agent named Tom Freeman saved Dave's life, but not before they put a round in Dave's shoulder. He's going to be all right, though."

"What happened to the helicopter?"

"I sort of helped it land with a lucky shot. We know what the shooter looked like." Keone avoided mentioning the shooter's severed head. "He's a well-known hit man from New York."

"You're not hurt?"

"No. I'm fine. They kept Tom overnight for observation. He has a concussion from the explosion."

"Another explosion. What was it this time?"

"The helicopter. I told you I got in a lucky shot. So how was your day?"

"I filed for divorce. Don't be mad. Jan took me over to a lawyer friend of hers. I was perfectly safe. We came straight home afterwards."

Keone felt a complex array of emotions, none of which was anger at Julie. But this did change things.

When they reached the condo, Keone jumped in the shower, while Julie laid out the goodies from Panda on the kitchen table. They ate in silence until Julie became uneasy.

"Okay. You're mad. I didn't follow your rules. I apologize. Just don't give me the silent treatment."

"What? Oh, no. I'm glad you filed for divorce. You were never my prisoner, you know. You did the right thing."

"Then what is it?"

"I have no justification for keeping you here, with Dave in custody. If you would feel more comfortable in a condo of your own, I know a guy here in the complex who's looking to rent a unit just like this one."

"Tired of having me around, eh?"

"No. No. I just, well, with you filing for divorce I thought you might be..."

"Ashamed of living with you? You've been a perfect gentleman ever since I met you. Maybe a little too perfect."

"It's not that I don't care, Julie. I like having you here. I like talking with you, being with you, smelling you. Oh shit. I'm messing this up."

Julie laughed and began removing his belt. When he resisted, she said, "You ass. I'm in love with you, too," and slipped the straps of her sundress off her shoulders. When the dress hit the floor Keone stared at her lovely, naked body. His nights on the couch were over.

Part VII: Resolutions

"It's no use talking about it," Alice said, *looking up at the house and pretending it was arguing with her. "I'm NOT going in again yet. I know I should have to get through the Looking-glass again—back into the old room—and there'd be an end of all my adventures!"*

So, resolutely turning her back upon the house, she set out once more down the path, determined to keep straight on till she got to the hill. For a few minutes all went on well, and she was just saying, "I really SHALL do it this time—" when the path gave a sudden twist and shook itself (as she described it afterwards), and the next moment she found herself actually walking in at the door.

Lewis Carroll, author

RICK LUDWIG

Chapter Forty

Wednesday, June 5, 7:00 AM

"Hello, Sam. Welcome to our humble abode. This is my wife Diane."

Sam gave Diane a hug, in true Maui style. "I've known your husband since college. He was the first person to nurture my love of astronomy and astrophysics. I even considered a career like his, but practicality won out. I'm an accountant."

"Sometimes I wish Brad was an accountant." Diane sounded serious. Sam was impressed by her soft voice and lovely face.

"I'm gonna to take Sam down to the lab and force him to drink a few Bloody Marys while we reminisce about the good old days."

"Why not stay up here? I'd be interested in knowing what you were like in your youth."

"That's precisely why we're going to the basement. Alone."

Despite Brad's effort to make everything sound light, Sam sensed Diane wasn't kidding and neither was Brad. He imagined the life of a research scientist's wife was no picnic, especially when the scientist was away all night, every night.

Brad's basement was crammed with scientific equipment. With this much here, Sam wondered how extensive his set-up was at the observatory.

"I was kidding about the Bloody Marys," Brad said, placing

a cool mango iced tea in Sam's hand. "You'll need a clear head for this discussion."

"Your wife is lovely. Where did you meet?"

"As you could probably tell, Diane is Chinese. Not a Hawaiian of Chinese ancestry, either. She was born in China. We met in Shanghai, when I worked with her father."

"Is he an astrophysicist, too?"

"Yes, one of the finest in China." Brad seemed uneasy with this conversation.

"Has he visited you here on Maui?"

"No. We no longer collaborate."

Sam sensed he shouldn't push any farther. Maybe Diane's father had been against the marriage. If so, it was none of his business.

They sat, sipping their tea, on a couch at the far end of the lab. Sam wasn't surprised to see a white board, a required tool for all scientists, opposite the couch where a big screen HD TV might be in anyone else's basement.

Between the couch and the board was a large computer display table. On it was a detailed map of the Hawaiian archipelago. Numerous sites were noted with times and dates. Sam's eyes scanned over to the area near Ma'alaea Harbor on Maui to find the time and date of his encounter with the bubble duly noted. Looking around the rest of the lab he saw all of the complex electronic equipment he expected. He also spotted a solvent cabinet, which seemed out of place in an electronics lab.

Taking a deep swig of tea, Sam asked, "Why a solvent cabinet? Do you do chemistry here?"

"No, but I do need to keep all of my electronics clean and conductive, a real problem with all the dust and wind up here."

He walked over and opened the cabinet. "See, acetone, chloroform, ethanol, and ether. I only keep small, sealed vials for use in that fume hood in the corner."

Sam watched as Brad closed the cabinet, then turned to pick up a document from a lab bench. He also noted Brad forgot to re-engage the lock.

"I finished reading your journals covering the time since the crash. Here's the original copy." Brad handed it to Sam like it was a rare manuscript.

"Well, did you discover any contradictions?"

"None. While there are obvious contradictions between your account and the explanations the doctors have cobbled together, there are none between your vivid memories and what actually happened."

Sam stared at his friend.

"You've crossed over, my friend. You are the first confirmed traveler between parallel universes." Brad's smile was contagious. Sam could tell this man, unlike his doctors, had no doubts about what happened to him.

Sam had also come to believe Brad's explanation for his experiences. Since their visit at the observatory, Sam had read everything he could find on the multiverse hypothesis, even plowing through some of Brad's original papers that he found on scientific websites. He'd also had the same nightmare about his children and Julie—every night. He now accepted Brad's theory as fact.

Sam also knew he couldn't let anyone else know. No one could suspect that his fragile acceptance of Drayton's explanations for his condition had been shattered.

"Brad. I believe you. I know inside that I'm not from this world. I've known it since the accident, since before the accident. I knew it when I passed through the bubble and everything changed. I knew it when I couldn't erase the vivid memories of my children. I need to go back home. Can you help me?"

Carvell again looked uncomfortable. He thought for a long time before answering Sam. "Oh, Sam, I thought you knew. The energy spikes I recorded are way beyond anything our current technology could produce. It's not possible for me or anyone else to send you back."

Sam just sat there staring at the half-full tumbler of iced tea. He felt lost.

"But, Sam, although I can't recreate the effect, I believe I can do more than just measure it. I'm developing a predictive tool."

Sam looked up. "A predictive tool?"

"The Hawaiian archipelago is a hot spot for this phenomenon. I believe other spikes, like the one that brought you here, are inevitable. The tool I am developing will allow me to predict where and when one will occur. By placing you at that precise spot at the proper moment, it's possible you could return home by the same kind of transposition event that brought you here."

Sam struggled with this, but admitted it would be worth a try. "Okay. How soon will you be able to predict the next spike? Then how long will it take to forecast one with the proper characteristics to get me home?"

"I am confident I could develop a functional predictive tool in less than ten years. But I have no idea how frequent an event such as yours occurs. It could be decades or centuries. The peak that brought you here could be the largest in a series or the smallest or anywhere in between."

"So I'm kind of back to square one." *Except now I know I don't belong here and am unlikely to be able to leave anytime soon.*

"I'm truly sorry, Sam. I will keep studying this phenomenon. If I discover anything new, anything at all, I'll call you."

"Thank you, Brad. It's better to know than to suppose. Say, could you spare a few books or articles about the multiverse. I think I should continue my education on the subject."

"Certainly, I'll just be a minute." Brad bounded up the stairs.

Sam did want to read more, but he also wanted Brad out of the lab long enough for him to slip a few vials from the solvent cabinet into his jacket pocket. He also engaged the lock that Brad had neglected. He didn't want Brad to have an excuse to check inside—at least not right away.

Brad returned to the top of the stairs with his arms full and called down, "Let me carry these out to your car for you."

"Thanks." Sam joined him at the top of the stairs, with his

journal in his hand. "Maybe studying these will help me to accept my situation and avoid making a terrible mistake."

Once Brad had stashed the books and reprints in the backseat of Sam's car, the two friends embraced. Sam drove away without another word but with the seeds of a plan germinating in his mind. If Janet succeeded in her efforts on his behalf, he could start implementing that plan tonight.

Wednesday, June 5, 9:00 AM

"Hey, Julie, it's Jan. How's everything going? As if I didn't know."

"I can't lie to you, Jan. I've never been so happy in my life. Keone is the man I should have met years ago. He's everything Dave isn't, strong, quiet, caring, and naturally passionate. Nothing Keone does is ever for show. He's the real deal."

"I'm so happy for you. You deserve to be happy after all you've gone through."

"Thank you. You deserve to be happy too, Jan. How are things with you and Sam?"

"Great. He's starting to remember things at last. He says they're just images. But they're from his life with me, before the accident. And, Julie, he kisses me each morning before he goes off to work."

"Honey, that's wonderful."

"He's even returned to an old hobby, astronomy. He went on a tour of the observatories on Haleakala with an old friend from college who works there. Ever since then he's been reading all kinds of stuff about astrophysics from the library and on the web. He's spending this morning at the guy's house. I tell you, Sam Loftus is a new man."

"I know that must be a huge relief for you."

"Oh, yes. We discussed something yesterday evening that he thinks could help slam the door on his old delusions and you and Keone can help."

Julie felt her defenses coming online. "What did you

discuss?"

"Well, now that we know Sam never had any romantic feelings for you, he suggested I ask you and Keone over for dinner."

He suggested. "Do you really think that's a good idea? We wouldn't want to do anything to delay his recovery."

"No. I talked with Dr. Drayton and he thinks it's a wonderful idea. He's even coming to observe the interaction."

Damn. "When is this get-together?"

"Uh...tonight. I know, short notice, but please say you'll come. It would mean everything to me, and Sam. I think he wants to apologize."

"Let me call Keone and see if it's even possible. What time?"

"Seven. I'll keep my fingers crossed until you call back. Aloha, honey."

Julie knew this was the next logical step in Sam's treatment plan and wanted to help Jan get her husband back. So, why did she feel like this was the worst idea ever? She remembered the way Sam had looked at her in the hospital. She'd seen passion and pain in his eyes that day and it had frightened her.

Chapter Forty-one

Wednesday, June 5, 7:00 PM

Keone checked to make sure that Dr. Drayton had arrived before parking his car. Julie had shared all of the great progress Sam had made with Keone, as Jan had with her, but Keone planned to reserve judgment until he'd seen this new Sam for himself. Julie rapped "shave and a haircut" on the door instead of ringing the bell. After a few moments two short raps from the other side answered, "two bits."

Jan opened the door and said, "Knock, knock."

Julie smiled and said, "Who's here?"

"Sam and Janet."

"Sam and Janet, who?"

"Sam and Janet Evening." Jan sang this to the tune of "Some Enchanted Evening" from *South Pacific*."

Keone realized this must have been an old joke the sisters shared before the crash stole fun from their lives.

"Hi, Keone, thank you for coming. It means a lot to us." Jan was trying hard to keep her eyes dry.

Keone gave her a bear hug. "Thank you for inviting us. I'm looking forward to meeting the new Sam."

"Actually, it's more like meeting the old Sam for the first time in a long while," Sam said as he joined them with a smile and two Longboards in his hand. Sam handed one to Keone as he took his coat and clinked a toast. Sam gave the other to

Julie, who handed him her wrap, a colorful shawl made from multiple silk scarves.

"Here's to really getting to know each other." Keone meant this at multiple levels.

Drayton and Jan led the small talk over cocktails before dinner. Sam nodded in agreement with everything they said about his progress and smiled at all the appropriate times. He seemed extremely comfortable when Jan described his acceptance of his illness and desire to get back to the life he'd led before. Sam gave her a squeeze as she said this. She smiled and returned the squeeze before heading to the kitchen to put the final touches on dinner.

"We've fallen in love again," Sam said. "Jan is the nicest person I've ever known. Her patience has been awe-inspiring, after all the pain I've caused her."

"She loves you," Julie said.

"And I'm so grateful. It's time I apologized to you, Julie. I know how hard it was to see me the way I was in the hospital. I hope you understand that everything I said was the result of my delusion. I'm deeply sorry for the pain I caused and will try my best to make up for it in the future."

"You don't need to do this, Sam. Jan explained everything to us," Julie replied.

"Oh, but I do. This apology is an essential step on my way back to a normal life." Sam looked at Drayton, who smiled and nodded. Even Keone sensed the honesty in Sam's words.

Jan had set the table for dinner as they talked. "No more about the past. Let's have a great time tonight."

The dinner was fabulous and the conversation light and funny. The men retired to the living room for coffee as Julie helped Jan clear up.

"Why don't you tell us about your renewed interest in astronomy, Sam? Janet told me you spend a lot of free time with your old friend at the observatory," Drayton said.

"Well, it's all part of the therapy really. You know, creating new memories to replace the delusions and reinforce the real ones," Sam replied.

"One of the observatories on Haleakala?" Keone asked, honestly interested. "How'd you get access? I've only been up there once when I was kid. The security wasn't so tight then."

"An old college friend of mine, Dr. Bradley Carvell, gave me a tour. He's also spent time bringing me up to date on things. He's a brilliant astrophysicist."

"That stuff's fascinating. I loved that *Cosmos* show that was on with Dr. Tyson. Did you see that, Sergeant?" Drayton asked.

"Call me Keone. I'm off duty. Yes. I saw most of it. Though I can't say I understood it all."

"What's Carvell's specialty?" Drayton asked.

"Mostly energy fluxes in space. A lot of the work going on now is to explain new discoveries in that area and determine how they fit with the theory of conservation of mass and energy. I like it because it's all based on mathematics. You know, I'm basically a numbers guy. Before I focused on business, I read a lot in advanced math. A lot of that stuff is central to astrophysics."

Keone could see why both Jan and Dr. Drayton were pleased with Sam's new interest, but he wondered if there might be another connection. "Those theories can be pretty astonishing. I remember Dr. Tyson talking about something called the multiverse. Do you or Dr. Carvell know anything about that?"

Sam looked directly at Keone for the first time. "No. I mean I don't. We haven't discussed that. Why do you ask?"

He's lying.

"Just curious. It sounded pretty cool when he talked about it, but I got lost after about two sentences." Keone laughed and Drayton and Sam joined in.

Drayton changed the subject. "Detec...Keone. I understand Mr. Walden has been transferred to a holding facility from the hospital."

"Yes. He's awaiting arraignment on multiple state and federal charges. I'm sorry about your friend, Sam."

"He's not my friend. He was once a long time ago, but

what he did to Julie..."

"I know. If it's any comfort, he'll be out of circulation for a long time."

"You know, he tried to involve me in his crooked activities when we first got here. I should have gone to the police then. But we had been so close for so long that I just said I didn't want to hear it."

"Keone, we've discovered that Dave's action may have been the tripwire for all of Sam's delusions. It was his mind's way of trying to save Julie by making her his wife instead of Dave's," Drayton added.

"That actually makes sense in a weird way. But you don't still have feelings for Julie, do you, Sam?"

"I feel she's a great sister-in-law, and I'm glad she's found a nice new...friend in you."

Keone saw a chance to test Sam. "We're more than friends, Sam."

Sam's smile never wavered, "Good for you, both of you."

Drayton smiled more broadly than he had all evening. Clearly, this was what he wanted to hear. It was what Keone wanted to hear, too. But, despite the honesty Sam tried so hard to display, it didn't ring true to his detective's senses.

"Does that mean you understand the children in your memories were delusions, too?"

Both Drayton and Sam tensed.

"Sam has made great progress, but this is a long process. We have to take one step at a time. I wonder when the ladies will join us?" Drayton said, obviously uncomfortable with this topic.

"Evan, tonight is about honesty," Sam said. "On an intellectual level I know that I imagined our children."

Keone detected the second blatant lie of the evening.

"But Cindy and Timmy are still very real in my memories, Keone. I have accepted that my future is with Jan and have truly come to love her. We've discussed my feelings of loss surrounding the children. She's suggested we look into adoption again as we did once before."

Keone saw Sam weaving in truth with the lie.

"I'm tempted to consider this option. But Dr. Drayton has raised some concerns about us doing so before I've effectively dealt with my memories."

"I'm confident we can work through this. I look forward to supporting any efforts Sam and Janet make towards adopting—at the proper time," Drayton added.

Now the ladies did return and the conversation for the remainder of the evening was light and friendly.

As they left, Keone could tell Julie was convinced of Sam's transformation. He wouldn't disturb her with reality quite yet. He wanted to talk to some folks up on Haleakala first.

Chapter Forty-two

Thursday, June 6, 9:00 AM

Sam held a lovely flowered shawl in his hand. He'd retrieved it this morning from between the sofa cushions where he'd stashed it after taking it from around Julie's shoulders. His performance went exactly as planned. Janet and Drayton still believed what they wanted to believe and Julie was convinced as well. That damn cop was still suspicious, but that wouldn't matter after today.

Sam opened his new cell phone and tapped in a number he'd copied from Janet's. "Hello, Julie? This is Sam."

There was a long pause before Julie replied, "Hello, Sam. Thank you for the wonderful evening. I look forward to having you and Jan here sometime." Her voice sounded strained

"We enjoyed it, too. Actually, that's why I'm calling. Are you missing a blue and yellow flowered scarf shawl-ly thingy?"

"Oh, yes. Dumb me. I forgot to collect it when we left." Julies voice was now relaxed.

"No problem. That's what Jan thought." Sam turned his face from the phone. "You were right, sweetie, it's hers. What? Okay I'll ask."

"Is that Jan?"

"Yes, she was yelling at me from the shower. She said I should ask if we could bring it by when I drive her to work. One of our cars is acting up."

"That's really not necessary. I can get it anytime." Sam knew Keone would be at work by now and suspected Julie wasn't anxious to face them on her own.

Again turning from the phone, Sam shouted, "She says we don't need to bother—Oh. Okay."

"She says it's no bother. I'll drive by and she'll run in with it. Do me a favor, Julie. Say yes. You know how she gets."

Another long pause. "Okay. I'll be here for the next couple of hours."

"Thank you, dear sis-in-law. We'll be by in about thirty minutes. Aloha."

"Aloha."

Sam was proud of himself. Proud that he'd convinced Janet to leave early for work. Proud that he'd remembered the nickname he used to call Julie according to his journal. And proud he was able to imitate a two-person conversation, when he was totally alone.

He grabbed a towel, the chloroform he'd lifted from Brad's lab, and a large blanket as he headed for the car.

Thursday, June 6, 5:00 PM

"Dr. Hassellbach, I appreciate you making time to talk with me. I asked for Dr. Carvell at the gate. But, after the guard checked in, he told me I needed to talk with you." Keone didn't try to hide his confusion.

"Please come into my office, Sergeant Boyd. I think I can enlighten you about Brad Carvell. And please call me Martin."

Hassellbach's office was good-sized but modestly decorated. Most of the walls were taken up with white boards filled with indecipherable formulas. They sat at a small, round desk covered with journals, many opened to specific pages. Hassellbach shoved them to the side so he could sit next to Keone with a yellow tablet between them.

Keone began the conversation. "Martin, I'm here because of the interaction between Dr. Carvell and a man named

Samuel Loftus."

"I'm aware of their connection. Brad brought Mr. Loftus up here once for a tour of the facility, shortly before I had to dismiss him."

This surprising news told Keone he was on the right track again. "Did the connection have anything to do with Carvell's dismissal?"

"Not directly—probably not at all." Martin Hassellbach seemed conflicted. "Sergeant, most of our work here is classified. But I think it's important that I explain why we had to let Brad go. And why it might be a good idea to keep Mr. Loftus away from him."

This wasn't enfolding the way Keone expected, but he was willing to roll with it. "Mr. Loftus is currently being treated for delusions associated with injuries he sustained in a car crash. Given his vulnerable state, anything you could tell me about Carvell would be helpful. And please call me Keone."

"Keone, I don't know how much you know about astrophysics, but there are thousands of theories involved in our research. A theory is validated by demonstrating that it is predictive of actual events. Such a theory remains useful until someone proves experimentally that it is flawed. Dr. Carvell was very interested in one particular theory and carried out experiments to see if he could measure evidence to support this theory."

"You mean like someone calculating that a comet will reappear at a certain time based on the physics then testing to see if it shows up when they predicted it would?"

"Yes. You used a very appropriate scientific term, testing. A scientist must be open to his hypothesis being either right or wrong. This is essential for effective scientific investigation. Some of the greatest scientific discoveries were the result of proving a promising theory wrong. Dr. Carvell carried out wonderful work at a number of institutions before he arrived here. That work involved testing hypotheses with strenuous data analysis and independent validation to assure the absence of bias. He disproved almost as many hypotheses as he validated. That's why I hired him."

"But something changed?"

"Yes. He had some evidence from his earlier work that the Hawaiian Archipelago was especially prolific in a certain type of energy flux and wanted to test that hypothesis with measurements closer to the site of these fluxes."

"And his earlier data was scientifically valid?"

"Yes. It had been peer-reviewed and accepted for publication in major journals."

"Doesn't sound like a problem."

"It wasn't—at first. But after he'd been here a few weeks, he started seeing fluxes everywhere. When I reviewed his data, I found it to be neither comprehensive nor reproducible. He was seeing connections that weren't there."

"What did you do?"

"At first, I mentored him and had him measure a larger spectrum of wavelengths, which he did. But he only looked for variations in those wavelengths most susceptible to false positive readings. In short, he was obsessed and no longer functioning as a dispassionate observer."

"I know things are classified, but I'm hoping you can answer one question for me."

"I'll try."

"Did Carvell's research have anything to do with transposition of objects between parallel universes?"

Hassellbach was clearly surprised. "How do you know about such things?"

"From two sources, the *Cosmos* program with Dr. Tyson and a conversation last night with Sam Loftus."

"I see. I can tell you that while the study of energy fluxes is of interest to this laboratory, we are not exploring parallel universes. However, speculation in this area could be extremely detrimental to someone suffering from delusions."

"Sam Loftus believes left is right and right is left and that his wife is his sister-in-law and vice versa. If Carvell provided him a specious alternative explanation for his situation, he could have set his therapy back months."

"I can neither confirm nor deny that this was the theory that Carvell was trying to prove." Hassellbach smiled. "But I can suggest you speak directly with him as soon as possible."

Keone got the message. "And where can I find him?"

Hassellbach wrote on the yellow pad and tore off a sheet. "He and his wife Diane live between here and Kula at this address."

"Thank you, Martin. I may need to call you if my suspicions are confirmed. I believe Sam's psychiatrist may need to get some clarification from you, as well. But I will never ask you to violate your secrecy agreement with the observatory or its sponsors."

"That's acceptable." He took the sheet back from Keone and added his cell phone number. "Call me anytime."

As a driver returned Keone to the second gate and his car, he formulated his interrogation strategy for Brad Carvell. He hoped the wife would be the one to answer the door. He had a few questions for her that would be best asked in the absence of her husband.

He also decided to call Julie's cell phone to give her a heads up. But after four rings he heard, "This is Julie Madison, please leave a message at the tone."

He thought about what message he could leave. "Stay away from Sam." Seemed a bit too scary. All he had was a theory so far. He decided just to say, "Call me as soon as you get this."

Unfortunately, Julie couldn't receive his message.

Chapter Forty-three

Thursday, June 6, 6:00 PM

Julie woke with a headache so severe she was afraid to open her eyes. She struggled to retrieve her most recent memories.

I answered the door and someone pushed a smelly cloth over my face. Someone knocked me out. Who would...? Sam.

Slowly opening her eyes, she noticed the room was in shadows. She was on her back on a lumpy bed, a sheet above and beneath her as well as a scratchy blanket. The linen smelled fresh but there was a musty odor beneath, probably from the mattress. She was pleased to find she was fully clothed before she reached out to bang her hand on a coarse surface. She ran her fingers along the wall and jerked her hand back after she picked up a couple of splinters.

The wall is made of rough wooden slats. I'm in a cabin.

She remembered Jan talking about a cabin that Sam's grandfather built past Hana and left to Sam after he died. Everyone tended to forget that Sam's mother was born in Hawai'i. But Jan told Julie that Sam was always fascinated as a child with his mother's stories about growing up here.

Julie tried to rise from the bed but was defeated by a pounding in her head and an overwhelming sense of nausea.

"You need to take it easy, sweetheart. Chloroform is a terrible anesthetic. Its only advantage is that it's easy to get."

Sam's voice.

She'd guessed right. But why was he doing this? He said he and Jan had fallen back in love. He said he was trying to erase the other memories. "Why, Sam?"

"Because I can never return home and I miss my family." Sam's voice was calm, almost tender.

"Sam, I am not your wife."

"No. You're not. Not in this universe. I accept that. Janet and I have grown very close."

Janet not Jan.

"I like having her as my wife. I had almost accepted Dr. Drayton's explanation of my condition, but then I learned what really happened to me. Let me share it with you so you'll understand what I'm trying to do and why."

Julie realized that Sam's insanity had progressed a long way from what he displayed in the hospital. He was probably capable of anything. Her best chance to get out of here alive was to agree to listen. "Okay, Sam. What really happened?"

"I was driving home from work with my friend Lee Marder. Right after we passed the marina entrance at Ma'alaea I passed through a transparent gateway between two universes and everything changed for me...."

Thursday, June 6, 6:15 PM

The Carvell home was as close as possible to the observatory without being in Haleakala National Park. Their view was breathtaking. Keone parked on the street in front of the house and walked up a gravel path to the front door. He was pleased when Diane Carvell, a small slim brunette with Asian features, answered the door.

"Aloha. How can I help you, Officer?"

Most of the time Keone preferred plain clothes, but he'd worn his uniform to help him gain access at the observatory. There'd been no time to change. "Aloha. I'm Keone Boyd with the Maui PD. I wondered if I might ask you a few questions about a man who may have visited your home."

"Should I get my husband? He is in his laboratory."

"I'd like to talk with both of you, but it's best to do so separately, okay?" Keone didn't want to frighten the woman. She already seemed to be under some emotional strain.

"Where are my manners? Please, come in. Would you like something to drink? I have iced tea, POG, and water."

"POG would be fine." As she went to the kitchen to pour a glass of the Passion Fruit, Orange, and Guava concoction popular with tourists and even some locals, Keone did a brief visual inspection of the living room. The decor was Chinese in style and very neat. There was a lovely contrast between different woods that gave the furniture a calming effect.

Mrs. Carvell placed two glasses on absorbent coasters bearing a bright floral pattern.

"Thank you." Keone took a large drink and made a point of sighing with pleasure, as though he'd just crossed the desert. "This is wonderful. Tell me, has your husband had a visitor recently named Sam Loftus?"

"Oh, yes. Sam was an old college friend of Brad's who liked math and astronomy. Brad has been bringing him up to date on astrophysics."

"Are you a scientist, too?"

"No. We met when Brad was on a post-doctoral fellowship in Shanghai. He worked with my father. My passion is art."

"Dr. Hassellbach said your name is Diane. I'm guessing Diane is not the name you were born with."

"You are right. My name in China is *Daiyu*. It means black jade. My father called me his precious gem. He always supported me in my dream of becoming an artist."

"You must enjoy Maui. So many fine artists have made the island their home."

"Oh, yes. My mentor is one of them. She displays my work in her Makawao gallery beside her own lovely paintings. I am very happy here."

"Is your husband happy, too?"

"He was—at first." An echo of what Hassellbach had told him. "Now he spends most of his time at work either here or at the observatory. Mostly here for the past month."

"Did he tell you he was dismissed from the observatory?"

Tears filled her eyes. "No. But I guessed as much. Do you know why he was dismissed?"

"I've spoken with Dr. Hassellbach. He explained about your husband's...extreme devotion to a particular theory."

"Contact between parallel worlds. He believes he has measured the residue of these events here in the Hawaiian Islands. He shouts about how his colleagues are all ignorant fools—including my father. They no longer speak to one another. I am afraid Brad might be ill." Now the tears and sobs broke through.

Keone felt compassion for this nice, quiet woman. He handed her a handkerchief and gave her a moment to collect herself. "I'd like to talk with your husband now."

"Let me show you to the laboratory."

A conventional basement door bearing no locks led to the laboratory. Keone thought of the contrast between this and Dave Walden's hidden lab.

At the bottom of the stairs, Diane called out, "Brad. You have a visitor."

There was no response. Keone moved past Mrs. Carvell and into the impressive laboratory. The walls were filled with electronic equipment and a huge computer display table filled the center of the room. Keone could see a number of locations along the Hawaiian Archipelago marked with dry erase markings. The largest of these was in Ma'alaea, near the point where he first bumped into Sam Loftus, literally. "Could your husband be upstairs, Mrs. Carvell?"

"I do not think so, but I will look."

Keone didn't think so either. He looked around the lab and found a phone with an answering machine. He noticed it had a different number from the phone in the living room, as Mrs. Carvell returned.

"He is not upstairs, and his car is gone. But I did not hear him leave."

Keone had noticed the sharp incline from the street to the

garage.

He probably coasted to the road before starting the engine.

"When did you last see him?"

"We ate lunch together, upstairs, about one."

That was four hours ago.

"Mrs. Carvell, is this telephone on a separate line from your home phone?"

"Yes. He uses it for contacting the observatory and other scientists."

"There's one message on the answering machine. It came in at quarter after one, probably when your husband was upstairs. I would like you to listen to the message. It could help me locate your husband so I can talk with him. Would you do that for me?"

"He would not want me to. He is very private."

"I can get a warrant, but that will take time. I know you are worried for your husband. So am I. Time lost now might be critical to helping him."

She still hesitated.

"I think the call might be from Mr. Loftus. I also think he may be in serious trouble."

She pushed Play on the answering machine. They heard Sam Loftus's voice, "Hello, Brad, I have her at the cabin. I want you to explain to her about how I crossed over into this world. I'll give you directions, but leave as soon as you get this. That curious detective she's living with will probably discover she's gone pretty soon. Anyway, you take the Hana Road through Hana and past the 'Ohe'o Gulch, then...."

Keone was scribbling the directions down as fast as he could. It was obvious the "she" Sam mentioned was Julie. That's why she hadn't returned his call.

Knowing Julie was in the wilderness past Hana with one insane man and another on the way was beyond a nightmare.

Chapter Forty-four

Thursday, June 6, 7:30 PM

Julie listened to Sam's wild tale of living in a world that was a mirror image of hers. He told her of his near acceptance of his delusions after reading his journals. He discussed the bond that had developed between him and Janet. He went into great detail about Dr. Carvell's discoveries and how they helped him understand the reality of his situation and the irreversibility of his transposition into her world. She felt sorry for him. He had come so close, only to have Carvell impose his own delusions on Sam.

What disturbed her the most was the way Sam changed when he talked about the impossibility of getting back to his— their—children, Cindy and Timmy. He nearly came apart when he described the hopelessness he felt. Then he described the plan he had to solve his problem.

"Janet and I have discussed adoption. She's fine with the idea."

"I agree, Sam. That sounds like the perfect solution."

"Not quite, but it could be. You see, my children represent aspects of my DNA and their mother's. I can't return to their mother, but you represent the next best thing."

"Sam. I don't—"

"You must let me finish." He raised his voice for the first time and Julie simply nodded and tried to maintain her composure.

"I don't expect you to love me. I don't expect you to leave Keone. I just want you to do me a favor. You could even close your eyes and imagine you're with Keone. Janet and I would raise them as our own. I'm sure this can work for everyone."

So that's it. He wants us to recreate his non-existent children. What? Right here on this moldy, lumpy mattress?

Sam continued talking, but it was almost as though he was talking to himself. "I'm not asking for a deep emotional commitment, just a few minutes of your time."

"Uh, Sam, I believe the process of bearing children takes a bit longer than that. You know, like nine months of my life—twice."

"Of course, you're right. It is a lot to ask of you, Julie. But remember, you'd be doing it for Janet, too."

"You honestly believe Jan would want you to do this?"

"Oh, no. She must never know. I'll work everything out through my lawyer so she will never be able to find out who the mother is. I'll pay for you and Keone to travel around the world during your pregnancies. I'll even take a large insurance policy out on you and make sure you have the finest doctors."

Julie knew Sam was beyond reasoning with, but had to think of some way to put off the inevitable until Keone could discover she was missing and rescue her.

"My memories of Cindy and Timmy are as real as you and I sitting in this cabin right now." Sam looked off into space as he continued. "Cindy, the older one, bosses me around terribly. She's the one who broke me of my borderline OCD by showing me how silly I was behaving. She taught me to enjoy fantasy and playing games. Timmy is the comedian of the household. He can make expressions with that rubber face of his that make you laugh until your sides hurt. They both have lovely singing voices. I can remember them singing *There's a Hole in the Bottom of the Sea*, all the verses.

There's a hole in the bottom of the sea,
there's a hole in...."

Sam went into a fugue state as he softly sang the words of the song. It was over five minutes before he spoke again. He shook his head, as if to clear his thoughts. "Well, that's my story, Julie. Do you understand now why I reject the delusion theory? I'm not angry with Dr. Drayton, you know. The real explanation was just beyond his understanding. I hope it's not beyond yours."

Julie knew that she needed to keep Sam talking. "It is a lot to take in all at once, Sam. I'm sure Dr.—"

"Carvell?"

"Yes, Dr. Carvell. I'm sure he explained it very clearly to you, but it's a little harder to accept second-hand."

"I thought you might feel that way. That's why I invited Dr. Carvell to meet us here and explain it to you directly. He should be here in another hour or so."

"That was very thoughtful of you. Maybe we could have a cup of coffee or tea and a bite to eat, while we wait."

"Certainly. You like Earl Grey with milk and one level spoonful of sugar, right?"

"That must be the same in both worlds." Julie smiled, though inside she was a jumble of fears and hopes. The clock displayed 7:30 PM. Even if Keone got home at his usual time, found her missing, and somehow discovered where Sam had taken her, he would still be hours from Hana. Sam seemed calmer now. But she knew she had to keep his mind occupied until Carvell came or he might decide to get busy re-creating their imaginary children.

"Sam, you told us last night what you discovered about the Dave in this world from reading your journals. Was that true?"

"Yes. But there were a lot of gaps between our disagreement on the kayaking trip and when I discovered he was hurting you." Sam brought the tea and some sandwiches on a wooden tray.

"Would you like me to fill in the gaps for you? I can even fill in the gap when we were on Maui and you and Jan were still in Indy."

"I'd be very grateful." Sam sipped his tea and gave Julie his full attention.

"As you know, Dave and I were married in Indianapolis and left immediately after the reception for our honeymoon on Maui...."

Thursday, June 6, 8:00 PM

Keone had driven as fast as he could across the island and on the initial leg of the Hana Highway, but even with lights and siren, he couldn't go much over forty on the narrow winding roads with one-lane bridges that comprised the largest part of the route to Hana.

While he waited for a large truck to finish making its way across one of the one lane bridges, Keone realized how stupid he was being. He could call ahead to the Hana Division police station and have them detail the actual route to the Loftus cabin, before he arrived in Hana.

I've got to start acting like a police sergeant and not a panicked lover.

He didn't use the radio in his squad car to contact Hana but called Sergeant Angela Beyers' cell phone number. He'd loved working with her in the Hana district, during his rotation. She was sharp as a tack and knew Hana like the back of her hand.

"Hey, Keone. What do you need on this side of the island?"

"This may sound funny, but I need some directions and maybe your best ATV."

"It's eight o'clock at night. Are you lolo?"

"No. I'm on a case."

"What kind of case?"

"An abduction and probable kidnapping."

"Why haven't I heard about this? I've been monitoring the police band, like I always do in the evening."

"Because I haven't told anybody. Look, this case is so damn complicated with all kinds of twists and turns, like this damn road I'm driving on."

"You're on your way over here? At this time of night? You

really are crazy. Okay, this has got to be good. Tell me the whole story and I'll give you what you need. But we'll have to report what's going on when you reach the station over here. Deal?"

"Deal."

Chapter Forty-five

Thursday, June 6, 9:00 PM

"So you see, Mrs. Walden, Sam had no delusions. He arrived here suddenly from a parallel universe, where things were as he remembered them. The power flux that I showed you matched precisely the time and location of that displacement. Unfortunately, we're not able, with available technology, to return Sam to his point of origin. It's only natural for Sam, under the circumstances, to seek an alternative method to rejoin his children."

Clearly Carvell was as loopy as Sam. But she knew Sam wouldn't try anything in front of him. "Dr. Carvell, thank you so much for clarifying what Sam tried to explain to me earlier. I have a few questions, if you don't mind."

"Not at all. Ask anything."

"As a scientist, I'm sure you studied fields other than astronomy and physics."

"Yes. I took courses in biology and chemistry, as well as in math, physics, the history of science, English composition, and philosophy. I'm fluent in French, Spanish, German, Italian, and Russian and can read ancient Latin and Greek."

"During your courses in biology, did you study genetics?"

"Yes. I took classical and molecular genetics courses."

"If Sam and I produced an offspring now, in this universe, what's the probability that such a child would be identical or even resemble the child Sam sired with the other Julie in the other universe?"

"The odds of creating an identical child would be many millions to one. However, any child you produced together would very likely have some similarity to a potential sibling in the other universe. Just as a second child you conceived would have some similarities to the first."

"Can you guarantee we would produce a boy and a girl?"

"Of course not. But I can guarantee each would be either a boy or a girl."

Thank you, Doctor Obvious.

"I understand you're working on technology that might enable you and Sam to predict the time and place of another *bump* between two universes."

"That's right. But the development of the technology could be a decade or more away and then we'd still have to predict a rare event."

"I understand the problems. But, even if you had the technology and you predicted an event accurately, can you be sure Sam would return to his starting point? Couldn't he just be transported to another parallel universe?"

"Sam never asked me that question."

Sam broke into the conversation. "And I don't plan to now. Thank you, Brad. You've been of great help. I'll walk you to your car."

Sam hustled Carvell out the door before Julie could protest. But she knew she'd made her point.

Carvell is obsessed with his interpretation of coincidental events and Sam's riding Brad's unicorn to la la land.

At least it was nine o'clock and there was a chance Keone could be here in a few hours.

Do I have a few hours? Does Keone have any idea where I am?
Don't go there. Not now. Hang on. Keone will come.
I have to be ready when he does.

She had to be careful. She must make Sam see the flaws in his plan without pushing too hard. His hold on reality was becoming more fragile by the minute.

"I'm sure now you understand exactly what happened to me." Sam returned and sat beside Julie on the musty bed.

This was way too creepy for Julie, but she retained her composure. "Dear, dear, Sam. I can imagine what you've been going through. I want to talk openly with you about everything, but I'm afraid I need to use the restroom first. Do you have some tissue?" Knowing Sam's interest in hygiene and neatness, Julie knew this would give her some breathing space.

"Certainly. It's in the outhouse. I'll walk you out there. I need to stretch my legs, too."

Sam still tried to act as though they were just there to discuss important matters. He avoided words such as kidnap and prisoner, but Julie knew exactly what was going on. Once in the outhouse, she refused to sit on the disgusting splintered plank that bore an ancient circular hole. Luckily, decades of disuse had made the stench inside endurable for a short period She would use that time to develop a plan. If it failed she'd have no choice but to run.

Thursday, June 6, 10:45 PM

Even using his siren all the way to Hana, Keone took hours to reach the small coastal town. He stopped at the Hana Division Police Station to find Sergeant Angela Beyers standing beside an imposing four-wheel ATV. He was pleased to see the vehicle had an ample backseat.

"Howzit, Keone? You blast that damn siren all the way?"

"Pretty much."

"Well, I've got some good news for you and some more good news for you."

"Shoot."

"Your man Carvell stopped at the gas station across from the Hasegawa General Store. He asked Clyde Kahala for directions and topped up his tank."

'What time?"

"Eight-fifteen."

Keone looked like he'd swallowed sour milk. Carvell had two and a half hours' head start.

"Cheer up, Big Guy. I got you covered. There's only one way in or out of that cabin. I've got one of my boys up at the turn-off. Nobody can escape. And you've got the best guide and the best possible ride to get you there." Angela opened the passenger door to the monster vehicle and motioned to Keone to hop in.

"I love you, Princess. You da one."

"Then Queen might be more appropriate."

"Your Majesty," Keone said as Angela punched the gas and tore out of the station parking lot. "Don't you have a report to make?"

"I will. When we get back."

Fortunately, the turn onto the dirt road wasn't too far from the end of the state road. Angela waved at her colleague as they turned in. Keone would have wasted precious time trying to find it without Angela, given the number of similar dirt roads that came off of the main highway in this area. He also would have played hell making any kind of time in his clunky police cruiser. During the trip down the narrow, dark path, Keone marveled at Angela's control. He also decided it was time to tell her more about the case.

"Angela, there's a personal aspect to this case."

"I wondered when you were going to level with me."

"The girl being held in the cabin, Julie...I'm in love with her."

"And the guy holding her is married to her sister?"

"That's right."

"I'm guessing you want to go into that cabin alone so your future brother-in-law doesn't accidentally get kind of shot up. Am I right?"

"Yeah. But I won't hesitate to take him down if I have to."

"I know you won't, Keone. But I'm gonna have your back."

"I know you will. Just kinda from out of sight, okay?"

"If I can." Angela concentrated on the road ahead, which

was filled with holes the size of watermelons. Angela knew her way and avoided numerous trip-ending craters.

Keone was starting to wonder if Carvell had made it, when Angela suddenly shut off all the lights and the engine. In the distance he saw lights approaching. As they drew closer, he saw Brad Carvell behind the wheel of a Range Rover.

Angela flipped on all of the spotlights causing the blinded Carvell to hit the brakes.

Keone exited the ATV with a shotgun locked and loaded in his hands. "Dr. Carvell, this is Sergeant Boyd of the Maui Police Department. You need to turn off your vehicle, exit with your hands over your head, and immediately kneel down on the ground in front of your headlights, where I can see you. If you do anything other than what I just told you. I will shoot you with a very large-bore shotgun. You will not survive."

"Don't shoot. Please don't shoot. I was just visiting a friend," Carvell shouted as he turned off the engine and exited the vehicle, arms flung high in the air. When he knelt in front of the headlights, Keone could see the urine marks from his groin down the legs of his jeans.

Angela cuffed the good doctor, read him his rights, and put him in the back seat, then backed Carvell's vehicle off the road and into dense foliage.

"Hey, Carvell," Keone yelled to the back seat, "did you see any weapons in Sam's cabin?"

Carvell was still shaking from their encounter but managed to mumble a few words, "A rifle, over the fireplace."

"How'd he get the girl here?"

"Chloroform on a hand towel. But Julie was completely attentive when I spoke with her."

Good for her. Julie was playing this just right. He prayed he could reach her, surprise Sam, and take him into custody, without anyone getting hurt. But he wouldn't risk Julie's safety. If he had a clean shot at Sam he'd take it. He didn't care how crazy the bastard was.

Chapter Forty-six

Thursday, June 6, 11:30 PM

Sam had become increasingly restless since they returned from the outhouse. Julie tried to have a normal conversation with him, but he kept turning the discussion to his imaginary kids. Julie decided to confront Sam with facts. She was tired of this rodeo and wanted to leave.

"Sam, I want to tell you exactly what I am thinking right now, okay? Then you can decide what you want to do next."

"All right, but you know what we need to do. It won't take long. I can use more chloroform if that would help."

"No. That won't be necessary. I am curious about one thing you haven't talked about, Dave. My husband was once your friend in this universe. Did his life turn out as badly in yours?" She felt this question would accomplish two things: keep Sam talking and lull him into a false sense of control.

"Dave is a wonderful person in my universe."

"Did he use drugs?"

"He experimented with pot at IU, but most people did. He only tried uppers once, in Grad School, not long before we met you and Janet. After he met Janet, he didn't dare. They moved to Maui before us, because you had to finish Medical School. It was five years before we moved here, but Dave and I picked up right where we'd left off. We started kayaking and he taught all of us how to play golf.

"Dave worked hard at his practice and was well respected. His focus was property law and estate planning. He made friends with a lot of the well-to-do but did a lot of pro bono work, too. When Janet's income made work unnecessary, he handed the high-income clients to his many protégés but continued to do pro bono work. He started a scholarship program to help young Maui College students afford law school on O'ahu. He even taught courses to prepare them and established the first four-year Political Science program at UH MC."

"How about Jan and me?"

"You were even closer than you are here. We did everything together. We took cruises to the Caribbean and the Greek Isles, before the kids got old enough to want to come along."

Julie sensed danger and steered the conversation away from the kids. "You said I was a doctor in your universe?"

"You were the best—are the best. All the parents want you as their pediatrician. You care so much for the whole family. Last month they made you the Head of Pediatrics for the hospital and you still maintained a full practice. You refused an appointment at the medical school on O'ahu because you wouldn't be separated from your patients or our kids."

"Sam, the Dave you just described is nothing like the Dave I know. And your Julie is nothing like me. You know I no longer love Dave, but I do love someone."

Sam looked confused.

"Listen to me, Sam. I'm not the Julie of your universe. I love Keone Boyd. I'll never love you. And I'll die before I let you touch me."

Sam reacted as though she'd punched him in the gut. Doubled over and staring at the floor, he appeared catatonic.

After a couple minutes, Julie rose and padded to the door. She slipped the latch and eased the door partway open without making a sound. Sam hadn't moved. She realized this was her one and only chance and took it.

Silently closing the door, she ran barefoot toward the

shelter of the dense jungle foliage. The welcome darkness was a few steps away when her head was jerked violently backward. She landed hard on the gravel.

Julie's butt struck the rocky surface shortly before her shoulders. Pain messages assaulted her brain. She'd instinctively tucked her head into her chest, which kept her from being knocked unconscious. Sharp rocks pierced the backs of her legs and buttocks. Then a huge weight dropped onto her hips and chest. It was Sam. He must have come to his senses, caught up with her, and grabbed her by her hair just before she reached the jungle.

"If you can't love me, you can at least give me back my children. I'll be gentle if you let me. Don't fight me or I'll have to hurt you."

Julie couldn't believe the calm, quiet man who spent so much time and effort trying to convince her of his sanity was about to rape her. She looked into Sam's eyes and saw a rage that threatened to petrify her.

Somehow she kept her voice calm and asked, "Are you going to rape me now, Sam?"

Sam's face transformed from the bestial sneer of a wild man to a look of utter surprise and confusion. He looked like he'd suddenly realized he was stark naked while being presented to the Queen of England. While Sam froze and stared into space, Julie didn't wait to think things over. She summoned all her strength and jammed her knee into Sam's groin. "Get off me, you crazy son of a bitch!"

With Sam writhing on the ground, Julie sat up to find Keone's gun pointed at Sam's back. "Your kick saved this bastard's life."

Keone kept his gun pointed at Sam.

From the other side of the clearing, a policewoman took handcuffs from her belt and walked over to kneel beside Sam. "Samuel Loftus, you are under arrest for the kidnapping, assault, and attempted rape of Mrs. Julie Walden. You have the right to remain silent. If you give up the right to remain silent, anything you say can and will be used against you in a court of law. You have the right to have an attorney present for any questioning. If you desire and cannot afford an attorney...."

Julie struggled to her feet and started to follow Keone.

"Julie, I want you to sit here and wait for me. I'll be right back. I promise." His voice was as gentle as it was caring.

Julie painfully lowered herself to the ground, clutched her knees in her arms, and waited patiently for the man she loved.

Keone was back in moments. He lifted her from the ground and cradled her against his chest. When they reached the ATV he set Julie in the middle of the front seat and climbed in beside her.

"Julie, the wonderful woman guiding Sam over here is Sergeant Angela Beyers. Without her I would never have made it in time."

Angela gave her a nod as she placed Sam in the back seat next to Brad Carvell. She climbed in front beside Julie. Angela leaned over, hugged Julie, stroked her bruised head, and gently placed it against Keone's chest. She straightened back up behind the wheel, started the ATV's engine, activated the spotlights, and took them back up the gravel road.

Feeling safe in Keone's arms an exhausted Julie let her eyes close.

When they reached the highway, Julie's eyes flickered open. "Where's Keone?"

"He's right behind us driving Carvell's Range Rover. He'll follow us to the station. I'm Angela, by the way."

"Keone told me. Thank you for saving me."

"Looked to me like you saved yourself. You were truly amazing. Keone knew you could hold out as long as you did, but I didn't think it was possible."

"How did you find me?"

"At the observatory, Dr. Hassellbach told Keone about Carvell's dismissal. Keone went on to Carvell's house to interview the mad scientist and his wife, but Carvell had already left to come here."

She heard Carvell start to chuckle in the back seat then abruptly stop

"Luckily, he neglected to delete Sam's voicemail that explained what he'd done and where to find you. Keone broke the land speed record getting here. That boy loves you, you know."

"I know. That's what kept me going. I really don't know if, at the end, Sam would have raped me, but I couldn't take the chance. Did I do the right thing?"

"Hell, yes. Keone wasn't kidding back there. If you hadn't kicked Sam off, he would have shot him in the brain. And if he hadn't, I would have."

Julie heard the sound of vomiting from the back seat and smelled the rank result.

Carvell rasped, "I'm sorry about that."

Angela glanced in the back seat and then at Julie. "Nothing I love more at the end of a long grueling night than cleaning some lolo haole's puke."

Part VIII: Commitments

*"If you set to work to believe everything, you will tire out
the believing-muscles of your mind, and then you'll be so weak
you won't be able to believe the simplest true things."*

Lewis Carroll, author

Chapter Forty-seven

Friday, June 7, 7:00 AM

Sam Loftus and Brad Carvell sat uncomfortably on metal chairs bolted to the floor. The table in front of them was the only other furniture in an interrogation room at police headquarters in Wailuku. Keone and Julie gazed through a one-way mirror at the two troubled men.

They waited for Dr. Evan Drayton and Dr. Martin Hassellbach. On the way back from Hana in his patrol car, Keone called both gentlemen at their homes and asked them to meet him at the station at 7:00 AM. Glancing at Julie, Keone marveled at her strength. During the past twenty-four hours she'd been chloroformed, kidnapped, assaulted, and spent hours enduring indoctrination in a wild theory by two mad men, before one of them tried to rape her. Despite all this, she looked so beautiful he could hardly contain his desire to take her in his arms and kiss her. She looked over at him and seemed to sense his desires.

"Soon," she said.

Keone wondered what she meant. *Soon, this would be over? Soon, they could go home and sleep? Or, soon, they could...?*

Then she winked and he knew.

Drayton arrived first and was ushered into the viewing room with them.

"Morning, Sergeant Boyd, Mrs. Walden. I can't tell you how

terrible I feel that I misjudged Sam's condition so completely. Julie, I'm so sorry this happened to you."

"Evan, none of this is your fault. Sam and I talked a lot in that cabin. He had accepted his delusions and wanted to create a new life for himself with Jan. But the dreams of his children continued to haunt him. "

Drayton looked confused. "I knew all of that, but I thought I could help him through it."

"You might have succeeded if it hadn't been for Carvell," Keone said.

Drayton looked through the glass at the scientist who had derailed his carefully constructed treatment plan. "How?"

Keone stepped in. "I want you to hear it directly from him. That's why I asked Dr. Hassellbach to join us."

Hassellbach had just entered the room. "I'm Marty Hassellbach, and you're Sam's psychiatrist?"

"Evan Drayton. Pleased to meet you. Are you an astrophysicist like Dr. Carvell?"

"My expertise is in the area of celestial mechanics with emphasis on singularities—black holes. I oversee the operations of the observatories on Haleakala. Dr. Carvell reported to me before he was dismissed."

Again, Keone took control of the conversation. "Gentlemen, I asked you here to meet with Sam and Brad and to hear them describe, in their own words, what they believe is happening to Sam. I want you to listen and ask clarifying questions, but not contradict or challenge what they have to say. After you're done, we will excuse them and Julie and I will tell you what we've observed.

"When that's over, I have a few questions for both of you and I'm sure you will have questions for each other. By the end of our discussions today I would like a recommendation from both of you as to the appropriate disposition for both cases. In Dr. Carvell's case, I'm uncertain as to whether any laws were broken, although his home laboratory could violate some safety and licensing regulations. Sam's situation is different. He definitely committed an act of kidnapping, at least two acts of assault and battery, and attempted rape."

Keone led the two doctors from the viewing area and into the interrogation room. An officer followed with two folding-chairs.

"Mr. Loftus and Dr. Carvell, I would like you to honestly tell these two gentlemen everything you told Julie and me about your understanding of the events that have taken place from the moments before the collision on March fifteenth to the present. Your openness and honesty in this session may well determine what actions this department takes in your individual cases.

"You both know Dr. Hassellbach, I believe."

Sam and Brad nodded.

"But I believe, Dr. Carvell, this is your first encounter with Dr. Evan Drayton." The men shook hands. "Dr. Drayton is the doctor who has been in charge of Mr. Loftus's treatment regime since shortly after the collision. Please be seated, everyone. I am going to leave the room. Standard procedure requires that I keep the door locked. When you've finished, either Dr. Hassellbach or Doctor Drayton can knock on the door and I'll rejoin you. Is everything I said clear to everyone?"

Four nods signaled it was time for Keone to leave the room.

Keone brought two chairs into the viewing room for him and Julie. The discussion went on for two hours, with Hassellbach interrupting only occasionally with non-threatening questions. Sam and Carvell were very forthcoming about their opinions and actions. They seemed totally comfortable with their justification for behaving as they did. The only exception was when Sam described his attempt to prevent Julie from escaping.

"I shouldn't have pulled on her hair. But it was the only way I could see to keep her from disappearing into the jungle. I was shocked when she hit the ground. I'm relieved it ended there."

"What happened next?" Drayton asked.

Sam's eyes stared into space. "That's the last thing I

remember until we arrived here at the police station."

Hassellbach looked at Carvell.

"I was in the back of the police car at this point. I didn't see Sam until they put him in beside me. He appeared out of touch with his environment at that point."

Hassellbach and Drayton exchanged glances before Drayton walked to the door and knocked. Seeing Drayton approach the door, Keone hurried to be on the other side by the time he heard the knock. He waved two officers into the room with him.

"These officers will take Mr. Loftus and Dr. Carvell to a holding area so we can discuss what you've heard." Once Sam and Brad were gone, Keone beckoned at the mirror and Julie soon joined them.

"Before either of you say anything, Julie and I need to provide our testimony of the same period. Some of this will be redundant for each of you, but we're recording this entire session and we need all of the testimony."

Drayton and Hassellbach nodded.

Keone began the retelling of every interaction and investigation related to Sam Loftus. Julie joined in with her own impressions of various interactions at the appropriate times. Keone only touched on Dave Walden's actions as it directly related either to Julie or Sam. When they were finished another hour had passed.

Drayton had the first question, "Could someone explain to me whether these parallel universe speculations have any basis in established scientific fact?"

Hassellbach explained the theoretical basis of Carvell's obsession to Drayton in much the same way he had to Keone at the observatory. Keone noticed Julie paying very close attention as well.

"What about the energy fluxes?" Julie asked.

"The wavelengths Brad used to support his hypotheses were in a region with extensive noise. None of the events he identified would have survived peer review," Hassellbach said.

"Do you think he was seeing what he wished to see?"

Drayton asked.

"Almost certainly," Hassellbach replied.

"Other questions?" Keone asked.

Drayton and Hassellbach exchanged glances, before Drayton spoke. "No more questions. But I have to compliment you, Mrs. Walden and Sergeant Boyd, on how you handled every aspect of this dangerous situation. Sam Loftus had what we call a psychotic break. We could have lost him for good if you two had performed any differently."

"I can confirm that Dr. Carvell's home lab was licensed and violated no safety standards. The observatory staff regularly inspected it. Most of the equipment was analytical in nature and represented no inherent danger," Hassellbach added.

"If I may, Marty, I'd like to give the sergeant my psychiatric evaluation of your colleague."

"Of course, Evan. We both know he needs help."

"Dr. Carvell is displaying a pronounced obsessive behavior. When he re-established his acquaintance with Sam, significant damage to both subjects occurred. They reinforced each other's delusions. This is what led to the extreme actions of the past twenty-four hours. Both men are mentally ill and require treatment. Having worked with the police, I know what's required to establish that an individual needs to be held for a period of time in the Molokini ward of Maui Memorial. Both men meet these requirements. I believe this is the best course of action for the present. The decision is yours of course, Sergeant Boyd."

"What prognosis would you suggest at this point for each man? I won't hold you to it, I'm just interested," Keone said.

"Carvell's prognosis is very good, I should think. This is the first evidence of a problem and it's exceptionally treatable. I would expect him to be completely functional in a month or two with outpatient sessions to follow. But Sam, dear Sam, has a long difficult road back just to reach where he was when Carvell intervened. I can give you a better idea in a month or so," Drayton said.

"Any comments, Dr. Hassellbach?"

"I defer to Evan's expertise. I'm encouraged about Brad's chances for recovery and am happy to help in any way."

"All right. Here's what we're going to do. Since no charges have been filed against Carvell, I'm going to get his wife down here to talk with Dr. Drayton. I'm sure she'll co-sign the commitment papers with you, Dr. Hassellbach. As for Sam, I've arranged a meeting for Dr. Drayton and me with Judge Fernandez at 1:00 PM. It's twelve-thirty now.

"Dr. Hassellbach, if you wouldn't mind dropping Julie by our condo, Dr. Drayton and I should have just enough time to prepare the paperwork."

"It would be my pleasure."

Julie wrapped her arms around Keone and kissed him long and hard. "Get home as soon as you can. I'll be waiting."

Friday, June 7, 2:00 PM

Judge Fernandez granted the commitments for observation of Sam Loftus and Brad Carvell to the Molokini ward of Maui Memorial Hospital after a short discussion with Keone and Dr. Drayton. After thanking Dr. Drayton and bidding him aloha, Keone decided to stop by Lieutenant Alcala's office to debrief him.

Karen was standing behind her desk when she saw Keone approach. "He's not here."

"Do you know where he is?"

"With Chief Watanabe. He said for you to join them as soon as you finished with Judge Fernandez. I was just going down to wait for you."

Keone started to leave.

"Keone." He turned. "Be careful in there. You're in real trouble this time."

"Mahalo for the warning, Karen."

Keone reviewed in his mind the rules he'd probably broken in the last twenty-four hours. The list was substantial. He was not authorized to investigate Sam Loftus, thus his interviews with Hassellbach and Mrs. Carvell and what he heard on Carvell's answering machine were tainted. Luckily, they wouldn't be necessary to bring criminal charges against Sam for kidnapping and assault. He was not authorized to chase after Carvell, or Sam for that matter. He should have reported his findings to Alcala and stepped away from the case. He did contact Angela, but that was outside the normal chain of command. She shouldn't get any flack, but he was way over the line. Taking Carvell and Loftus into custody should be a clean bust for her. Besides they weren't going to jail, just to the Molokini ward for observation.

Keone identified himself to Chief Watanabe's assistant and took a seat outside the chief's office.

"You can go in now," the assistant said after a very brief phone call to the chief.

Inside the office, the chief sat behind his desk and Lieutenant Alcala stood to the side. Neither person looked happy.

"Detective Sergeant Boyd, do you know why you are here?" the chief asked.

Keone considered saying, "A commendation for my amazing detective work isn't necessary, sir."

Instead, he said, "My tactics on the Loftus case were unorthodox, I know, but—"

"The only Loftus case I'm aware of was closed some months ago. Is there another of which I'm unaware?"

"Yes, sir. A kidnapping, sir. But we've captured the perps and they will undergo psychiatric evaluation."

"Sergeant, both Lieutenant Alcala and I are pleased that you and Sergeant Beyers were able to rescue Mrs. Walden before she sustained further harm."

"Thank you, sir. Sergeant Beyers did an outstanding job."

"Other than the result, Sergeant, everything involved with this action has brought shame on this department."

Keone remained silent.

"Would you tell us the location from which Mrs. Walden was abducted?"

"She was in protective custody."

"Where?"

"My condominium in Ma'alaea."

"Were you aware of this, Lieutenant?"

"No, sir."

"Sergeant, don't you think your direct superior would have been interested to know that you were playing house with a material witness, when he was led to believe she was in an authorized safe house?"

"I never actually lied, sir."

"You withheld critical information from your supervisor and this department. You disregarded multiple policies of this department—which are not merely guidelines, by the way. You performed an unauthorized investigation of a man who was of no known interest to this department, before he even committed a potentially criminal act. You carried out multiple illegal searches tainting potentially valuable evidence, and you allowed yourself to fall in love with and have intimate relations with a material witness in an important drug prosecution involving multiple agencies of our government as well as Interpol. Do you take issue with any of the offenses I've just enumerated?"

Before Keone could say anything, Alcala spoke. "You are allowed to have a representative of the Hawaiian Police Officers Association present before any further discussion takes place. You are currently suspended pending a hearing to be held on June fourteenth. You will turn in your badge and sidearm."

Keone placed his holster and sidearm on the chief's desk along with his badge, then stood at attention.

"Go home, Sergeant," Alcala said. "A representative from the Association will be in contact with you tomorrow. You're dismissed."

Chapter Forty-eight

Thursday, June 13, 7:15 AM

For Keone, the last week was the worst and most wonderful of his life. The freedom to drop all of his barriers around Julie was more than a relief—it was a rebirth. He always hated it in movies when a man or woman would say, "You complete me." How corny can you get? But living with Julie made him realize that he'd always been missing something in his life that Julie provided. It wasn't a dependency. He felt more independent than ever and knew she did, too. It was a wholeness. But he knew neither he nor Julie would ever say something as corny as that.

"So, you ready to protect us Mauians from harm, mistah detective?" Julie teased.

"I will be once I get my pants on."

"Carrying a concealed weapon, eh?"

"You know it. I'll try to get home at a reasonable time tonight."

"I've started writing again."

Keone was surprised at how good those words made him feel. "About time you started earning your keep around here."

Julie punched him, hard, in the gut. "Watch that trash talk, buster."

Keone lifted her off the ground, kissed her gently, and said, "I'm so proud of you."

"You know it. I'm the best damn thing that ever happened to you and don't you forget it."

Keone had downplayed his suspension and hearing to Julie, making it sound like a common thing after an unusual case like her kidnapping and assault. As for her still living with him, he saw no need to close that barn door as all of the farm animals were clearly out in the open. Julie wouldn't need to testify at the hearing tomorrow. But he knew Frank Kulima would be there with a shit-eating grin on his face.

He had an excuse for going to the station today, as he would be meeting with his appointed representative in preparation for the hearing. He knew from their earlier meetings that a loss in rank was the minimum he could expect. The chance of complete discharge from the police department was a real possibility.

He was glad to be out of the condo for another reason. It would help hide his despair from Julie.

Thursday, June 13, 8:00 AM

When he reached the station, Keone found a voice message on his desk phone. "Keone, this is Rich Hopkins with the Federal Prosecutor's office. I just thought you should know Dave Walden is starting to become annoying. His new lawyer advised him to stop being so accommodating and trade what he knows for a ticket into witness protection. We aren't opposed to a deal. But he's starting to piss us off. He's even trying to contest his divorce from that wife he beat the crap out of and almost blew up. I thought you might find a subtle way to remind him what playing hard ball with us could mean for his longevity."

Keone deleted the message and called Rich back on his cell.

"Richard Hopkins, United States Prosecutor's Office. How may I help you?"

"It's me, Rich. I got your heads up. You might want to be around our lock-up at about twelve-thirty this afternoon. I'm planning to give a singing lesson just before then to a very unfortunate gentleman."

"I'll be there. Aloha."

Keone had to call a few friends to make sure his lesson was unobserved and unrecorded. He was certain he and Mr. David Walden were going to have an open and productive discussion around lunchtime. Keone had very little left to lose.

Thursday, June 13, 5:00 PM

"Well, I'll be damned. You're home early. Is there no crime left to fight?" Julie asked, as Keone came through the door.

"No. I took care of all the bad guys, today. Including one you may know."

"What has my notorious ex gotten into this time?"

"Nothing much. He just made a faulty assumption about a simple physical law called leverage. But we discussed it over lunch in his cell and he's become educated."

"Can he walk?"

"Oh, yes. There's not a mark on him. He has learned some facts about food placement that will be of value in the future. I know he enjoyed the Mexican food we served today. Dave has agreed to provide important evidence against his former good buds on the Eastern seaboard and elsewhere. He also signed these." Keone produced some papers from behind his back with his left hand while keeping his right hand hidden in his pocket.

"He signed the divorce papers? You are good."

"My friend Judge Fernandez has offered to fast track the paperwork. How do you feel about a Fourth of July wedding?" He produced a small box from his pocket.

Julie's eyes went wider than he'd ever seen them as she slowly opened the box to display a four-carat diamond ring in a platinum band. "Did you rob a bank?"

"No. When the insurance money arrived I thought, 'Who needs another Morgan Roadster?' I found something I love much more. So, Julie Madison..." He slowly descended to one knee. "Would you—"

Julie cut him off. "Of course I would, dumbass. Get up here where I can kiss you."

Julie pulled Keone to his feet and covered his face with kisses. "Did you remember to save anything for the honeymoon?"

"How about a cruise of the Greek Islands?"

"You're on."

Chapter Forty-nine

Friday, June 14, 1:30 PM

"Hello, Sam."

"Hello, Dr. Drayton."

"Where are you today, my friend?"

"I'm not sure anymore."

"I saw Brad Carvell a little while ago. He told me to tell you how sorry he is about everything. He's making excellent progress in his treatment."

"I'm glad for him."

Drayton didn't show his frustration, but he felt it. They had come so far. "Sam, we're going to get you back to where you were before you visited the observatory, but to achieve that we have to use the two tools that helped us last time, your journals and Janet."

"No. I've hurt her enough. I'll re-read the journals, but I couldn't bear to let Janet down again.."

"Sam, she's been here every day. It hurts her when you turn her away. She is the best friend you have in this world."

"This world." Sam smiled.

"Sam, you can't go on believing that craziness Carvell was spouting. Even he doesn't believe it anymore."

"I know. It's just that I want to believe it. I need to believe it or Cindy and Timmy won't exist. I can't let that happen. I won't."

"We lose people in the real world, too. Think about when your mother died."

Sam did remember those days. She was only sixty and died without warning. "It hit me very hard. I didn't cry until after the funeral, but then I broke down in our bedroom. In both worlds my wife came and comforted me. It helped."

"Losing the two children your mind created will be hard, too. Don't you want your wife with you to help you through that?"

"Yes."

"Now answer honestly. Knowing you're in this world and not the one from your memories. Which wife would you like that to be?"

Tears filled Sam's eyes. He didn't understand the Julie in this world. She was foreign to him. She'd even hurt him. After a long pause, he whispered, "Jan."

"Okay. Then you need to let her come."

"Give it one more week. If she still wants to come then, I'll see her. We both need more time."

"That's reasonable, Sam. I'll ask her to come on June twenty-first."

"But only if she wants to. Promise me."

"Only if she wants to. Now I want to introduce you to someone. I'll be right back."

Drayton left the room and returned with a young African-American man of about thirty. "Sam, this is Doctor Jude Miller. Dr. Miller will be filling in for me over the upcoming July Fourth holiday. My wife and I are visiting our son on O'ahu."

"Your son the architect."

"Yes. That's right."

Miller stuck out his hand and Sam shook it, "Nice to meet you, Doctor. Maybe we can watch fireworks together from the roof."

Miller smiled. "Maybe we can. I'll leave you and Dr. Drayton to continue your session."

Sam knew Miller would be watching them through the one-way glass that looked like a small mirror in the session room. But he didn't mind. He didn't mind much of anything these days. He felt hollow. He could function but couldn't care much anymore.

Drayton addressed this exact point. "Sam, there are only two paths for you now. You can decide to come back to your life here or you can withdraw from it. My work going forward is to remind you of everything this world has to offer you. You know at every level that you cannot return to the world of your memories. Don't you?" Drayton almost shouted these last two words.

"Yes. If it's a delusion, there's nowhere to go. If it's not, there's no way to get there." Sam had known this when he took Julie.

"You also know that you cannot recreate the same children you remember in this world. Don't you?" Again Drayton put emphasis on the last two words.

"I know."

"But you can have children. You and Janet could adopt."

"Do you really think she would do that for me? After all the crap I put her through?"

"She would do it for both of you. But you can't wait too long. This week I want you to envision a life with Janet. A life completely open to any possibility: children, travel, new home, new job, new hobbies, anything."

"I will, Doctor. I'll try. But I'm so sad sometimes—and so weary."

"The new medicine will help you with that. Just take one day at a time. Sam, to me you are more than a patient. You're a friend. Do you know that?"

"I do, Evan."

"Please help me keep my friend."

"I'll try. I'll really try."

"That's all anyone can ask."

Chapter Fifty

Saturday, June 15, 6:00 PM

"You two have made me happier than you can imagine," Jan said, as they sat around her dining room table drinking champagne and enjoying luscious appetizers in celebration of Julie and Keone's engagement.

"Jan, these *pupu* are fantastic. Are you sure you don't have some Hawaiian blood in you somewhere?"

"I wish I did, Keone. I've had to work hard to learn. Our neighbor, Mrs. Kanaloa, taught me everything I know. But I'm looking forward to having you and your brothers teach me how to do real Hawaiian barbeque, Maui style."

"We'd be delighted."

"You'll taste the best in the world at our wedding. We have to have it in the morning so all the boys can compete at the rodeo. I'm afraid you may need to lend a hand with preparations," Julie added, giving her sister a squeeze.

"Try and stop me."

"Would you like one of my handsome brothers to accompany you to the wedding?" Keone said.

"Very tempting, but I have someone in mind to take me. We've only been dating for a few days, but it's been very special."

"What about Sam?"

"I visited every day for the first week and he refused to see me."

"The Sam we brought back from Hana was pretty worn down. He may just need some time," Keone said.

"I understand. I do. But Sam lied to me. I know there was a time during his recovery when he'd honestly decided to learn to love me. I know Carvell derailed his recovery. But I also know Sam lied."

"I understand. The lying was the worst part with Dave, too," Julie said.

"Julie, you're the one person who truly gets it. I'm not sure if Sam learning to love me is enough anymore. Although we've only been dating for a few days, I've known Michael Fowler for years. I decorated his home and helped him through the death of his wife. I don't know about love, but I do know he likes me for who I am. And I like the way he makes me feel. We're so happy when we're together. I guess I'd rather be someone's first choice than a consolation prize."

"Dr. Drayton told you long ago that you have grounds for divorce from Sam. You helped me get my divorce from Dave started. I'd be happy to return the favor."

"Thank you, dear. I may take you up on that. I just want to give things a little time. I loved my old Sam. I even learned to love the new one, for a while. But he grew out of his love for me. He's continuing to grow as a person. And, damn it, so am I. I don't want to make him worse. But I can't live my life trapped in his treatment plan."

"I know you'll do what's right. Make sure it's what's right for you," Julie said.

"Now. Tell me about this cruise you have planned. And don't you dare spend it all in bed." Jan's expression looked suspiciously like a leer.

Saturday, June 15, 9:00 PM

They had barely left Jan's neighborhood when Keone's phone began playing the theme from *Cops*, "Bad Boys." Keone knew it would be Tony Alcala with the review board's decision.

"Hello."

"Keone, it's Tony."

"How bad is it?"

"It could be worse. You're still working for me."

"But the sergeant stripes are gone, right?" Keone thought back on how hard he'd worked to make sergeant. He also remembered Frank Kulima's damning testimony during yesterday's hearing.

"They would have been, if not for an unexpected turn of events."

"What?"

"A key witness's testimony is now inadmissible."

"What key witness?" Keone felt a faint ray of hope.

"Former Detective Sergeant Frank Kulima. It seems he had another employer in addition to the county of Maui—a Mr. David Walden. He was named along with Roger Walker from West Maui and a guy from Kihei division as being on the take. Walden even admitted to paying him to follow you around after the crash."

"Where's Kulima now?"

"Maui Memorial. When the officers arrived to arrest him he tried to shoot himself in the head. The dumbass missed and shot his right ear off."

"So what is my punishment?"

"You have a two-month suspension, starting immediately. And when you return you will rotate through all of the districts again to demonstrate that you have learned how to obey department policy in every possible contingency."

"Tony, thank you. I know I would have been out on my ass if you hadn't gone to bat for me. I won't let you down again. I know I screwed up."

"But you'd do it all again to save Julie. Hopefully, now that you're making an honest woman of her, that situation will never arise again. By the way, I got you permission to leave the country during your suspension. You damn well better have one hell of a honeymoon. Aloha."

When the call ended, Keone didn't try to hide his tears from Julie. He planned to never hide anything from her, ever again.

"How bad?" she asked.

"No demotion. It turned out Kulima was working for your ex-husband. Two months' suspension followed by a year rotating through every division before I return to work in CID."

"You risked everything for me."

Keone started to interrupt, but Julie held up her hand. "No, don't talk. It's my turn. I want you to know I understand what you risked to love me. We'll spend the rest of our lives making that risk worth it for both of us."

By this time they were home and parked. Keone reached over and gently stroked Julie's cheek. "It's already worth it."

They kissed in the car, then in the living room, then in the bedroom. They spent the rest of the night providing each other more joy than either could have imagined possible.

Chapter Fifty-one

Sunday, June 16, 1:30 PM

"Hello, Martin. Are you visiting Brad today?" Evan Drayton liked the observatory director. They'd kept in touch after that harrowing morning in the interrogation room. Drayton made sure to keep Hassellbach up to date on Brad's progress.

"Hi, Evan. Diane suggested I come. She's very happy with his progress and wants me to see the results of your treatment regime." Hassellbach was dressed casually in shorts and an Aloha shirt.

"He's doing very well. I'm sure he'll be ready to leave here next month."

"That soon? I'm impressed. Has he talked about returning to work?" Hassellbach's face showed concern.

"I'll let him tell you. I think you'll be pleased. Stop by on your way out, would you? I'd like to discuss something."

"Sure, Evan. I'd be happy to." With that, Hassellbach entered his former colleague's room.

"Hello, Marty. I'm so glad you stopped by. I think you'll find me a little less loony than the last time we spoke."

"Hi, Brad. I hear good things about your recovery."

"Dr. Drayton is a fantastic doctor. The hardest thing to accept as an educated individual is that something like this obsession of mine could have grown so obvious to everyone else and been totally invisible to me. He let Diane bring my laboratory notebooks from home. There is absolutely no reasonable evidence of a power flux in any of the measurements I analyzed here on Maui. I was seeing patterns in noise."

"The fact that you realize this tells me that you and Dr. Drayton are making progress."

"I still have a ways to go, but Drayton confirms the obsession is gone at last. I have a lot of repair work to do on my life, my marriage, and my career. I also have to accept and work through the damage I did to my old friend, Sam."

"I know you can do it. I'd like to help in any way that I can." Hassellbach felt relaxed with this Brad Carvell. He reminded him of the energetic scientist he'd initially interviewed for the project. But he also knew Brad would never be allowed to work on a sensitive project like that again.

"You can help, Marty. You can help a great deal. I need a recommendation from you."

Hassellbach remained silent.

"Don't worry. I know I can't go back to what I was doing. I'm a security risk. I've discovered a need in our community for a person with my background to lecture to high school and college students on Maui. Once I'm certified as recovered by Dr. Drayton, I'm going to apply for a teaching position at UH Maui College, with adjunct duties in the high schools. I wondered if you could recommend me for such a position. There is absolutely no research requirement. I've decided I'm destined to be a teacher."

"Of course, I'll write you a recommendation. I'll even find a way to get your students some time in the observatory. I think you're making a great choice." Hassellbach's relief was evident."

"Thank you. I'm very grateful. I have another, more personal, request, if you're willing."

"Sure. What is it?"

"I'd like you to take all of these lab books, all of my raw data, and the equipment in my home lab back to the facility and use them as you see fit. Just promise never to let me see any of it again."

"Of course."

"Diane can show you where everything is. I want to turn my basement into a den. I think a pool table and a large HDTV should fill the space amply." Brad smiled.

Hassellbach rose and stuck out his hand. "I'm proud of you, my friend."

Carvell shook the offered hand and said, "Now get out of here. No one should have to see a grown astrophysicist cry."

Drayton was waiting outside the door.

"You've done wonders, Evan."

"Thank you, Martin. I hope you support his decision to go into teaching."

"One hundred percent."

Drayton paused as if making a decision. "Would you do a favor for me?"

"You want me to talk with Mr. Loftus, don't you?"

"Yes. I know it's a huge imposition. But Brad's not ready to face Sam. He needs to know the details of Brad's obsession and how a respected scientist would evaluate his conclusions. He also needs to hear Brad is improving from someone other than me."

Now it was Hassellbach's turn to pause. "He may not believe me. He doesn't know me terribly well, you know."

"Sam is nothing if not logical. If you present the information to him in a logical manner, I believe he will accept it. I certainly believe it's worth a try. Sam is at a very pivotal point here. You could help him decide to get better."

"I'll do my best."

Chapter Fifty-two

Thursday, July 4, 4:00 AM

Sam was not surprised when Dr. Drayton told him Janet had turned down his offer to visit, but was surprised when she changed her mind a week later. At their session yesterday afternoon Dr. Drayton told him she would visit the next day. Over the past two months Sam had let himself go, growing a beard and letting his hair grow long. In preparation for Janet's visit, he decided to get a shave and haircut and dress in his best suit. Unfortunately, he didn't decide this until the middle of the night.

"What is it this time, Sam?" Louie asked. Sam was glad Louie was on duty. He was one of the good ones.

"Louie, my dear friend. I feel like a shower and a shave. My wife is coming to visit today, and I need to look my very best."

"Sam, you know I love ya, but it's 4:00 AM."

"Then the shower shouldn't be busy and you probably have time to give me a shave. Look, it will be two less things you have to do in the morning. And I need my suit, a dress shirt, a tie, and my nice leather shoes. You can wait to tie them until she gets here, so you won't break the suicide prevention rules. Come on, Louie, I really need this."

Louie looked torn about something then said, "Sam, This is my last night here. I waited until Dr. Drayton left for the holiday before giving them my notice. I was afraid he'd talk me out of it. But, my new job is great and I don't have to work nights."

"That's wonderful, Louie."

Louie smiled at Sam. "OK, Sammy, just this once. Consider it a going away present from me."

"Oh, and bring some scissors. I could use a haircut."

Thursday, July 4, 2:00 PM

When Dr. Martin Hassellbach entered the visiting area and notified the attendant in charge that he wished to see Mr. Sam Loftus, the clock displayed 2:00 PM on July fourth. In fifteen minutes Sam entered the room and sat down across the table from Hassellbach.

"Dr. H., I'm so glad you picked today to visit. I always enjoy seeing you. But today is very special for me. My wife, Janet, has agreed to visit." Sam's excitement was obvious but so was his anxiety.

"I'm happy to hear that, Sam. I've asked you to call me Martin."

"Sure, Martin. Did you visit Brad today?"

"Yes, I did. It's a special day for him, too. He gets to go home."

"I'm happy for him, and for Diane. They're such nice people. Is he cured?"

"Nearly. He's well enough to go home. He's hoping to teach this fall at UH Maui College."

"That's great. I'm going to ask Janet to forgive me. I've decided I want to live with her again. It's the right thing to do."

Hassellbach was disturbed by Sam's rapid responses and disjointed comments. He preferred the quieter, more thoughtful Sam he'd experienced on previous visits. "Is everything all right, Sam? You seem a bit hyper."

"I'm just excited. I think Brad's release today is auspicious. Do you realize today is Independence Day? How appropriate."

"Yes, Sam. It is appropriate for Brad. He sees it as the day he's declaring freedom from false things. We've discussed many times why he misinterpreted his data and how sorry he is that he misled you. How do you feel about it all, today?"

"I understand and accept that Brad was obsessed and shared his obsession with me. But I know he bore no animosity towards me. He honestly thought he was helping me."

"He'll be very glad to hear that." This sounded more like the rational Sam he'd been visiting.

"I look forward to having him and Diane over to our home, when all of this is behind us. I'd like us to be friends."

"He'd like that, too."

"I have to get changed for Janet's visit. But I'm so glad you stopped by. Even though Brad's going home, will you still visit me, you know, on weekends and holidays like you've been doing?"

"Of course, Sam. I'll see you this weekend. I hope your meeting with Janet goes well. Aloha."

"Aloha."

Thursday, July 4, 4:00 PM

At precisely 4:00 PM, Sam was brought back to the visiting room. He'd washed his face, combed his now-short hair, and applied deodorant and after-shave before donning his sharply pressed suit and shiny wingtips. Sam entered with a spring in his step and a smile on his face. Janet was already seated on the other side of the table and had a manila folder in front of her.

"Hello, Jan. It's wonderful to see you. I'm sorry it took so long to pull myself together enough to let you visit. Dr. Drayton told me how you came every day for the first week I was here."

"Sam, we have to talk." Janet seemed tense, but that was natural after the things he'd put her through.

"I know, sweetheart. I hope you can forgive me for all I put you through. I know you understand it was this crazy illness that made me do what I did. I'm ready to begin again. We made so much progress before Brad sidetracked me. I was never faking my affection for you. My fondest wish is to get well so I can come home and live with you, like we did before. Please say you forgive me."

"I do forgive you, Sam. I know you're sick and can't control what you do. I also believe the closeness we achieved before you went on that tour of the observatory was real."

Tears came to Sam's eyes. "I won't let you down this time, Jan. I promise."

"I believe that, too. But something else has been added to our situation." Janet paused to summon the strength to continue.

Sam jumped in. "I've decided we can adopt. We can have the family I dreamed of together."

"No, Sam. We can't. Another man has entered my life, a wonderful man, who makes me happy. His name is Michael and he loves me for who I am. He doesn't need to learn how."

Sam's face fell, but he didn't try to escape from reality this time. He knew his dreams of winning Janet back had little chance of success, but had still hoped.

"Too little, too late. You do deserve better. Your forgiveness will have to be enough for me. I'll never forget your patience and caring when I came home. If I could have stayed on track, we might have made a nice life for ourselves. I blew that chance. I hope this man provides you a more complete life than I could have. I hope you understand that I do love you and want what's best for you."

"I do, Sam. I hope you find a path to happiness as well." She looked down at the folder in front of her. "There's one more thing."

"Yes."

"I need you to sign these documents." Janet handed him the folder.

"I suppose these are divorce papers. You probably didn't need my signature to get a divorce given my condition. But it means a lot to me that you're asking for it anyway."

"I'm glad you understand."

"May I ask you one last favor, Janet? Could you give me twenty-four hours to come to terms with this, before I return these to you signed?"

Janet obviously hadn't expected this and hesitated.

"I promise I will sign them. Just give me the time I need to grieve over this lost opportunity."

"All right, Sam. I owe you that much. I will be here at 4 PM tomorrow to pick up the papers. But we won't meet again."

"I understand. Thank you. Goodbye, Janet."

"Goodbye, Sam."

RICK LUDWIG

Part IX: Another Looking Glass

"He was part of my dream, of course -- but then I was part of his dream, too."

Lewis Carroll, author

RICK LUDWIG

Chapter Fifty-Three

Thursday, July 4, 4:30 PM

Sam stumbled back to his little room, clutching the divorce papers to his chest. He knew Janet needed her freedom. Even he couldn't pretend he was the best possible husband for her. Still, what were the implications if he found a way to return to his world someday? Would signing the papers here mean his doppelganger in the real world did the same for Julie there?

Once again he'd convinced everyone, Drayton, Hassellbach, even himself to some degree, that he accepted his memories as delusions. But inside he never really had. He knew Brad's conclusions were flawed. He knew he could be wrong. But he could never completely let go of the belief that his memories described his real life in another place. He knew Cindy and Timmy were real.

He struggled with his thoughts, alone in his room, for hours. It was nearly midnight before he finally did what he knew was best for everyone else and scratched his name on the documents. He even made the point of writing in the manner of this world and not his own. As he changed for bed, he felt a sense of relief. The covers seemed warming as he pulled them over his chest and sleep came quickly to wash his remaining concerns away.

Friday, July 5, 2:00 AM

Hours later Sam awoke refreshed, though he could tell by the darkness that dawn was still hours away. Lying on his back, he gazed up at the ceiling and wondered at how blurry it appeared. It was like...

...like looking through a soap bubble. The portal had returned and looked just like it did when he was in the car. The bubble moved ever closer to him until it enveloped him and produced a loud pop.

Startled, he jumped from his bed and ran to the table where the divorce documents still lay. Was he finally back home? One look at the documents would tell him, but he was afraid. Finally forcing his eyes to scan the pages, he smiled broadly. The words were no longer in mirror writing and the plaintiff's name was Julie Loftus.

Somehow, he'd made it back home.

He had a huge task ahead of him. He would have to convince Julie, who would surely be the wife who came this afternoon, that he was himself again. She must have spent as many days with the mirror-Sam as he'd spent in the mirror world.

He tore the divorce papers to shreds and banged on his door to get the night attendant's attention.

"What is it this time, Sam? Hey, where's your beard?" Sam was not surprised that the attendant was a stranger. It reinforced his belief that he was home.

"I'm a new man. Yesterday I decided to return to the real world. Now I feel like a shower and a shave. My wife is coming to visit today and I need to look my very best."

"Sam, you know I love ya, but it's 2:00 AM."

"Then the shower shouldn't be busy and you probably have time to give me a shave...."

Chapter Fifty-four

Friday, July 5, 4:00 PM

When he came into the visitor's room, Sam was not surprised to see Julie there. Julie, on the other hand, was positively shocked to see Sam.

"Hello, sweetheart," Sam said.

"What, you're talking again? What happened to the caveman look and the wild eyes and the drooling? Who are you?"

He looked deeply into her eyes and said, "I'm your husband and you're my wife. I've been lost to you for too long. I'm back and ready to go home."

"After all you've done, how can you expect me to believe you? You hurt me, Sam. You hurt Jan and everyone around you again and again and...." She dissolved into sobs.

He took her face in his hands. "That man wasn't me. I've been away."

"I've heard Dr. Carvell's theory. I know his boss, that policeman, and a number of others—including you—believe it. But I don't. I rely on Dr. Drayton. He says you're severely damaged and are destined for a life in an institution."

"If Dr. Drayton pronounced me cured, would you consider having me back?"

"Why should I put myself through all of this again?"

"Because we love each other more than anyone else can

ever understand. I won't try to explain what happened to me. But you are my Sweet Jubilee and always will be."

His use of this term of endearment—one that he hadn't used since the accident—forced Julie to look up and search his eyes for the truth. "I have to go now, Sam."

Sam dropped his head to his chest. "You have to do what you think best, sweetheart."

"I'm willing to let the doctor decide if you've actually recovered. If he tells me you're back, I'll consider believing you."

As Sam looked up at Julie, his Julie, the tears began to flow. "I can ask for nothing more."

Saturday, August 10, 4:00 PM

After a full month, which included extensive tests and a period of re-acquaintance between Sam and Julie, it was finally time to leave the hospital. Dr. Drayton was there and both Sam and Julie gave him big hugs and their eternal thanks for making Sam well again.

As they pushed through the clear glass doors, Keone and Dr. Carvell were both waiting for them.

"Dr. Drayton knows I'm sane, now. According to Julie, you two always knew. I can't thank you enough. I want to get to know these versions of each of you."

Dr. Carvell gave him a hug and showed him a printout displaying the energy flux that occurred in the wee hours of July fifth.

Keone shook his hand, leaned in to his ear and whispered, "I told you we'd solve this mystery."

Sam and Julie left their two new friends behind and walked to the car. The kids were standing beside the car and Sam swept them into his arms for minutes of hugs and kisses. After placing everyone in their appropriate positions in the car, Sam allowed Julie to drive them home.

"Do you think Janet came back for mirror-Sam in that

other world?" Sam asked.

"I'm afraid he was too far gone. Let's just be happy that you and Cindy and Timmy and I are all together again."

He nodded and looked outside of the car to see everything was written in the way he found normal.

He looked at Cindy and Timmy in the backseat playing "I touched you last" and laughing.

He noticed Julie's medical bag in the backseat, before she brought his attention forward. "I've invited Dave and Janet over tonight. I hope it's not too soon."

"You know I love those guys. I can't wait to see them again."

"Were they that different in the other world?"

"Dave was horrible there. But Janet was pretty much the same."

"What was I like?"

"Still beautiful, of course, but tougher. Dave was hard on you. You weren't a pediatrician, though." Sam didn't want to talk about the other Julie. He felt guilty about what he'd done to her.

"I'd hate that. I love taking care of kids. Did I work?"

"You were a writer—a famous one. You wrote children's books."

"That sounds better."

Sam began to notice his wife was running all the red lights. Then when they neared home, a red light changed to green and his wife stopped dead.

"Why did you stop?"

"I always stop for green lights, silly."

From the back seat Timmy and Cindy sang, "Green means stop and red means go. The yellow light means go real slow."

Sam realized he wasn't quite home after all, but it was close enough for him. He smiled broadly and relaxed back into his seat, ready to explore another new world.

Chapter Fifty-five

Saturday, July 6, 5:00 PM

Dr. Drayton peered through the small one-way window into Sam's cell. Sam sat in the far left corner of the tiny room, where he had remained, motionless and gazing into space, since the day after he signed the divorce papers Janet had presented him during their last visit.

As he continued to observe his patient, life returned to Sam's face for a brief moment. He didn't move or speak, nor was he aware of his surroundings. But his eyes were bright and the expression on his face pure contentment.

Dr. Drayton said aloud to no one in particular, "Why is this man smiling?"

"Because, in his mind, he's returned home."

"Sergeant Boyd, I didn't hear you come in. How was the wedding?"

"Wonderful. Julie was so happy Jan could be her matron of honor. Jan is a different person since Sam agreed to the divorce. Her boyfriend came, too. I really like him. He's part Hawaiian, you know."

"Did you finally solve all your mysteries?"

Keone stared at Sam's peaceful face, sitting alone in the corner of his tiny room. "In our own way, I guess each of us did."

The doctor patted Keone on the shoulder and left to see

other patients. Keone continued to gaze at Sam until he heard someone come up behind him and turned.

"Pitiful, isn't he?" Dr. Hassellbach approached the window.

"Oh, I don't know. He seemed to be smiling a minute ago. I just told the doc that I think Sam may have made it back to his own reality, in his mind, at least."

Hassellbach seemed to ponder this. "In his mind, yes, or...."

"What?"

"Oh, I don't know. Sam needs better hygiene, don't you think? How long do you think it's been since he's been shaved?"

"It looks like at least a few weeks. I'll talk to the orderly about giving him a shave and a haircut, too."

"Good idea. You know, something you said when we first met got me thinking. I went back and reviewed the data on the energy surges that Carvell reported."

"You said he'd made them all up." Keone felt uncomfortable.

"Yes. He did make his up. I saw nothing in the range he'd measured. But I analyzed a broader spectrum of electromagnetic radiation than he did."

"Go on."

"Just as I'd suspected, there were no surges on any of the dates and times he'd recorded–except one."

"The one when Sam was supposed to cross over."

"Yes. I also discovered one surge since Carvell ended his study."

"When was that?"

"Precisely 2 AM on the morning of July fifth."

"Just a coincidence."

"Of course, you're probably right. But something else is bothering me. I've been visiting Sam every weekend and holiday for almost a month. I first stopped by out of curiosity but found I really enjoyed talking with him. He seemed to enjoy my visits, as well. On every other visit he seemed perfectly normal, always expressing his deep regret for the actions that got him committed. Now he's catatonic."

"The nurse said he signed the divorce papers during the night of July fourth and was like this when she came in on the fifth."

"That could certainly explain it. But how do we know which Sam we have in there?"

"What do you mean which Sam? Sam Loftus, of course."

"Oh, yes. But which Sam Loftus?"

"You're not considering Carvell's crazy parallel universe story, are you? You're the one who told me the idea was extremely theoretical and impossible to prove. "

"I know. It's not possible. It's just that I visited him two days ago, on Independence Day...."

"So what?"

"He'd just had a shave."

MIRRORED

ABOUT THE AUTHOR

James R. (Rick) Ludwig, Ph.D. spent over forty years in the academic, health care, biotechnology, and pharmaceutical industries. Rick also maintained a writer's journal since his junior year in high school and populated it with short stories, poetry, and essays throughout his career.

Although a published author of multiple scientific papers and book chapters, writing for a popular audience presented a unique challenge. Rick spent the first year of his retirement, converting all of his writings, including his journal, to digital format. Since then, he has written full-time and completed three manuscripts. *Mirrored* is his first published novel. His second novel, *Something More*, will follow in 2015.

Rick participated in the 2009 Hawai'i Writers Conference in Honolulu, Hawai'i, served as Volunteer Coordinator for the 2013 Aloha Writers Conference in Kapalua, Maui, and attended best-selling author William Martin's Retreat workshop during that conference. Rick participated in best-selling author William Bernhardt's Level 1, Level 2, Level 3, and advanced writers' workshops between 2010 and 2014.

Rick is married with two grown children and lives in Maui, Hawai'i with his wife of thirty-four years, Christy, with whom he is learning to relax and enjoy the game of golf.